Souls of a Feather

Jan 6, 2013

To Daniel –

It was nice to meet you.

Bnb

Souls of a Feather

Charles W. Shirriff

Writers Club Press
San Jose New York Lincoln Shanghai

Souls of a Feather

Writers Club Press
an imprint of iUniverse, Inc.

For information address:
iUniverse, Inc.
5220 S. 16th St., Suite 200
Lincoln, NE 68512
www.iuniverse.com

ISBN: 0-595-20626-3

Printed in the United States of America

Dedication

To my wife Wilma for her tolerance and support, my children Anita and Ken for helping with editing and keeping me focused, and Henry and Kathryn for their input and encouragement.

Also, to Frances Young who is in her 95th year, and to my granddaughters Sydney and Emma just for being themselves.

The earth is but one country, and mankind its citizens.
—*Bahá'u'lláh*

Contents

List of Illustrations

Preface

Although this novel is a sequel to *Spirits of a Feather*, there is no need to have read the previous one. Each book is a self-contained, albeit related, story.

The previous novel, *Spirits of a Feather*, documents the first six months in the life of a young man named Jay as he learns the joys and pitfalls of a big city. The events of his daily life force him to develop a personal identity within his peer group.

This book, *Souls of a Feather*, follows Jay's life for the next year and a half. During this time, he begins to search for spiritual foundations within himself and in the life around him.

For readers who prefer a bit of background information the following brief introduction of the main characters, common to both novels, may be helpful.

Jay—a seventeen-year-old boy who leaves his dysfunctional family in northern Manitoba to search for a new life in the metropolis of Winnipeg. The city of Winnipeg is the capital of Manitoba and is situated straight north of Fargo, North Dakota. Jay's search for his biological father takes him to California by the end of the first novel.

Phil—the man who befriends Jay when he first arrives in Winnipeg and provides him with moral support and a place to stay. Phil is on disability leave from the police force until such a time as he is able to get his periodic bouts of aggression under control.

Steve—one of Phil's friends who is a travel agent during the workweek and a flamboyantly gay man on the weekends. He helps Jay overcome his homophobia and eventually becomes one of his trusted friends.

Sue—Jay's girlfriend until her wealthy father decides their relationship should end before Christmas.

Helen and George Parkington—Sue's parents who live in an affluent area of Winnipeg.

Cam, Jamie, and Tiffany—Phil's friends from his high school days. Although heterosexual, Cam likes to dress up and go with Steve to gay bars and clubs for entertainment. Cam and Jamie live as friends in the same apartment. Tiffany is supported by her parents while she searches diligently for a permanent boyfriend.

Becky and Jimmy—friends who have lived together in a shaky relationship for two years. Jimmy was a smalltime crook and is a former drug user. They are friends of both Jay and Sue.

Tanya—A New Age sort of girl who floats in and out of Jay's life, invariably upsetting it.

Han Sing—owner of a small restaurant and bar called the Red Dragon. Jay gets his first job there and lives in a room above the establishment.

R.B.—an old native (First Nation) shaman who also lives in a room above the Red Dragon. His full name is Running Bear but everyone calls him by his initials. He helps Jay to look within himself for spiritual strength, and beyond himself for meaning in his life.

Arrow—R.B.'s old dog and companion.

Acknowledgements

Thanks to the many people who took the time to discuss my previous novel, *Spirits of a Feather*, with me and encouraged me to write this sequel.

Special thanks to all those, including my Internet friends, who provided me with suggestions and counsel as the work progressed.

Extra special thanks to the members of the First Nation, Bahá'i, and Hutterian Brethren, communities for the time and effort they gave so generously to ensure that the portrayal of their lives and philosophy was as authentic and realistic as possible.

~ *1* ~ _____

I LEFT MY HEART
IN…WINNIPEG?

Jay flopped into the middle seat on Air Canada flight 836 from San Francisco to Winnipeg. He leaned back and closed his eyes in an effort to relax. He tried to visualize his girlfriend's ready smile that would light up a room when she walked in and the way her eyes used to twinkle with humor at the slightest provocation. However, his mind insisted on going back to the phone call he had received earlier in the day. The words of his girlfriend's mother kept echoing in his mind:

> "Her dad brought in the best specialists he could get. They say they need to do more tests. She won't tell the psychiatrists anything. She says you're the only one she'll talk to."

"Excuse us, please," a voice said.

Jay remained lost in his thoughts. A tap on his shoulder caused him to open his eyes.

"Could you, like, skootch over to the aisle seat so my boyfriend and I can sit together?"

Jay looked up at a young couple leaning over him and said, "Sure."

The man was a well-rehearsed California beach god: Costa del Mar sunglasses pushed up into his sun-bleached hair, face tanned from the sun and wind, physique toned by the gym and the surf, a Marcuzza "Circle of Waves" T-shirt, and a wooden big-bead Hawaiian necklace. She was a casual petite bundle of enthusiasm with Irish-red hair.

"Troy and I booked this aisle seat and the window seat, too. That way we'd have, like, you know, extra space if the middle one stayed empty. I'm Misty."

"My name's Jay. The aisle seat is great with me. I was glad to get any seat because I had to leave in a big rush."

Troy smiled, showing a flash of straight, shiny white teeth as he settled into his seat. He nodded a curt acknowledgment, "Dude," before slipping on a set of headphones.

"You're, like, going home for New Year's Eve?" Misty asked.

"I guess so."

"Cool. You were, like, visiting friends in San Francisco?"

"Looking for my dad," Jay said.

"Awesome. You were going to be together for the holiday?"

"I was hoping to find him."

Misty frowned and said, "Is he lost?"

"I've never met him. He left Mom before I was born."

"You know what he looks like, at least?"

"No. Nothing. Until I get to meet him, it's as if a piece of my life is missing. I don't have a family history."

Misty sat for a moment, trying to think of an appropriate response to this unexpected revelation of Jay's feelings.

"You have your mother's history. Maybe you could live with that," she said.

"I'm more like my dad than my mom," Jay said.

"How do you know, when you've never met him?"

"I know I'm not like my mom."

"Like, how come you're here instead of still looking for your dad?"

"I'm going home to see my girlfriend. Actually, she's my former girlfriend, I guess."

"You don't know for sure if she's your girlfriend?"

"Her father doesn't approve of me. I haven't seen her since before Christmas."

"Well that sucks, not to be with your girl at Christmas. Her father doesn't like you at all?"

"I think he likes me as much as he'd like any of Sue's boyfriends. It's more a wrong side of the tracks thing. I don't fit into the family picture."

"Because…?"

"They have money. My family has no money. I'm part native. He's white. Totally white, if you get my meaning."

"You don't look native."

"That's why I think I must be more like my dad."

"Except for your eyes."

"What about them?"

"They are such a solid, dark brown. You must have got them from your mother."

"Why do you say that?"

"Native people have such deep, passionate eyes," Misty said.

"Is that good?"

"It's good to be passionate."

"I do feel things deeply, if that's what you mean," Jay said.

"You're, like, so amazingly honest about yourself."

"My friend, Steve, taught me that you need to be true to yourself and not try to hide who you really are."

"He sounds very wise."

"It's more his years of experience in coping with being gay."

"Oh," Misty said, looking toward the window while she tried to find the right words for an appropriate reaction. "Oh, look. We're going to takeoff."

"Good. Now, stop with the questions until we get into the air, eh? I need to concentrate on getting this lumbering behemoth off the ground," Jay said, pulling on the armrests and pushing back into his seat as if by sheer willpower he would raise the plane's nose.

"Everybody says I, like, talk too much. I guess it's because I'm such a shy person," Misty said.

After the plane had risen sharply into the afternoon sky, Jay exhaled with a sigh of relief. "Okay. Now we can talk."

Misty leaned over and looked intently into Jay's eyes. "Tell me like, everything. I love other people's stories."

Jay took a deep breath. "I'll start from the beginning. But promise me you'll stop me if I'm boring you."

"Cool. People say I'm a good listener."

"I used to live in the bush, way up in Northern Manitoba, with my mom, sister and brother."

"Why did you leave?"

"I got fed up with the isolation. That and her live-in boyfriends."

"Sounds like you didn't get along with them."

"It was okay. I got beaten on some by a couple of them."

"How awful."

"They thought everything I did was weird."

"Bummer. Like what?"

"They constantly made fun of me and found ways to put me down."

"Really?"

"They called me names and made fun of me for reading everything I could find."

"That doesn't sound very serious."

"It's like that oriental thing, death by a thousand cuts. Each cutting comment is nothing by itself. If you get enough of them, it'll kill you."

"So you just packed up and left?"

"There wasn't any future there for a guy like me. Now, tell me about you and your friend, eh," Jay said.

"Oh, cool. We're kinda, you know, like, almost married. Troy took a course in San Jose on how to do computer special effects for movies. He landed this job with some sort of film company in Winnipeg."

"That's a big move."

"We had to choose one of Vancouver, Montreal, or Winnipeg. They're all active in film things."

"I don't suppose you chose Winnipeg because of the weather. Manitoba is a colder province than either British Columbia or Quebec."

"Apparently it has some great locations for making films. Wasn't there some movie with Rob Lowe in it that was partially filmed in Winnipeg?"

"I was there when they made the Portage and Main area look like New York. US postal stickers on the mailboxes and everything. You'd think it would have been easier to go to New York," Jay said.

"There's a firm in Winnipeg called Frantic Films. They do computer-generated special effects for TV and movies. That's what Troy's trying to get into."

"Have they done anything I might have seen?" Jay asked.

"They did the digital blizzard in Storm of the Century, for one. Swordfish for another. Troy has always been fascinated by special effects in movies."

The creation of computerized visual effects is a time-consuming process. To produce the scene in Swordfish that Misty was referring to required fifteen people six months to program a 42-second explosion.

"I'd like that kind of work but I don't have any education or training or anything. I like hanging around where they're shooting films. Maybe someday I'll get chosen as an extra," Jay said.

"Do they shoot a lot of films in Winnipeg?" Misty asked.

"Some. Most of our actors go to Los Angeles where the real action is."

"I didn't know film stars came from Winnipeg."

"Our most famous ones were in the movie, Hannibal."

"I don't believe that. You're, like, handing me a line."

"It's true. Some of those fourteen tusked boars came from near Winnipeg."

Misty laughed. "You're funny. One movie doesn't qualify them as stars."

"They went from there to be in Crocodile Dundee III. Doesn't that make them stars?"

"I bet they have a better life now than they had in Winnipeg. It isn't going to be cold up there, is it? Everyone says it will be. And there'll be, like, you know, snow all over the ground?"

"It'll be freezing. Let me guess. You've lived in California all your life, haven't you?" Jay asked.

"Yeah. Like, we've never been anywhere. This is such a cool adventure."

"It'll be cool, all right. Especially if you didn't bring warm clothes. And there will be piles of snow. We don't call it, 'Winterpeg Manisnowba' for nothing. At least you won't have to worry about mosquitoes for a while."

"What's a mosquito?" Misty asked.

"Little flying insects that bite you."

"Gross. They have teeth?"

"No. A long needle-nose they use to suck blood out of you."

"Yuck."

"Only a drop or two. They itch for a while afterward. Wood ticks are much worse."

"How could they be worse?"

"A wood tick buries its little head into your skin and injects a toxin into you that relaxes the muscle. That way, it can suck the blood out more easily."

"Yuck."

"My mom told me about the moose up north in the bush. They'd get so many wood ticks on them they'd collapse. If the ticks aren't removed, the moose will become paralyzed and die."

"You're, like, playing with my mind again, aren't you? Those things don't exist, do they?"

"Oh they're real. Fortunately, they only live in trees or long grass. Lots of city people have never seen one. You're lucky to live in California where you don't even need to have screens on your windows."

"You mean you have to, like, live with these things all year?"

"Heavens, no. Just during the summer time."

"So, that's what? Six months?"

"Our summer is more like three months."

"And the rest of the year is winter? I'm going back home."

"Spring and fall are nice. Some years it seems that winter is six months, but it really isn't," Jay said.

"We don't have spring and fall. California has six months summer and six months cool rainy season," Misty said.

"I like talking with you. It takes my mind off Sue."

"Maybe it would help if you, like, talked about her," Misty said.

"What do you want to know?" Jay asked.

"You sound worried about her."

"Her mom says she's in the hospital."

"She's, like, really sick, then?" Misty asked.

"I don't know. Her mom found her semiconscious on the bathroom floor."

"That's scary," Misty said.

"She couldn't talk or anything, so they took her to the hospital. They're doing tests."

"It sounds serious."

"She's such a great girl. I'm really worried."

"Isn't there anything they can do?"

"I won't know until I get there."

"You must know just everything about Manitoba, Jay. Tell me about it."

"I'm afraid I don't know all that much," Jay said. "Only what I read in magazines and the newspaper."

"Like what?"

"Like Manitoba grows the best marijuana in the world. It's one of our major exports. People say it's better than the best Jamaican."

Troy looked over with sudden interest. "Dude. I thought Vancouver was the drug capital of Canada. That's where B.C. Bud comes from. It's our most common pot."

"The police estimate that Canada grows something like 800 tons of illegal marijuana a year. It may be British Columbia's biggest cash crop, however, for the home-grown designer stuff, Manitoba's the place."

"Marijuana's illegal in Canada, isn't it?" Misty asked.

"Except for some medicinal uses."

"The way they walk it across the border in gym bags you'd think nobody cared."

"Is it that easy to get it across?" Jay asked.

"They have to walk through the bush areas and then get picked up on the other side," Misty explained. "But yes, there's a constant flow of marijuana going one way and cocaine the other."

Troy pulled off his headphones. "Suppose I had this killer backache. Could I buy pot legally?" he asked.

"You'd have to get a photo I.D. so you wouldn't get arrested for possession."

"So, if I have an I.D. I can buy all the pot I want on the street?"

"You'd have to buy it from the government. They have strict rules about who's sick enough to qualify. You need two doctors' signatures. There are only about three hundred people in all of Canada who been approved to use marijuana medically."

"I'll bet that number will go up in a hurry once the word gets out. Where does the government get it? From the drug dealers?" Troy asked.

"That'd be too easy," Jay said. "Originally the law allowed the patients to grow it themselves or get someone else to grow it for them."

"That sounds unrealistic. If they're sick, they probably don't need that kind of hassle."

"It's a new idea. I'm sure they'll come up with a better one."

If Jay had known all the facts, he would have told Troy about the Federal Government's experiment in growing legal marijuana. A deserted mine shaft under Trout Lake in northern Manitoba near the town of Flin Flon was adapted for the hydroponic growing of marijuana under strict security and a thousand meters of solid granite. A five-year contract worth almost six million dollars was awarded to a gardening firm to produce a trial crop of some 600 grams of legal marijuana the first year, making it undoubtedly the most expensive pot on the planet. The project is kept under a high level of security measures. Why anyone would want to steal government-produced marijuana with a THC content of 6 percent, when the supply currently available on most street corners is 16 percent, has not been clearly explained.

"What else is Manitoba famous for?" Misty asked.

"It's probably the world's hog capital. Besides the boars for Hannibal, Manitoba farmers raised five million pigs last year and plan to produce

10 million next year. We'll have at least four times as many pigs as people."

"Unreal. It must stink like a…well…a pig sty," Misty said.

"It's a big province. I guess the stench blows away. The sewage dis-
posal is always in the newspapers as a big problem in the country."

"I'd never even heard of Manitoba before Troy got his job there,"
Misty said. "In fact, I didn't think there was much of anything in
Canada."

"We have the longest recreational pathway in the world," Jay said.

"The what?"

"The Trans-Canada Trail. It's 16,000 kilometers of paved biking path.
Right across Canada. Coast to coast."

"What a cool idea," Misty said.

"I guess when you can't sit on the beach or ride the waves you have to
come up with some sort of imaginative things to do," Troy said.

"We do a lot of winter sports, like skiing, ice skating and snowmobil-
ing," Jay said.

"San Francisco is a radical area for sports. We've got the ocean on one
side and mountains for snow on the other."

"It must be great to live in San Francisco," Jay said.

"Oh. We don't live there. We live way south. In San Luis Obispo. It's
halfway between San Francisco and Los Angeles," Misty said.

Jay perked up.

"Do you know a place called Solvay or something like that?" he
asked.

"Maybe you're thinking of Solvang. It's close to Los Angeles."

"That's where I think my dad lives now. What can you tell me about
it?"

"It's well known as a Danish community. It's been all done up to look
like Denmark. Lots of tourists go there. That's all I know. I've never
been there."

The flight was uneventful, with Troy listening to his headset and Misty reading a romance novel. Jay wondered why Misty was served a different lunch from everyone else, but he didn't ask. He preferred to keep his thoughts on Sue and the memories of good times spent with her.

SNOW, SNOW, GO AWAY

Troy and Misty crowded together to look out the tiny window as the airplane began its descent to Winnipeg.

"It's pretty with all those lights," Misty gushed.

"Dude. There's nothing there but a bunch of lights sitting on a plate of snow. What's with all the nothingness around it?"

"See those tiny groups of lights?" Jay asked. "They're farms."

"Those highways go out in all directions but they don't go anywhere. They just disappear into the night," Troy said.

"There are towns," Jay said defensively. "We just can't see them."

"They must be miles apart. We have wall-to-wall towns where we come from," Misty said.

"The rest is farmland. Southern Manitoba is mostly grain and vegetable farms," Jay explained.

"We'd better set our watches ahead two hours," Misty said to Troy.

"Dude. No wonder it's so dark."

In the airport immigration area Misty and Troy went to a one booth and Jay to another. Jay was one of the chosen few to have his luggage inspected.

"Where's your luggage?" the inspector asked.

"I don't have any except this bag I carried on," Jay replied. "I had to leave suddenly."

The inspector looked up with interest. "You had to leave suddenly?"

"My girlfriend's in the hospital here in Winnipeg."

The customs inspector peered at Jay, stamped his form and said, "Oh. Go right on through."

Jay hustled through the exit door and was jogging up the stairs when he heard a voice call, "Jay. Over here."

He looked back and saw Helen, Sue's mother.

"Mrs. Parkington. What are you doing here?" he asked.

"I came to meet you," answered the neatly dressed, middle-aged lady, as she fussed with her gloves.

"How could you have known I was coming? I didn't have time to phone. I'll bet R.B. sent you a message. Like he did to me."

"Who's R.B.?"

"His name is really Running Bear. We call him R.B. for short. I don't think you know him."

"No. Who is he?" Helen asked.

"He's the native shaman I met at the Red Dragon restaurant when I started working there. If it wasn't R.B., how did you know?"

"Your friend, Steve, phoned me from California. He said to tell you he'd pick up your stuff from the hotel and bring it with him when he comes back. I brought you my husband's overcoat. In case you've forgotten, Winnipeg is cold in December."

Helen handed Jay the overcoat.

"Thanks. Anyway, as soon as I got the message I knew I had to come quickly."

"The message from R.B.?"

"Well, not directly from him but I'm sure he had something to do with it. It's a bit complicated. I was on the beach and an eagle feather fell to the ground at my feet. When I picked it up, it spoke to me. Well, it didn't exactly speak, but somehow I knew I had to phone you. This vision comes to me sometimes. It's as if R.B. talks to me through the spirit of my guardian eagle. He told me that Sue needed my help. It sounds crazy now but it was totally real at the time."

"Whatever it was, I'm grateful. However, you should have taken time to pack."

"I have a bad feeling about Sue. Is she any better?"

"The medical tests haven't found any physical problem. She just lies there staring into space. It's as if she's in a trance. They keep doing more tests every day. Maybe they'll tell us something soon," Helen explained.

"Can we go to the hospital right now, please? I need to see her."

"Certainly. It's past visiting hours but I'm sure they'll let us in. When you've financed an entire research wing they're willing to bend the rules a bit for you."

"Your husband did that?" Jay asked.

"In a way, yes. His father started it, so he felt obligated to carry it through to completion."

"I'm impressed by his generosity."

Sue's mother paid the parking ticket at the machine near the door. Misty and Troy stood nearby, discussing their next move.

"Is there any way we could we give those guys a ride?" Jay asked. "They're new here, and they look a bit lost."

"Sure. Anything for friends of yours, Jay," Helen said.

"Hey, Misty," Jay called, "would you guys like a ride?"

"Dude," Troy replied with enthusiasm. "If it's not too much trouble."

Helen looked at Troy and Misty. She noticed their California clothes and gloveless hands.

"Why don't you two wait here with the luggage," she said, "while Jay and I get the car? We'll stop at the curb just outside the door."

Jay and Helen went out to the parking lot and climbed into her silver BMW sedan.

"Cool wheels," Jay said.

Helen guided the car gently onto the street. "I insisted my husband, George, get me the M5. Of course, he wanted to get me a big 750iL like he drives. He goes for show and luxury in everything. I like a car that handles well. Besides, this one cost about half as much as his."

"It still must have cost a fortune," Jay said.

"Not really. However, they did charge something called a gas guzzler tax, whatever that means."

Helen pulled the car around to the loading zone. Troy and Misty quickly loaded up the luggage and hopped into it.

"This is like, so nice of you guys," Misty said, blowing on her fingers to warm them. "It's colder than we expected."

"We didn't make arrangements or anything," Troy said. "Can you, like, recommend a hotel? Nothing too expensive. This is my first real job and we're low on cash."

"And we'll be even lower before the first payday rolls around," Misty added.

"I have an idea," Jay said. "I used to stay with this guy, Phil. My old room is probably still empty. Maybe you could stay there. Do you want me to check with him for you?"

"We wouldn't want to impose on him," Troy said.

"Trust me. He'll enjoy the company. He was pretty down about my leaving."

"Why did you leave, then?"

"I got hired at this restaurant on the other side of town. I moved to a room upstairs there so I'd be closer to work. You could stay with me except it's only a tiny single room."

"It would be way cool to stay with someone who knows the city. Maybe you could phone him and, like, check it out?" Misty asked.

"I have to see Sue first. If you don't mind waiting at the hospital I'll phone him afterwards," Jay said.

"You can use the car phone," Helen suggested.

Jay took the phone. "What's the security number?"

"2137."

Jay smiled.

"What's funny?" Helen asked.

"That's your house number."

"I use the same number for everything. It makes life so much easier."

Jay spoke into the phone:

"Hi Phil."

" . . . "

"I'm back in Winnipeg."

" . . . "

"It's a long story. I'll tell you later."

" . . . "

"Yes. I came back to see her. You've talked to Steve?"

" . . . "

"I have a couple of friends who are looking for a temporary place to stay."

" . . . "

"They're your kind of people." Jay turned around and winked at Troy and Misty.

" . . . "

"Well, they're Californians. He's going into film work."

" . . . "

"We'd be coming over after I see Sue."

" . . . "

"Think about it. I'll give you a call before we come over."

" . . . "

"It'll be good to see you again, too."

Jay and Helen went into the hospital waiting room. They were met by stark white walls, a polished tile floor, and a vaguely antiseptic odor. It was deserted except for the nurse on duty.

"Let me talk to her," Helen said to Jay as they walked over to the desk.

After a brief but intense discussion, the nurse led them down an empty hallway. Their footsteps echoed eerily in the silence as if the whole building were deserted. The nurse opened a door for them and with a curt nod indicated they could enter. The hospital room was empty except for a single bed in the middle. A private nurse sat near the door, blankly staring into space through half-closed eyes. Troy and Misty waited outside the door.

Jay felt his chest tighten with nervous anticipation. His breathing became shallow and rapid as he peered at the solitary figure lying on the bed, hidden by a sheet.

Helen whispered into Jay's ear as they walked toward the bed. "We got a private room for her and she has nursing care twenty-four hours a day. She's getting the best care money can buy but she doesn't seem to be responding."

Jay stood by the bed without speaking, looking down at Sue's wan face. He took her hand and held it gently between his. Her blank stare moved to his face. Their eyes met, then locked in a silent, intense embrace. The seconds stretched into minutes. Jay sat gently on the edge of the bed. There was no reaction from Sue except for a small tear working its way slowly down her cheek.

Jay reached over and brushed the tear aside. "I love you, Sue," Jay said. "I'm back now and I'll look after you. Things will be all right, you'll see."

"What should we do?" Helen asked. "It's as if she's paralyzed."

"I don't think it's as much physical as it is mental," Jay said.

Jay looked back at Sue. "Trust me. I'll make everything all right for you," he said to her.

"We'd better go now," Helen said.

Jay leaned over and kissed Sue a gentle goodbye. "You just rest. I'll be back soon."

They walked toward the door.

"I think we should get her out of here," Jay said.

"The psychiatrist says she'll be going on some medication soon. She'll have to stay here for observation. They'll want to talk to her," Helen said.

"This isn't the right place for her. I think you know that. We have to get her out of here so she gets some mental stimulation. She needs to be with me so I can look after her."

"She's getting the best care money can buy here."

"It's not medicine that she needs," Jay said. "I want to take her out of the hospital even if we have to kidnap her. It's the only way she can get the understanding and support she needs."

"You can't do that, Jay," Helen said.

"I think it would be the best thing to do. She'll just stay in her shell if we leave her here."

"We'll have to see what George says. He's her father and what he says is law."

"I'm sure he'll understand," Jay said.

"Let's get these two friends of yours looked after first," Helen said.

Jay and Helen joined Troy and Misty in the hallway.

"How is she?" Misty asked.

"It's hard to know. She doesn't say anything," Helen said.

"Give me a minute to check with Phil, again," Jay said, heading toward the pay phone.

"Jay's like, such a caring guy," Misty said to Helen. "Sue's a lucky girl."

"You're right. I used to think he was a bit flaky but it does feel good to have him here now."

"He's one righteous dude, for sure," Troy said.

Jay returned from phoning. "Phil says to come on over. I knew he wouldn't let us down."

Troy, Misty and Jay knocked on the door of Phil's apartment. The man who opened the door had the look of a typical Harley-Davidson biker: husky, a bit thick in the stomach, with a bushy red beard. His piercing bright eyes, deep-set beneath shaggy red eyebrows, surveyed them with an air of apparent suspicion.

"This is a pleasant surprise, Jay," he said with a friendly smile that belied his gruff bearing and raspy voice.

"Troy, Misty, this is Phil. He's my ersatz mother," Jay said. With a wide grin he added, "It's my new word-of-the-day."

Misty said, "Hi, Phil."

Troy said, "Dude," and flashed a friendly smile.

"I hope you don't mind my suggesting they might stay with you until they get settled. You did such a great job looking after me, I thought you might like to help them out a bit."

"And what made you think that?" Phil asked.

"It's more like I felt guilty about leaving you the way I did," Jay said. "Maybe it doesn't make sense now that I say it. It just seemed like a good idea."

"This is the living room," Phil said, waving toward the area beyond the threadbare hide-a-bed. A white leather recliner, sitting in front of the small TV, looked out of place in the rundown surroundings. The flowered wallpaper was faded and cracked. There were no pictures on the walls.

"Jay's room is still empty and I do like company," Phil said.

They stepped into Jay's former room. "Cool. A waterbed," Troy said, sitting on it and bouncing up and down.

Jay picked up a set of keys off the timeworn wooden dresser that used to be his. He opened the closet door to display the few clothes hanging there.

"Use whatever you want. They were too big for me so they might fit you," Jay said.

"It isn't much but you're welcome to it," Phil said.

"Dude. It's great," Troy said. "However, you have to let us pay. We don't take charity."

"We can talk about that later. Did Jay tell you I'm vegetarian?" Phil asked.

"Way cool," Misty gushed. "I'm like, vegan, too."

"Well, I'm not a vegan. I eat eggs and milk but we should be able to work things out around that."

Jay interrupted with a grin. "Phil will look after you just like an old mother hen."

"How did the search for your dad work out?" Phil asked, happy to shift the conversation away from himself.

"I talked to a fellow who worked with him. From what he said I'm sure it's my dad. Apparently, he moved south to somewhere near Los Angeles."

"You feel better about it now?" Phil prodded.

"Not really. If anything, I'm more anxious than ever to find him now. I've got to meet him so I can see what I'm going to be like when I grow up."

"Children don't always grow up like their parents," Phil said.

"Maybe not but I won't be at peace until I know something about him."

"You're getting close. You'll find him."

"Sorry to run, but I left Sue's mother in the car. We're going over to talk to Sue's dad."

"Okay," Phil said. "Drop around soon, Jay. I want to hear more about your trip."

"Good luck. Let us know how things work out," Misty said.

"Dude," Troy called from the kitchen.

~ 3 ~

LIFE ON THE LEDGE

Sue's mother sat on the edge of the chair in her living room. Jay leaned back, sinking as inconspicuously as possible into the plush sofa. Sue's father, George, paced up and down, taking long pulls from his glass of Scotch. His shirt collar was unbuttoned, his tie loosened and his double-breasted suit jacket hung open.

"You're telling me she's just the same? No change at all?" George asked.

Helen replied, "She lies there, staring into space. I can't even tell if she recognizes me."

"The psychiatrist called it conversion disorder," George said.

"What does that mean?" Helen asked.

"He says it's severe hysteria resulting from trauma. They'll start treatment tomorrow," George said.

Helen's eyes opened in surprise. "Not electric shock, I hope."

"They don't do that any more," George said.

"I read that some hospitals are starting to use it again. I'd hate to have that for her."

"He'll use Pentothal to get her started talking. Maybe they'll try hypnosis but that will have to be later."

"I don't like the sound of that," Helen said.

George scowled in Jay's direction. "Why did you bring him here?"

"Jay thinks he can help," Helen replied.

"I'm sure he does. What could he do?"

"He thinks the hospital isn't the right place for her."

"Where does he think she should be? Up north on some Indian reserve?"

Jay cleared his throat. "I don't live up north anymore. I live here now."

"What are you suggesting?"

"We need to get her out of the hospital."

"Great. Where would she go? To that dive of yours above the Red Dragon? Never."

Jay swallowed. "There are people who would help us."

"Like your crazy old Indian friend?"

"Indians are people who came from India," Jay countered quietly. "We refer to them as first nation people."

"Don't get smart with me, kid," George said, glaring at Jay.

"R.B. is a respected first nation elder, and a shaman besides," Jay continued.

George went over to the solid oak sideboard, refilled his glass and muttered, "Whatever."

"Our friends would help us but I'm not counting on anyone else. I know I can help Sue because I've been there," Jay said.

"We've all been to the hospital. That doesn't prove anything."

"I didn't mean the hospital. I meant I know what she is experiencing," Jay said.

"How could you possibly know anything about this? You have no medical credentials. You haven't even finished high school."

"I may not have any formal credentials but I do know how to help Sue."

George frowned at Jay. "Do you think you know more than the best doctors money can buy? What do you know about the world? You're way out of your depth here. I put my faith in people with medical training and experience. You get what you pay for in this world."

"Doctors deal with the physical body," Jay said. "Sue's problem isn't physical. It's spiritual and emotional."

"What would you know about that? You don't have a degree in psychology," George countered.

"Maybe I'm not educated but I've had some experiences in my life. I try to learn from them."

"I pay attention to people who have credentials."

Jay's face betrayed his frustration and annoyance. However, he kept his voice low and calm. "You want credentials? I'll show you credentials," he said, taking off one of his shoes. Jay pulled off the sock, exposing his foot, ringed with a neat row of cigarette burns. "These are my credentials from when I was twelve. He said it was another notch on his six-shooter every time he did one. I never understood what he meant but I knew it wasn't good."

Jay pulled his T-shirt over his head and turned to expose the welts on his back. "And these are my most recent credentials."

"How horrible, Jay. Why would anyone do that to you?" Helen gasped.

"The latest of my mother's boyfriends tried to teach me how to behave. I didn't learn well. At least he cared enough about me to make the effort to teach me. It was better than being ignored. I appreciated the time and effort he spent. I'm sorry I could never please him. Sometimes I did try."

George returned from the sideboard with another drink, which he set on the table.

Helen absent-mindedly reached over and put a coaster under it.

"I'm sorry. It must have hurt terribly," she said.

"The physical pain soon goes away but the emotional effect lasts. It saps your spirit and will eventually rot your soul unless it's stopped."

"Can't you talk it out?" Helen asked.

"Who can you tell? There's no one who would understand, even if they did believe you. Soon you feel guilty about keeping secrets from those you love. You come to feel that it must somehow be your fault. If it weren't, you should be able to talk about it."

George plopped heavily into his armchair. He took a long pull on his drink and set the glass down, missing the coaster. He wiped his salt-and-pepper mustache with the back of his hand.

"It's too bad about the things that happened to you but it has nothing to do with Sue. We know she hasn't been beaten or abused," he said.

"There doesn't have to be anything physical. It can be an emotional conflict that the person is trying to resolve. Starting to talk about it can be hopelessly difficult," Jay said. "I've had the experience of sitting with someone who is ready to listen, but the words don't come. We'd end up talking about the weather or sports."

"It's like making it rain," Helen said.

George rolled his eyes. "Here we go again."

Helen continued. "When they try to make it rain they seed the clouds with potassium iodide crystals. This makes a nucleus for the moisture to condense around and to form a rain drop."

"That's surprisingly accurate," Jay said. "There needs to be a beginning point to break through the wall."

"Like when they put a little nick in the cellophane peanut packet so…"

"Stop already," George interrupted.

Helen looked thoughtfully into space. "I've heard of soldiers in the war whose arms become paralyzed. They can't hold a gun and have to be sent back home."

Jay continued. "In Sue's case her brain shut down to protect her from having to deal with something."

"What could it be?" Helen asked.

"It doesn't matter so much what it was. It was important to her and that's what matters. If we don't act quickly, the wall will get thicker and it'll become harder to get through to her."

Helen looked at George. "Maybe it's like people who become temporarily blind after witnessing a gruesome accident. Or a person who develops amnesia because…"

George interrupted again. "I still don't see how this has anything to do with Sue."

"It isn't something you can explain to people who haven't experienced it. When I look into her eyes I see fear and pain sapping her spirit," Jay said.

"Sue's getting the best treatment money can buy."

"She doesn't need medicine or treatment. She needs someone who understands her feeling of isolation."

"We pay psychiatrists to do that. What do you think you can do that they can't do?" George asked Jay.

"I'm what's called a wounded healer. In matters of the spirit the healer needs to have experienced the emotional pain himself in order to understand it."

"It's like a white man can never totally understand the feelings of an oppressed black man," Helen said.

"He can only treat the physical symptoms and hope the spirit will heal itself," Jay continued. "The symptoms may disappear but the sickness in the spirit remains to fester and corrode the soul."

"It's like if you've never lived on a reserve…"

George interrupted, "We get the idea, Helen. Jay, you don't mean to sit there and tell me you want us to take Sue out of the hospital and away from all medical treatment, do you?"

"I know that she needs to feel safe enough to be herself. She needs to feel acceptance without having expectations placed on her. This won't happen in the hospital but I can give her that."

"What makes you think that will help her?"

"I know what it's like to curl up in a corner with the blanket over your head, wishing for the world to go away. I was lucky because there was nobody to take me away to some friendly, antiseptic hospital where everyone would take care of me and look after my needs. Eventually, hunger and the smell of stale urine forced me to come to grips with my own reality."

"She could come here. Surely she'd feel safe here," Helen said.

"Physically safe, yes, but you'd expect answers from her. She needs to feel safe enough to cry without having to explain why."

"We wouldn't pressure her," Helen said.

"You wouldn't intend to but the expectation would be there. It's as if Sue is standing on the edge of a cliff. She's afraid to move for fear of falling. You'd want to help so much that you might push or pull and make her lose her balance. She needs someone to walk beside her. To be there if she needs a hand to hold but not trying to help."

"It's like helping a blind man," Helen said. "You never take him by the arm to guide him. You offer your arm for him to take so he's in control."

"What's the difference whether you take his arm or he takes yours?" George asked. "Help is help. Sue needs help. She needs to face reality."

"There will be a time for that but right now she needs to come to grips with her emotions in her own way. A different environment would make it easier for her," Jay said.

"Maybe we should tell Jay what we think was troubling Sue before we found her on the bathroom floor," Helen said.

"No. It's a family matter. We don't discuss family with strangers."

"Jay's not exactly a stranger, George. They did go steady for several months and even you must know how upset she was when she and Jay broke up. He's the only person who is offering us any real hope for helping her."

"You don't need to tell me anything," Jay said. "Sue needs help on a feeling level not a factual level. Maybe it's better I know nothing other than what she chooses to tell me."

George poured himself another drink. "If we let you take Sue out of the hospital, and I'm not saying I will, where would she go if she doesn't come here?"

"I have friends who would take us in. We look after each other like family. Any of us would put his own life on hold without even being asked to help. That's what true friendship is all about."

"I won't have her in some slum like that Red Dragon place where you live," George said, setting the glass down beside the coaster.

"There isn't room for her there, anyway," Jay said.

"Jimmy and Becky's place isn't much better. Besides he's a crook, a convict and a drug addict."

"He's given up drugs."

"His kind can never give up the drugs and anyway that doesn't make him any less of a thief."

"He's served his time. Now he's following the red road."

"What's a red road?"

"Sorry. You'd say the 'straight and narrow'. Red road is the term native prisoners use."

"He's an Indian too, is he?"

"No. He picked up the expression when he was in jail. I like the term red road better than the straight and narrow. It sounds less restrictive, more positive and flexible."

"How's that?"

"It offers the opportunity to smell the flowers along the way, and to romp in the meadows, so long as you are headed toward the right goal."

"None of that makes him less of a crook. He's a *no-goodnick.*"

"Jimmy's a caring guy who'd share anything with his friends."

"That doesn't say much when he doesn't have anything to share."

"He's been a good friend to me. I trust him. He and I share everything we have," Jay said.

"Big deal. Neither one of you has anything of value and never will. He'd steal the milk out of your tea if you weren't watching him every minute."

"He never steals from people he knows."

"That doesn't help me much. He's a *shmuck.* By the way, don't forget to get his watch back," George said.

"What do you know about his watch?" Jay asked with interest.

"I know you pawned it to get the cash to go to California. Never pawn an old Rolex like that. It's worth way more than they'll give you for it."

Jay looked thoughtful. "You're probably right," he said automatically.

George continued. "Steve at least has a job and a decent apartment but he's a flaming faggot. His place is probably a hangout for all kinds of gay orgies. I don't want Sue around with those kinds of people."

"Steve's still in San Francisco."

"Phil's place is decent but he's emotionally unstable. That's why they fired him from the police force. I wouldn't want anyone to find out I'm having my daughter stay with a crazy man."

Jay looked confused. "How do you know more about my friends than I do? Did you have me investigated while I was dating Sue?"

"Certainly. What's the use in having money if it doesn't buy you the information you want? Knowledge is power. Not as powerful as money, however, because money can buy knowledge."

"Money can buy information," Helen corrected gently, "not knowledge."

"What about Cam and Jamie? Accountants are respectable and their apartment is decent. Or don't you like them because she's pregnant?" Jay asked.

"My man never mentioned any Cam and Jamie. Who are they?"

"Friends."

"Great. I pay that guy a small fortune and he still doesn't do a proper job. He'll never work for me again. Come to think of it, he didn't report on Tanya, either."

"There's nothing to say about Tanya."

"Sue told us you went out with Tanya. She was jealous about that. That wasn't very gentlemanly of you."

"Tanya has absolutely nothing to do with anything," Jay said, a bit too loudly.

George looked sternly at Jay. Jay's gaze dropped to the floor.

"You protest too much. You're still interested in her, aren't you?" George asked.

Jay opened his mouth to reply but was interrupted by Helen. "What about a hotel? That would be respectable."

"She should be here with us where she belongs," George said, refilling his glass.

"She's nineteen years old and can do what she wants," Helen said.

"Not in her present condition she can't."

"Maybe Jay does know what she needs. Why don't we give him a chance?" Helen asked.

"I don't plan to give him a chance to do anything. I don't want that *klutz* anywhere near my daughter."

"You know she won't talk to anyone else. We have very little choice."

George looked at his drink. Jay stared at the floor. Helen looked back and forth between the two.

Finally, George drained his glass. "I'll make a call to the Birchwood Inn. You know the one. It's close by, just over the Moray Street Bridge. It's one of Winnipeg's prestige hotels."

"If it doesn't work out she can always go back to the hospital," Helen said.

"However, I want you to understand, young man, that I'll be reserving a two-room suite and I expect you and Sue to be in separate rooms."

"Oh, George," Helen exclaimed. "It's insulting when you talk like that. You need to learn to trust people more. Besides, the Birchwood's now a Holiday Inn."

"I didn't get to where I am today by trusting every *momzer* who comes along in hopes of latching onto our daughter and our money."

"I understand what you mean, sir. You may not know me well enough to trust me, but I do love Sue. I can assure you Sue's well-being is, and always will be, foremost in my mind."

"And no psychic stuff or Indian mumbo-jumbo."

"It's settled then?" Helen said. "We'll pick her up tomorrow."

"Right now, please," Jay pleaded. "Time is important."

"I don't drive at night," Helen said. "We could go now if you'll drive, Jay."

"I'd be happy to. I'll drive carefully," Jay said, looking at George.

"Take Sue's Mustang, Helen," George said. "I don't want anything to happen to your new BMW."

"Do you need your overcoat back, sir? I'd like to keep it for a day or two until Steve brings me my parka from California, if you don't mind."

"Why would you take a parka to California?"

"I wore it to the airport and didn't know what else to do with it except to take it with me."

"Whatever," George said, heading back to the sideboard.

Jay and Helen talked as they drove to the hospital. "Is George Jewish?" Jay asked.

"No. Why do you ask?"

"What's with those strange expressions? They sounded Jewish."

"It's Yiddish he picked up from the neighbors. A lot of Jewish people have moved into the neighborhood. Unfortunately, George is fascinated by some of their less complimentary terms. He tries to be sociable but he doesn't have much in common with them. It's his attempt to bond with the neighbors. I try to keep him from using them but when he gets a bit too much to drink he likes to insult people in Yiddish. He thinks he can get away with it because people won't know meaning of the words."

~ 4 ~

THE GREAT ESCAPE

The hospital waiting room was still empty except for the nurse behind the desk. "You go and sign Sue out while I go and get her," Jay said.

"This is crazy, Jay. It's after 11 o'clock. They'll never discharge her at this hour."

"You go talk to the nurse. I'll be right back."

Jay went down the silent hallway to Sue's room. He tiptoed past the private nurse who was dozing in a chair beside the door. Taking off his borrowed overcoat, he wrapped it around Sue and scooped her up in his arms.

He got as far as the hallway before a nurse challenged him. "Hold on. What do you think you're doing?"

"Checking out," Jay replied.

"You need a wheelchair to move a patient."

"Of course. Would you get us one, please?"

While the nurse went in search of a wheelchair, Jay continued out to the exit with Sue in his arms.

"She says the doctor has to sign the release form," Helen said.

"Fine. Tell her the doctor will do it in the morning," Jay called from the doorway.

Helen joined Sue and Jay in the car. "What are you doing to me? I've never done anything like this before in my life. We could get in trouble for this, couldn't we?"

"A person has to do what seems right at the time. Maybe we'd better get going before they call the police," Jay urged.

"Can they charge us with kidnapping?" Helen asked.

"I doubt it. After all, you're her mother. Besides, if they don't catch us, they can't arrest us. There's a Sev. Do you mind if I pull in there, please?"

"A what?"

"A 7-Eleven store. I'll pick up a snack and some stuff for breakfast. Can I get you a Slurpee?"

"A what?"

"A Slurpee. You've never had one? They're a crushed ice sort of thing."

"It's wintertime. I doubt they're selling crushed ice this time of year."

"Sevs sell them all year long."

Jay got back into the car with a bag of supplies and a Blue Raspberry Slurpee. He passed it to Helen. "Try it."

Helen took a tentative sip. "Mmm. Sweet." She took a long drink. "Oh. It's great."

"Don't drink it too fast or it'll freeze your head," Jay warned.

Helen gave Jay a quizzical look, and took another long drink.

"I'm not kidding," Jay said, taking the drink from Helen. "It can give you a major brain freeze. They don't last long but they really hurt."

"You're so protective, Jay. I like that."

"You mean to tell me you've never had one of these before?"

"Never. George and I don't spend a lot of time in 7-Eleven stores."

"Manitoba is probably the Slurpee Capital of the World."

"You're making that up, aren't you?" Helen asked.

"Macleans newsmagazine reported that Manitoba 7-Eleven stores sell almost twice as many Slurpees a month as the Canadian average. There are some 30 million sold in Canada every year."

"That's a lot."

"Well, that's only one per year for each Canadian," Jay said.

"I doubt that everyone buys one."

"It works out. I buy enough to make up for those who don't."

"You're quite the source of trivia, aren't you?" Helen said. "How do you remember things like that?"

"Whatever I read just seems to stick in my head," Jay said. "Maybe it's because my head was empty for so long."

He drove to Portage Avenue and turned left.

"This isn't the way to the Holiday Inn, Jay. You need to turn right," Helen said.

"We're not going there."

"Are you kidnapping me, too?"

"It depends entirely on your reaction to what's happening. We're going to Steve's apartment. He'll be in San Francisco for a few more days. I have a key. If you don't want to come with me, then I guess I'm kidnapping you. If you don't mind, then I'm not. The facts are unimportant. It's your reaction to what's happening that is real."

"It's like the Polynesians say: the world is what you think it is," Helen said.

"I guess so," Jay said. "In many ways our minds do create our own reality."

"What's wrong with the Holiday Inn?"

"Nothing. I'm sure it's a fine hotel, and it would be better than the hospital. Still, it's a stagnant environment. There's no feeling of life in a hotel. The rooms are cheerless and static, with no hope of a future nor memory of a past."

"Like a rain cloud without a nucleus."

Jay let Helen's simile float by. "Steve's place pulsates with vitality and life."

"We should go and check you into the Holiday Inn to keep George happy. He'll be angry if he phones there and finds you're not registered. You don't have to stay there, just so long as you're signed in."

Jay made a U-turn and they drove to the hotel.

"Maybe we should tell your husband what we're doing," Jay suggested.

"I don't want to get into a hassle with him about it right now."

"I'll tell him, if you want me to."

"No. What he doesn't know won't hurt him," Helen said.

"You know best, but I'd rather we tell him."

"You and Sue can wait in the car. I'll go in and look after the room."

Helen started toward the hotel, then stopped and returned to the car.

"This is embarrassing. I don't know your full name," Helen said.

"Jay Winston Maytwayashing."

"Oh, dear. Maybe it would be simpler if I register it under my own name."

Helen came back to the car after registering. "If you decide to use the room, it's number 305. You might as well take me home and keep the car. There isn't much more I can do now."

"Thanks for all your help. I couldn't have done it without you," Jay said.

"Drop me at the door. I'm not going to tell George anything except that we got a room at the Holiday Inn. I hope he doesn't try to phone you or we'll both be in his bad books."

"I still think we should be honest with him."

"If I have to, I'll tell him in the morning when he's sober."

Helen leaned over and kissed Sue.

"Her eyes followed me," Helen said to Jay.

"Don't tell me. Talk to her," Jay said. "She needs to have people talking to her, not about her. She needs to regain her place in the world."

Helen put her mouth to Sue's ear and whispered intently for a moment.

"Here's my American Express card. Use it for whatever you might need, Jay. The PIN number is the same as the security alarm for the house. You remember what it is, don't you?"

"It's the same as your house number, right?" Jay asked with a grin.

"I know it's not smart but it's the easiest way for me to remember. Take as much money as you need. All I ask is that you be good to my daughter. Give me a call in the morning."

Jay fumbled for his key in the foyer of Steve's apartment, trying to keep Sue protected from the cold with her father's overcoat, and all the time carrying on a rambling monologue.

"I'll have to put you down for a minute until I get the door open. Man. It's cold. I wonder why anyone would leave California to come to a place like this. Here we go. The door's open now."

Sue lifted her bare feet off the cold floor, one after the other, until Jay scooped her up again and carried her to the elevator. "We're going to be staying in Steve's apartment. I don't think you've ever been here before but I know you'll like it."

With his arm around Sue's waist, Jay guided her to the apartment door. The dull gray hallway carpet ended abruptly at the doorway. Sue's toes curled in and out of the apartment's plush white carpet, luxuriating in the soft texture, like a happy pussycat making itself comfortable.

They walked past the blue chintz-covered furniture and glass-topped dining room table surrounded by sculptured black metal chairs. The stark black and white posters portraying nude male figures caught Sue's attention as they walked to the kitchen.

"Sit here while I get you a robe," Jay said.

He returned and slipped a dressing gown over Sue's shoulders. The expensive silk felt smooth and sensual against her skin. "It's lovely, isn't it," he said. "You have to watch out because it has a mind of its own and it'll slip open if you aren't careful. Silk's like that. Here's a glass of milk and some cookies for a late evening snack. They're Oreos. Your favorite. I have to make a quick phone call, and then I'll be back."

Jay spoke into the phone:

"Hi Jimmy. I need you to do me a favor."

"..."

"What I need right now is for you and Becky to move into the Holiday Inn for a few days in case anyone is looking for Sue or me."

"..."

"It's all taken care of. If anybody questions you, tell them you're me."

"..."

"No, we aren't hiding out. I'll explain later."

"..."

"It's that fancy one on Portage Avenue. It's called Airport West, I think."

"..."

"You can charge meals and stuff to the room."

"..."

"No, you can't. Food and necessities. Nothing else."

"..."

"I suppose in your case a few beers could be considered a necessity."

"..."

"Whatever you think is fair."

"..."

"If anyone phones tell them I'm out and I'll call them back later. Then phone me here at Steve's place."

"..."

"Yeah. I had a good time. I'll tell you about it later. I've got to go now."

Jay ended the conversation and returned to Sue. "We'll play a quick game of Snakes and Ladders and then get you to bed. Sorry there isn't a better choice of games. Steve doesn't go in much for board games. Somehow, I don't think Truth or Dare is what we would want to play right now."

Jay rolled the dice, moved the pieces for both of them and carried on an animated dialogue with himself throughout the game. Occasionally he miscounted moves to ensure Sue stayed ahead of him.

"You win," Jay said with enthusiasm. "That means you get to have me carry you to the bedroom as your prize."

Jay tucked Sue into bed, gave her a gentle, loving hug, and slid under the covers on his side of the bed.

~ 5 ~

BATTLE OF THE VEGGIES

As usual, Phil got up early to do some baking and to prepare vegetables for the day's meals. He tried to work quietly so as not to disturb Troy and Misty who were still sleeping in their room.

"Dude. That smells good," Troy said as he came into the kitchen. "We, like, had a totally awesome sleep last night, dude. That waterbed is one wild ride."

"Just like riding the surf?" Phil asked.

"As if. But it's way cool."

"Glad to hear that," Phil said.

"And speaking of water, your toilet is, like, wicked."

"It's a regular toilet. Aren't they all the same?"

39

"No way. Five years ago, our toilets had their water cut in half as a conservation thing. Their flushes are way wimpy now. Yours are, like, totally emphatic."

"Maybe you could start a business selling them in California, eh?"

"I'd make a fortune. But I'd rather become famous in the film industry."

"How about breakfast? I usually make crepes but they have eggs and milk. You did say you were a vegan, didn't you?"

"Misty's vegan. I usually, you know, go along with whatever she wants because she does the cooking. I'm cool with anything. When I'm by myself, I'm a total carnivore."

Misty came in. "I eat plant products only. Since you're already, like, vegetarian, it's only a matter of cutting out the dairy stuff. You know, like milk and butter."

"And eggs," added Troy.

Troy sat across the table from Phil. "You're such a righteous bro, Phil. We're most appreciative of your killer hospitality."

Phil smiled broadly. "It's great to have you here. I love your company, and your accent."

Troy and Misty exchanged looks and laughed.

"We were saying last night you Canadians have such a cute accent. What's with the 'eh' thing, anyway?" Troy asked.

"It's a general question expression. Canadians don't like to be too pushy, so when make a statement we soften it by making it into a sort of question. The French do the same thing with their *n'est-ce pas* at the end of a sentence."

"You Canadians, like, speak French, then?" Misty asked.

"Some of us, but not me. They say Canada is a bilingual country but it's mostly French in the East and English in the West."

"So officially there are two languages?"

"Well, sort of. We have our laws and cereal boxes in both languages. Except for the province of Quebec, of course. They actively promote French and discourage English as a way of preserving their culture.

Businesses in Quebec are required by law to have the English on their outdoor signs no more than half the size of the French."

"What a relief. I was afraid I might have to, like, learn French when I moved here," Troy said.

"Not unless you plan to work in Quebec."

"Cool. What kind of vegetarian are you?" Troy asked. "Ovo? Lacto? Ovo-lacto?"

"Ordinary garden variety. I eat eggs and dairy products."

"What about fish?"

"I'm a simplistic vegetarian. I don't eat anything with a face," Phil said.

Misty frowned. "You aren't a true vegetarian, then."

"I thought I was. My doctor said my cholesterol level was too high, so I started cutting out red meat. From there it gradually expanded to include all flesh."

"Not eating meat doesn't make you a true vegetarian. Being a vegetarian is a lifestyle and a philosophy. It's not only a food thing."

"I don't understand what you mean," Phil said. "It's how I eat, not how I am."

"We vegans are pro animal-rights. We oppose inflicting cruelty and pain on animals for economic gain."

"Whoa, Misty. Don't start with your preaching again. Phil can live his life any way he wants. We're his guests and we should be nice."

"It's all right, Troy," Phil said. "I relish a good discussion. I'm opposed to the killing of animals, too. I don't wear leather or fur because I don't want to be responsible for the needless death of an animal. However, I don't see what's wrong with drinking milk or eating eggs. It doesn't kill the animals to produce them."

"They raise chickens in tiny wire cages. They are nothing more than egg-producing machines. Male chicks are slaughtered and discarded because they are of no value in producing eggs."

"Would it be all right to eat free-range eggs?" Phil asked.

"In a perfect world it might be. Nevertheless, it's wrong to use chickens or any other animals for our own purposes when it isn't necessary. It's doubly wrong to make them suffer in order to increase the profit margin for the producers."

"What about milk? Cows produce milk naturally."

"Some cows are raised for the sole purpose of producing milk," Misty said.

"They are?"

"I don't know for sure. I've never even seen a real live cow. However, that's what I'm told. They should be free to live their lives as nature intended. Besides, do you know what happens to the calves produced as a byproduct of their pregnancy?"

"No."

"They're force-fed an inadequate diet to produce tender, light-colored meat and then slaughtered for sale as veal. This isn't what God intended when he created the world. I refuse to drink milk because of the pain and suffering associated with its production," Misty said.

"Besides, she's lactose intolerant," Troy added with a wry look.

"I have cereal but I don't know what you'd put on it," Phil said.

"Soy beverage is way cool. We drink a lot of it," Misty said.

"I tried it once a few years ago but it was gray, thin, and tasted like bitter beans," Phil said.

"It's totally excellent now. They even make different flavors, like vanilla, strawberry and chocolate. More like a milkshake than anything else."

"That sounds like an improvement since when I tried it," Phil said.

"I can eat the bran flakes dry or with water if you don't have milk. However, if you have orange juice, that would be the greatest. Bran is good because it's high in iron, and I always have orange juice with it because Misty says I should. I try to always do what she says."

Misty added, "The vitamin C makes plant iron easier to assimilate."

Phil looked at Misty. "I'll remember that. It's good to know even if one isn't vegan. Doesn't a vegan diet cause nutrition problems?"

"We have to watch out for a shortage of vitamins D and B12."

"Vitamin B12 is hard to come by if you don't eat meat products," Phil said. "I'm always concerned about getting enough B12."

"In California, we spend our time baking on the beach. That gives us killer amounts of natural vitamin D," Troy said.

"Manitoba gets a lot of sunlight. We call it sunny Manitoba," Phil said.

"Dude. With all your cold weather, nobody in his right mind is going outside. I'm surprised you aren't all suffering from a vitamin D deficiency," Troy said.

"Everybody's milk is fortified with vitamin D," Phil said.

"Soy beverage is too. In fact it's fortified with a wild assortment of vitamins and minerals like calcium, phosphorus, iron, and zinc to fill in almost anything you might be missing."

"I'm convinced. I'll pick up some this afternoon. For now, would tofu sausages and toast be all right?"

"Fine for me, thanks," Troy said. "You'd better ask Misty about the toast."

"Oh. Right. It'll take me awhile to get into the swing of this no-egg and nondairy thing."

"We usually make our own food. It's either that or spend hours reading labels."

"How about some honey for your toast?"

"I don't eat honey," Misty said.

"You've lost me again," Phil said. "What constitutes bee abuse?"

"It's a philosophical issue. It's not how they are raised, it's the reason for their life that's important."

"They make honey. We just steal some of it," Phil said.

"They're raised to make honey, and then sometimes they're killed at the end of the season."

"You mean, if instead of killing them off, they were left to die during the winter then it would be all right?"

"Not at all. They shouldn't be born in the first place if it's only for the pleasure or profit of people. They should be allowed to live and die in the fulfillment of their own destiny."

"That sounds like a rather fine line to me."

"Besides some poor little bees get accidentally squashed when the lids are put back on the hives," Misty added.

"That's an accident. It's not as if they're being deliberately killed."

"It's an accident that wouldn't happen if they weren't being raised for their honey in the first place. It's a needless death."

"I'll have to think about that. Let's get on with breakfast. Coffee?" Phil asked.

"Do you have tea?" Troy asked.

"Caffeine free," Misty added.

"You're in luck. I love herbal teas."

"Cool. We'll do a bit of grocery shopping later, but this is totally adequate for now."

"Give me a bit of time and I'll come up with some recipes for us," Phil said. "I've become pretty good at modifying regular recipes to make them vegetarian. Making them vegan shouldn't be too much more difficult."

"You'll find it surprisingly easy. A good way to start is to use soy beverage in place of milk or yogurt in all your usual vegetarian recipes. It sort of replaces butter, too."

"What about eggs? Most baking calls for eggs," Phil said.

"You can replace an egg with two tablespoons of corn starch or with a banana."

"This vegan cooking sounds like an interesting challenge," Phil said.

"I don't suppose you've ever used wheat gluten?" Troy asked.

"When I was a boy on the farm we used to take a handful of wheat and chew it until it got rubbery like gum."

"I wouldn't know about that. It's called 'seitan' in Asian food stores," Troy said.

"I have an idea," Phil said. "I'm planning to have people over for New Year's Day. Maybe we could use some wheat gluten in our dinner. It'll be a great chance to show you off to some of our friends."

"Dude. Way cool. That's a totally awesome idea. Misty and I have, like, no plans. Speaking of your friends, what's the deal with Sue and Jay? It sounds like Sue's in bad shape."

"Sue and Jay were an item last fall but her dad broke them up before Christmas."

"They take it hard?"

"I didn't think so at the time. As far as Jay was concerned, he seemed to take it in stride. Although, he did always say he was going to get back with her eventually."

"What about Sue."

"Her friends said she seemed to be sick a lot. Nothing major, just sick to her stomach. They said she seemed worried about something. Then a few days ago, she collapsed and they took her to the hospital. I don't know what it's all about except it seems more psychiatric than physical."

"You think she was that upset about losing Jay?"

"There must have been more to it than that, but I wouldn't want to guess."

"It was good of Jay to shorten his holiday to help," Misty said.

"It doesn't surprise me. He always said he was going to marry Sue, someday."

Phil, Troy and Misty finished their rather Spartan breakfast and talked while they washed and dried the dishes. The apartment was filled with the spicy fragrance of Good Earth herbal tea.

"You and Jay seem to be close friends," Misty said.

"He's more of a soul mate than anyone else I've ever met," Phil offered.

"He said you met by accident."

"We happened to be on the same bus to Winnipeg. Somehow, we recognized we needed to have each other in our lives. It was some sort of synchronicity."

"Dude. You lost me on that one. Excuse me, but I'm going to get cleaned up a bit," Troy said.

"That'll take the better part of an hour," Misty said to Phil. "He's totally particular about his image. Honestly, sometimes I think he must be gay or something. Sorry. What were you saying?"

"You know how things work by cause and effect?"

"Sure. One thing is the cause of something else. If I drink too much beer it will cause me to throw up."

"Well, synchronicity is like that except the two events occur simultaneously instead of one after the other."

"If they occur at the same time, one can't cause the other. Doesn't that make it a coincidence?"

"It's as if some cosmic plan makes the events happen together, for some reason we don't understand. You might say both the events cause each other."

"I get it. It's like Troy and I are here with you because we were assigned seats next to Jay on the airplane. If we hadn't been on the same flight, and had seats in the same row, we would never have met. Then we wouldn't be here with you now."

"Right. My life and yours are being affected by Jay, although he isn't directly the cause of any of it. Therefore, it isn't cause and effect. None the less, it's because of him we are having this conversation. It's synchronicity."

"Isn't it simply a coincidence?"

Phil replied, "It would be if it didn't have significant implications for us. Obviously, there are millions of events that occur at the same time. Only a few of these coincidental events are life changing. Jay's been a catalyst in my life and he still is. I think I've been an influence in his life. I consider that to be synchronicity."

"How would you try to prove synchronicity?"

"You can't prove something like that the way you prove cause and effect. Cause and effect is easy. If I drop something, it'll fall down."

"Unless it's a helium balloon. Then it falls up," Misty said.

"I meant in a vacuum."

"How often do you drop things in a vacuum?" Misty teased.

"Well, it's been done in the lab often enough. With things concerning humans, controlling conditions is hard. You can't put them in a lab. This is where the study of cause and effect breaks down when you try to apply it to people," Phil said.

"Maybe an example would help me."

"Everybody knows that people who have a cat or dog live longer, right?"

"Sure. Or maybe it only seems longer because you have to look after them and clean up after them."

"So you'd say that having a pet is the cause, and the person living longer is the effect, right?"

"Sure."

"How would you prove it? Would it be possible to do a lab experiment where you take a bunch of people and give some of them pets and others not? And then wait to see which die first?"

"We could do that. With difficulty. Why not compare people who have pets with people who don't? Just feed it into a computer and see what drops out," Misty suggested.

"It's simple enough, but you wouldn't know if having the pets was the cause or perhaps something else."

"Like what?" Misty asked.

"Like the personality of the people who have pets. The same characteristic that makes them want pets might also make them lead a relaxed life style. Maybe the personality characteristic causes both the liking of pets and the living longer. What you think is cause and effect might be two separate effects from some other single cause."

"Isn't there some way to get around that question?"

"You could select a random group of people who have pets and take the pets away from half of them. Then compare how long the members of each group live," Phil said.

"That could be a problem. Not everyone would want to give up their pet for an experiment."

"Exactly. Besides, if you did the experiment only with the people who were willing to give up their pet, you'd be back to the personality thing. It would no longer be an average group, and your experiment would be biased," Phil said.

"You're saying that in ordinary human life, cause and effect may be an illusion?" Misty asked.

"As a minimum, yes. It's highly questionable. Besides there's the problem of which is the cause and which is the effect."

"Isn't it obvious?"

"Consider the well-known fact that the rate of poverty for two-parent families is less than a quarter the rate for single-parent families. This means getting married is a good financial move, right? Getting married is the cause, and less poverty is the effect."

"I get it. It could be that having money is the cause, and getting married is the effect."

"Exactly. This is the big fallacy in a lot of computer-based research. It is easy for the computer to find relationships, but not as easy to interpret them."

"Can you prove synchronicity?"

"Synchronicity is one of those things in life that defies proof. It's a totally different way of looking at the interaction of human events. It requires faith, not proof."

"I'll try explaining it to Troy when he comes back. You may have to help me out. I'm the intellectual one. Troy's the kind of dude who would rather be on a surfboard than reading a book. Sometimes he can be super dense."

~ 6 ~

THIS IS NO PLACE LIKE HOME

Jay woke up feeling disoriented. For a moment he wasn't sure if he was still in San Francisco or back in Winnipeg. Then the events of the previous day slowly filtered back to him. He remembered getting Sue out of the hospital and realized that they were in Steve's apartment.

He rolled over to look at Sue. "Hi. You sleep well?"

Sue smiled and nodded agreement.

"We're going to have breakfast and then visit some of our friends. Anything special I can get for you?" Jay asked.

Sue smiled and nodded in agreement again.

"What would you like? Something special to eat?"

She shook her head from side to side.

"Something to drink?"

Sue shook her head again.

"I give up. What do you want? You'll have to tell me."

She mouthed a single word to Jay, "Clothes."

"Of course. Silly me. We'll go to your place and get some right after breakfast."

Sue shook her head emphatically and whispered, "No."

"I understand. I'll phone your mom and have her bring some over. We won't go anywhere until she gets here. How about you have a shower and freshen up while I get some breakfast ready. Do you need some help?"

Sue shook her head, climbed out of bed and went to the bathroom.

Jay popped two slices of bread into the toaster and phoned Sue's parents:

"Hi. Mrs. Parkington? This is Jay."

"   ..   "

"She's showering right now. We plan to go out and visit some of our friends today."

"   ..   "

"Well, yes. I suppose it's more my idea than hers but she seemed to be okay with it."

"   ..   "

"She needs some clothes. I can come over and pick them up if you'd rather not drive."

"   ..   "

"It's apartment 1605. You'll have to buzz from the entrance."

"   ..   "

"Sure. We'll save you some coffee. Bye."

An hour later, Jay answered the lobby buzzer. "Come on up, the door's open."

He met Sue's mother at the door and they stepped into the living room. She paused in front of the black and white photos, her mouth dropping open. "These are..."

"Surprising, aren't they?" Jay finished for her.

"That's putting it mildly. I'm not used to pictures of naked men on the walls. Or anywhere else as far as that goes," Helen said.

"I'm sorry if they offend you."

"They don't offend me. They're remarkably artistic, and positively resonate with repressed energy. Still, as you say, surprising. It's a good word for them. Surprising."

"Let's go to the kitchen. We've almost finished our breakfast."

"How's Sue?"

"See for yourself," Jay said.

Sue looked up from the newspaper she had been looking at. "Hi Mom."

"How are you, Sue?" Helen asked.

Sue shrugged her shoulders and gave a feeble smile.

"It's good to see you out of bed, but do take things easy," Helen said.

"We'll be careful," Jay said.

"I brought you some things," Helen said, handing Sue a sweater and a few other clothes.

"Oh good," Sue said. "My favorite sweater."

"I also brought some of your favorite bread for toast."

"We got bread from the Sev," Jay said.

"It's not like this. This is City Bread Company rye bread. Former Winnipeg residents always take some home after they visit. They ask for it as a Christmas present."

"What makes it so great?" Jay asked.

"Some say it's the Winnipeg water. Some say it's the elevation. Whatever does it, it's the best thing since sliced…uh…bread?" Helen ended lamely. She paused to think for a moment, and added, "That did-n't come out quite right, did it?"

"I'll pop some in the toaster right now, and then we'll see," Jay said.

Helen turned to Sue. "Jay says you're going to meet up with Becky and Jimmy. Are you sure you feel up to it?"

"Jay will look after me. He even cheated last night and pretended I won at Snakes and Ladders."

"You weren't suppose to notice," Jay said. "I shouldn't have done that. It wasn't being honest with you. Sorry."

"You meant well. It was a sweet thing to do," Helen said.

The bread popped up in the toaster.

"It does smell good," Jay said.

"I wonder what makes it so good," Helen said to herself.

"They don't add sugar, fat, or shortening," Jay said. "However, I think the reason it's so good is that it is sour dough bread."

"I thought you'd never heard of it before."

"I'm reading the fine print off the wrapper," Jay said.

"No wonder you always sound so smart," Helen said.

"It's not because I try to."

"I've noticed you're always giving little off the cuff lectures."

"Sorry. There always seem to be things in my head that just come out. I don't try to show off."

"It's cute," Helen said. "And quite informative."

"I don't even know what sour dough is," Jay confessed.

"It's what they used in the olden days before they had yeast," Helen said. "Like in the days of the cowboys."

"Is your husband happy about the present situation?" Jay asked, getting the topic back to his main concern.

"Maybe not happy. It takes a lot to make him happy, and even more to get him to admit it."

"Is there anything we can do to make him happier?"

"I've told him I think this is a good idea but he won't be satisfied until he has Sue back home."

"That's up to Sue."

"When are you coming home, Sue?" Helen asked.

"Soon," Sue answered, looking at the floor.

"I've got some errands to run for George. Call me if you need anything," Helen said. She gave Sue a big hug.

Later that afternoon, Jay and Sue sipped Cokes and nibbled at a plate of French fries in the Portage Plaza Mall.

"Jimmy and Becky said they would meet us here. You're going to be all right with them, aren't you?" Jay asked.

Sue nodded agreement.

"I'll take my cues from you. You can talk if you feel like it. If you don't want to, I'll fill in for you."

Sue nodded and whispered, "Okay. Do I look all right?"

"Beautiful," Jay smiled. "Don't worry about a thing. Remember we're all on your side."

Sue smiled.

"Here come Jimmy and Becky now," Jay said. "Hi guys."

Anyone could see that Becky was a practical person. Her jeans, sweater, sneakers, and short cut brunette hair all gave a clear indication that she was not one to be distracted by frivolous matters. She considered a rub of flavored lip-gloss to be more than enough makeup for most occasions, and expected her relationships with people to be similarly unembellished.

Becky sat between Jay and Sue. "Hi. We had a super swim at the hotel this morning. It's such a totally fantastic place. Thanks for letting us use it."

Jimmy looked unshaven, unwashed and unkempt. His clothes may actually have been clean but they exuded an aura of grubbiness that no amount of washing could remove. Tattered jeans can never look neat. Dirty-blond hair hung in a ponytail partway down his back. A few scraggly whiskers pretended, without success, to be a beard. He carried a half-smoked cigarette balancing precariously over his right ear.

"I hate these nonsmoking bylaws," Jimmy said.

"They're trying to give you a message, Jimmy," Jay said.

"Don't start with me."

"Just kidding."

"I've gotta thank you for the hotel."

"No problem," Jay said. "You're doing us a favor."

"It's the first time for me in a real hotel. Room service has got to be about the greatest invention ever," Jimmy said. "It's the best holiday. They even send beer to your room."

"You're taking it easy on the charges, I hope," Jay said.

"Oh sure. We only order what we need."

"How much beer would that be?"

"Jimmy's behaving himself," Becky said. "I'm making sure of that."

"Thanks for helping us out. Remember that if anyone phones for Sue or me, you tell him we're out. Then phone me and I can follow up on it. We're supposed to be living there, you know."

"Oh right," Jimmy said. "I forgot. Sue's dad phoned this morning."

"You're such a loser, Jimmy," Becky said. "Try to concentrate on the real world and get that drug-numbed brain of yours working."

"What did he say?" Jay asked.

"He wanted to know if everything was okay. I said it was. He said for you to call him at the office."

"I don't suppose you got the number?"

"You've got to be kidding. My brain doesn't hold numbers well."

"I know the number," Sue said.

Jay and Sue went to find a pay phone:

"Hello, sir," Jay said when Sue's father answered.

"   . . .   "

"Yes. Thank-you. The suite is more than we needed."

"   . . .   "

"I'll ask her," Jay said into the phone. He covered the mouth-piece with his hand. "Do you want to say hello to your dad?" he asked Sue. She nodded and took the phone.

"Hello."

"   . . .   "

"Yes."

"..."

"I'll be home soon."

"..."

"No. Not today."

"..."

Sue handed the phone back to Jay.

"Hello again," Jay said.

"..."

"Yes, sir, I will."

"..."

"Nothing right now. I'll phone if we need anything. Thanks."

Sue and Jay returned to the table.

"How was San Francisco?" Jimmy asked.

"It's the most beautiful city I've ever seen," Jay said.

"How many cities have you seen?" Becky asked.

"Lots on TV," Jay countered.

"You went there looking for your father, didn't you? Did you have any luck?" Becky asked.

"I'm getting close. He lives a day's drive south of San Francisco. I wouldn't have had time to see him on this trip, anyway. Besides, I needed to be here for Sue. She and I'll go and visit him sometime."

Sue stood up suddenly.

"I've got to go to the washroom," she said, hurrying away.

"Did I say something wrong?" Jay asked in confusion.

"I'll come with you," Becky said, running after Sue.

"Did I say something wrong?" Jay repeated.

"Not that I noticed," Jimmy said. "But then, I've been having trouble concentrating lately."

"Are you back on drugs?"

"No. I've been clean since you guys did that number of yours on me. What was it you called it? An intercession?"

"An intervention. I hope you don't think we were meddling, but as your friends we had to do something. Sticking ourselves solidly into the middle of your life forced you to choose between drugs and us. We couldn't sit by and watch you destroy yourself. If you hadn't given up on drugs, we'd have been forced to shun you totally."

"I couldn't have lived with that. When I saw I had to make a choice, it was easy. I'm lucky to have friends who put themselves on the line like that for me. What was it you asked me?"

"If you're on drugs again. You said you weren't."

"I haven't touched anything since the…"

"Intervention."

"Right. Well, okay. One or two joints to be sociable but I didn't inhale."

"Oh sure. You and Clinton."

"Honest. I've been having sort of flashback trips. They don't last long but they sure do mess up my head. They're from the acid, I think. They say it takes a long time to get your system cleared out. Ecstasy isn't supposed to do that sort of thing."

"Are you saying that ecstasy is a safe drug?" Jay asked.

"No. They say it causes brain damage and memory problems. Sometimes I don't concentrate well. I think I'm getting better but a lot of the time my brain is like Swiss cheese."

"So why do people use it?"

"It makes a person feel friendly and open to you can express your feelings. I hate it because you're always chasing a high."

"What do you mean by that?"

"The high is never as good as it was the first time you tried it. You keep increasing the dose trying to recapture that first experience. Then you try adding other drugs like LSD with it."

"Hang in there. You'll be getting a little better every day. The human body is remarkably resilient."

"I think Becky's getting fed up with me and my problems."

"Remember I'm always here for you if you need help to get through the night," Jay said.

"Thanks. That means a lot to me."

"Friends have to stick together. It can be a tough world, sometimes."

"Don't forget we have a deal to go to Montreal, eh?" Jimmy said, brushing his dirty-blond hair back over his shoulder.

"Count on it, buddy. Remember our deal. You said you'd give up smoking if I took you to Montreal."

"Maybe I did. There are a lot of things I don't remember. I know I've given up drugs. I might as well give up smoking, too."

"And then drinking?"

Jimmy glared.

"Just pulling your chain," Jay said.

Jimmy smiled with relief. "It's a deal. You take me to Montreal and I'll quit smoking."

"What's taking the girls so long?" Jay wondered out loud.

"Don't worry," Jimmy said. "Those two always have lots to talk about. When we heard Sue was in the hospital, we planned to see her but we didn't get around to it before you got her out."

"I wanted to get her out of there as quickly as possible."

Becky and Sue returned. Sue's eyes were red and moist. She was leaning on Becky's arm.

Jay looked at Sue. "Is everything all right?"

Becky answered, "No. We need to get Sue back to the hospital."

"Do we need an ambulance?" Jimmy asked.

"Take her other arm," Becky said. "She's bleeding inside."

"This'll be faster than calling an ambulance," Jay said, swooping Sue up in his arms. "Becky, you get the doors. Jimmy, you run and get the elevator."

The obvious urgency of the group cleared a path for them through the Food Court as they rushed down to the parkade. Jay was stopped by the tollgate. "This is a medical emergency. Open the gate. Never mind the change," Jay commanded, shoving a ten-dollar bill at the man in the booth.

The drive to the hospital was fast and silent. Jay concentrated on judicious lane switching to beat the yellow lights. Sue was looking pale and drawn when they checked into the emergency room. Becky spoke quietly to the nurse.

"Wait here, Jay," Becky said.

"I want to come with her," Jay protested.

"You can see her later. Trust me. This will go better without you."

Jay moved restlessly from chair to chair in the waiting room for half an hour before Becky returned.

"How is she?" he asked anxiously.

"They want to keep her here at least overnight," Becky said.

"I should never have taken her out in the first place. My stupidity could have killed her."

"Don't blame yourself. You had no way of knowing."

"Her dad was right. I'm just an uneducated, stupid nobody. If only I hadn't been so caught up in trying to be a hero," Jay said.

"You'd better come and stay with Jimmy and me tonight at the hotel," Becky said.

"I'll have to talk to Helen first. She and George need to know what's happening."

"We'll come with you," Jimmy said. "You may need some moral support."

"You guys stay in the car," Jay said, as he parked the Mustang in front of the Parkington's house.

"I think I'd better come in," Becky said.

"You're right. I don't know anything about what happened."

"I'll guard the car," Jimmy said. "Leave the keys so I can listen to the radio."

Helen opened the door for Jay and Becky. "Come in. George and I were having a cocktail. Can I get you something?" she asked.

"No thanks," Jay said. "I don't think you've met Becky."

"Why no, I haven't. Sue's talked about you often but we've never met. Nice to meet you."

"Mr. Parkington," Jay said, "I'd like you to meet Sue's friend, Becky."

"Is this a social call?" George asked.

"I'm afraid not," Jay said. "We had to take Sue back to the hospital."

Helen jumped up from her chair. "We have to go see her."

"I told you to leave her there in the first place," George said. "You should have stayed away from us and let the experts handle things."

"Is she all right?" Helen asked.

Becky moved over to sit beside Helen. "The doctor says not to worry. There was some internal bleeding so they want to keep her overnight."

"If you'd left her there in the first place this would never have happened," George said.

"I'm sorry, sir. You were right. It was a bad mistake."

"I hope you learned something from all this."

"Yes, sir. I should have listened more and been less impetuous. It was more important for me to be a hero than to respect the opinions of others. I'm sorry."

"Good. I'm glad you learned something."

"Yes sir. I did."

"Apparently there was no serious harm done," George said. "What you did was stupid, but it was a gutsy thing to do."

Jay looked confused. "You're not angry with me?"

"Of course I'm mad at you, and I expect you to listen to me next time. However, I do like it when people have *moxie*."

Helen interjected. "Your motives were good, Jay, and we appreciate that."

The three spent a few more minutes reviewing what little they knew and restating the obvious until finally Jay and Becky left to join Jimmy in the car.

"Damn fool kid," George said, settling down with the Financial Times. "We've got to keep him away from our daughter."

~ 7 ~

WELCOME BACK

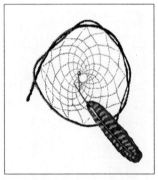

Early the next afternoon, Jay drove over to see Helen.

"I'm going to the hospital to see how Sue is. Would you want to come with me?" Jay asked.

"George and I talked to the doctors earlier this morning. The psychiatrist said he had a good talk with Sue."

"And?"

"There's no need for her to stay there. She can leave as soon as we want," Helen said.

"Did they say what the problem was?" Jay asked.

"It seems to be way her body reacts. He says teenage girls often react to emotional things with physical symptoms."

"But what's causing the stress?"

"He didn't say."

"Was he angry that I took her out of the hospital?" Jay asked.

"On the contrary. He said she is much better emotionally."

"Then why did they want to keep her there?"

"They always like to have a period of observation in a controlled environment. Now that they have done that she's free to go."

"Did he say anything else?"

"He said whatever you're doing, you should keep doing it."

"Do you think her dad will let her stay with me at Steve's place?"

"He thinks you'll be at the hotel. However, he's resigned to having you look after her. The psychiatrist was specific on that point. He says she feels safe with you. He also mumbled something about writing a paper on the therapeutic value of Snakes and Ladders, whatever he meant by that."

"Do you want to come with me when I pick her up?"

"I don't think so. I got the impression we should leave things up to you."

"I'm going to get her right now," Jay said. "I'll keep you posted."

"Make sure you get her appointment times with her therapist. The psychiatrist says she's to be scheduled for sessions twice a week."

Jay and Sue picked up burgers and fries from the nearby drive-thru and were back at Steve's place in time for lunch.

"Han Sing gave me time off until the New Year. Since I'm back, I think I should go in to work. We could use the money. If you can spare me for a few hours a day, that is," Jay said.

"I'll be all right. You should go to work."

"Do you feel up to coming with me to the Red Dragon?" Jay asked. Sue nodded.

"What about visiting Running Bear?" Jay asked.

"If you think I should."

"He's a great old guy, and an amazing shaman. I never know what he's doing but it works miracles for me."

They finished their makeshift lunch slowly and then drove down North Main Street. Jay found a parking spot in front of the Red Dragon.

"After San Francisco, Winnipeg seems tiny," Jay said. He looked over at Sue. "You can stay in the car or come in. It's up to you."

"I'll come with you," Sue said.

"All you have to do is relax and go along with whatever happens. I'll do as much of the talking as you want."

Sue took few deep breaths. "Okay. Let's go."

A wizened little man of Asian heritage looked up from his activity behind the counter. "Hi, sonny boy."

"Hi, Han Sing. This is my girlfriend, Sue."

Han Sing grinned. "You make a cute couple but I hope you don't intend to have her stay here."

"We're staying at Steve's. I wanted to see how you're getting along without me."

Han Sing laughed. "You think one week and the place will fall apart without you? You could take a pot of tea up to R.B. if you want to be helpful. And I hope you take Arrow out for a walk while you're here. I get tired of doing it every day."

Sue looked at Jay. "Arrow is Running Bear's dog," Jay explained.

Han Sing put the kettle on to boil. "I do a special little turkey dinner as a thank-you for my regulars and their friends before New Year's Eve. Usually a lot of people drop in and I could use your help."

"We'll be going to a friend's place for dinner. It'll probably run from eight o'clock until midnight, so I could come in anytime before eight."

Han Sing put the pot of tea and three cups on a tray. "It would help a lot if you could come in around four o'clock and help us get set up. Stay as long as you can. I don't charge for the meal, so there's no cash register to worry about, except for the drinks. It's the serving and cleaning up after that needs help."

Jay picked up the tray. "I always knew there was a soft heart beneath that tough exterior."

"Don't let it get out or these guys will be after me all the time for charity. Besides, some of them stay and drink until midnight. That pays for the meals."

Jay went up the stairs and gently pushed open R.B.'s door a crack. He called gently, "*Boozhoo.*"

An old first nation native sat cross-legged in the middle of the room, amid rolled up rugs, which created a circular living space in the middle of the room. Sage branches scattered around the floor filled the room with their pungent aroma.

"*Biindigeg!*" the old man said.

Jay and Sue sat on the hide-covered floor in front of R.B. The old German Shepherd beside him lifted his head and sniffed the air. The dog got up on his shaky legs and wobbled over, resting his head on Jay's knees.

"Arrow has missed you," the shaman said.

They sat for a few minutes of comfortable silence. R.B. looked at the floor most of the time, stealing only quick glances at Sue. Native men, like Jewish men, are expected by custom to refrain from prolonged looks at the fairer sex. To do otherwise is considered impolite.

He turned to Jay and smiled. "*Onizhishi giinimoshe.*"

Jay gave R.B. a questioning look. "What did you say?"

"Your girl is pretty," R.B. said.

Sue smiled shyly and looked down.

"I know only a little of the Ojibwe language," Jay said. "My mother taught me a few words. She said our language connects us to our ancestors and our culture, and that I am to be proud of being *Anishinaabe.* I'm not even sure what *Anishinaabe* means."

"*Anishinaabe* means I am a person. We take it to be the Ojibwe word for our people," R.B. said, and then began laughing quietly to himself.

"Why are you laughing?" Jay asked. "Back home people always laughed when they spoke Ojibwe. I never knew why. I thought it must have something to do with me, and they were making fun of me."

"Ours is an oral language. We listen to the sound of the words," R.B. said.

"How does that make it funny?"

"The words give a funny meaning in our language. The word 'Ojibwe' was the name given to our tribe by the other tribes because the seams of our moccasins were puckered on the outside. When I said that *Anishinaabe* is Ojibwe for us, I was actually saying I am a person who is puckered on the outside."

"I can see how it would be funny," Jay said.

"We often laugh because of our language. It speaks in words of action for naming objects. This gives unusual and vivid meanings which are often funny."

"Can you explain that?" Jay asked.

"Our ancestors had no need of a word for restaurant. The time came when we needed one. We made up the word *'wiisiniiwigamigoonsan'* from words we already had. Its real meaning is, 'he eats little house more than once' by which we mean restaurant. The separate parts are like a joke to me. It makes me laugh inside every time I hear it."

"Was my mother right that I should learn our language?"

"When the white man took our land and water, we could find other land and water. When the law forbade us to practice our traditional ceremonies, like the Sun Dance, we could do them in hiding. However, when they took our language, they took our culture and the heritage of our ancestors," R.B. explained.

"How were they able to take the language?" queried Jay.

"They put our children into residential schools. They were forbidden to speak their native tongue and were punished if they spoke anything but English. Ours was an oral language until the white man came. When our children grew up, they had no language to teach their children our customs and ceremonies. Our teachings have always come from the heart and our memories."

"Does this still happen?"

"We have our own schools now. Soon we will have native teachers to help our children regain our past. The first step is to teach our children the value of their language and their heritage. Our culture passes from generation to generation through the imagery of our own words. The white man's words do not have this imagery. If we lose our words, we lose our culture."

"Maybe that's what my mother meant by wanting me to be proud of being *Anishinaabe*," Jay said.

R.B. nodded solemnly. "Your girl has uneasy influences in her spirit."

"I brought something for you from California," Jay said, pulling a crumpled package from his pocket. "It's a mixture of Orrisroot powder, lavender, cedar chips, rose buds and sandalwood," he said, reading from the package. "They said it makes a good smudge. I hope you like it."

R.B. accepted the package. "What comes from your heart, I like."

He took his medicine bundle from a tripod of willow branches against one wall. Selecting a wisp of sweetgrass, he twisted it together, looked at it thoughtfully, and then put it back.

"We should use cedar," he said, whittling cedar shavings into the pan and then lighting them with the help of some crumpled paper. "Cedar connects with Grandmother Bear, who brings with her, courage and purification."

As the smoke began to rise from the cedar, he carried it in a clockwise circle around the room.

Having completed the circle, he looked thoughtfully at a pair of deer horn rattles. "Rattles are used to call the spirits. We do not need rattles because the spirits are already with us."

Selecting a small drum, he began a steady rhythmic beat. "Let yourself become one with the heartbeat of mother earth. She will be our guide."

Abruptly R.B. stopped the drum beating.

He carried the smoldering pan over and set it on the floor in front of Sue. "*Nookwezo*."

Jay explained, "He says to smudge yourself. When you breathe in, the smoke mixes with your thoughts, fears and desires. When you breathe out, they go with the smoke up to the spirits. You will be cleared of guilt and worry if you find favor with the spirits."

Jay used his cupped hands to waft the smoke toward Sue.

Arrow got up and moved away. R.B. began chanting softly in his native tongue.

R.B. looked into Sue's eyes. "You must let the world unfold following the rules of nature. We learn from our sacred animals."

Jay looked at R.B. questioningly.

"The wolf has always been our brother. It communicates with us and guides us."

"It talks to you? Do you talk to it?" Jay asked.

"Not in words. In thoughts and pictures in the mind."

"You mean by telepathy?"

"How else would you have known to phone Sue's mother?" R.B. asked.

"It was a hunch. Maybe I suddenly felt lonely."

"You may call it what you want."

Jay thought for a moment. "Who told you that I had phoned?"

"There are things that a person knows, without knowing how."

"I like to understand things. That way I have more control over my life," Jay said.

"There is no control over life and death. We must live our life the best way we can, and accept the world as it unfolds. Close your eyes and you will become one with Mother Earth and the universe. No other communication is necessary."

The cedar smoke curled gently up from the pan, filling the room with its sweet, restful odor.

R.B. continued, "Other than our dedication to sharing, our people have only one commandment. It is respect."

He stood in front of Sue and said, "The four faces of respect are, love of yourself and others." With this, he cupped smoke in his hands and poured it over her head.

He continued, "Patience with your place in the world," and poured smoke again.

"Discipline in your life," he said, and again poured smoke.

"And giving forgiveness freely." R.B. began chanting a soft, rhythmic Ojibwe prayer.

Sue sat with her eyes closed for a long time. Finally, she opened her eyes. The shaman looked into Sue's eyes. "Do not listen to the words of others. Put your trust in your inner spirit and follow the words of your heart, not your head."

Jay smiled at R.B, "Thank-you."

He turned toward Sue and asked, "Do you mind if I take Arrow out for a walk?"

She nodded. "I'll wait here for you."

Jay scooped the fragile Arrow into his arms and carried him easily out the door.

"I have something for you," R.B. said to Sue. He took a five-inch hoop of twisted red birch from the wall. A net of animal sinew, dyed blood red, formed a web with a small opening in the center. A leather lace hung from the opening, passing through a wooden bead to a dangling owl feather.

"Thank-you. What is it?"

"We call it *Bawadjige Ngwaagan.* Our people use it to protect our children from bad dreams. It will protect you from distracting thoughts, and from confusion in the night."

"That would help me," Sue said.

"The web catches the *bawadjigewin*, the bad dreams. Only the good *bawadjige* can escape through the hole in the middle of the web. They slide down the feather into the sleeper's mind. The owl feather adds wisdom to the dream."

"How do I use it?"

"It will hang above your sleeping area. When the morning light hits, the bad dreams it has caught will dissolve."

"It's beautiful. Thank-you. I'll cherish it."

"My great-grandson made it for my 70th birthday."

"I couldn't take your grandson's gift."

"It served me well at a time when I had need of it. Now it will serve you. I will have no further need of it."

"I'll cherish it, and think of you when I look at it."

"He made it in the traditional way. The willow is becoming brittle and the sinew is shrinking. It will collapse soon. By then it will have done its work and you will no longer have need of it."

Jay returned with Arrow. "What an awesome dreamcatcher," he said.

"Its eleven points are for each of the four winds and the seven sacred teachings of the grandfathers," R.B. pointed out.

"I know about the winds, but I don't know the seven sacred teachings," Jay said.

"The Wolf teaches humility. The Beaver, wisdom. The Turtle, truth."

"I know the Eagle symbolizes love. You taught me that, and it has served me well. I learned the hard way the teachings of respect symbolized by the Buffalo," Jay said.

R.B. continued, "The Bear gives courage, and the Giant which we call Sabe teaches honesty. These are the seven natural laws by which we live."

As Sue and Jay headed toward the door, Jay paused at a small wooden bowl half full of money. He took a ten-dollar bill from his pocket and dropped it on top of the other bills.

"You do not need to do that," R.B said.

"I owe it to you," Jay replied.

"You owe me nothing. I remember the time you needed money and my little bowl helped you. That is why it is there. My people respect others by giving to them what they need. I have little use for money. This is my way of sharing with those who have better use for it than I do."

"There is much I can learn from you," Jay said.

"Do not return the money to me. That would make the action nothing more than a white man's loan. It would break the circle of helping. Give to one whose need is greater than yours. In that way, the circle of respect will continue when he gives it to someone else. We come into the world with no possessions; we leave with nothing. While we are here, we should share what we have with those who have needs."

"I'm not breaking the circle. The money I took has already gone on to help another. I was hoping to start a new circle with this gift."

"If the bowl is empty, it will accept your donation gratefully. However, it is not empty now. Putting more money in it does not help anyone. You must find your own way to start a new circle of respect."

"I have to give help without expecting anything in return. Not even gratitude, right?"

"You learn quickly," R.B. said.

"I try," Jay said.

"Goodbye," Sue said.

"*Miigwech*," Jay said.

On the way out of the Red Dragon, Jay asked Sue, "What would you like to do now?"

"I'd like to be alone with you for a while."

"Do you want to talk?"

"No. I just want to be with you. Silence is comforting for me right now. We can exchange thoughts."

"You want to go back to Steve's?"

"Maybe drive around the city a bit and then go back to Steve's later, if you don't mind."

"It's your party," Jay said, pulling out into the light traffic. "Let's take a drive to the Forks and look through the shops. Then we can go to Osborne Village and shop or get a bite to eat. I'll cruise around the city until you feel ready to go home."

~ 8 ~

HOW'S THAT AGAIN?

It was early in the evening when Sue and Jay returned to Steve's apartment. The phone was ringing as they entered. Jay took the call.

"That was Jimmy," Jay said, hanging up the phone. "Your dad dropped over to the hotel. He wants us to go over to your place to see him."

Sue looked down at the floor.

"If you don't want to go, you can stay here. I'll go talk with him."

"Would you mind?"

"Of course not. I'll say you needed a nap. It'll be a piece of cake."

George ushered Jay into the living room and plopped himself into his favorite armchair.

"Where's Sue?" he asked.

"We drove around a bit and I'm afraid it tired her out. We thought it best if she rested a bit."

"You mean you thought it best that she doesn't talk to me."

"She wanted to rest."

"Why would she be tired? She hasn't been doing much of anything, has she?"

"Pain can be tiring."

"She hasn't been hurt, has she?"

"Not physically. However, any kind of pain is tiring."

"Helen says she seems to be getting better."

"Yes, I think she's doing well. She's a strong girl," Jay said.

"Strong enough to come home? Or do you plan to keep her hidden away forever?"

"It's only been a couple of days. I think we should leave it up to her to decide where she lives."

"I don't care what you think. Why did I let Helen talk me into this harebrained scheme of yours, anyway? Where did you take her today?"

"Mostly we just drove around," Jay said.

"Did you meet up with those two *schmucks* at the hotel?" George asked. He went to the sideboard, poured three fingers of Glenlivet Scotch from its crystal decanter, and took a long drink.

"Not since yesterday."

"What are they doing there anyway? That suite was for Sue."

"They're there to answer the phone and take messages. We didn't want you to think we had disappeared. We didn't want to give you any reason to worry."

"By we, I assume you mean you."

"I take full responsibility for everything, if that's what you mean," Jay said, shifting in his seat.

"I'm glad to hear you say that. Now you can explain to me why they are at the hotel and you aren't."

"Sue and I are staying at Steve's."

"You chose to disobey my wishes, then. And you lied to me."

"I didn't intend to do either. I only did what I felt had to be done."

"It was your idea, then, to pretend to be staying at the hotel and not to tell me?" George asked.

"I take full responsibility."

"And you went to see that sham Indian after I told you not to."

Jay looked thoughtful for a moment. "You've had us followed?"

"What else would you expect after the hotel manager reported to me that those two imposters were staying there? This time I've got a good guy. He doesn't miss a thing."

"How long do you intend to keep us under surveillance?"

"Whatever it takes. Do you expect me to pay a hundred and fifty dollars a night so your friends can *shmaltz* it up?"

"I'll pay for the hotel, if you want me to," Jay said.

"When are you bringing Sue home or do I have to have you arrested for kidnapping?"

"I'm leaving it up to her."

"You know she'll do anything you say," George said.

"That may be true, sir. However, she knows what she needs and I listen to her. She tells me what to do."

"You expect me to believe that garbage? How can she tell you what she wants when she barely talks?"

"There are other, and sometimes better, ways of communicating than by words."

"I live my life by words. Preferably notarized."

"I think I should get back to Sue," Jay said, getting up from the sofa.

"Whatever."

George went to refill his glass.

"Do you mind if I keep the Mustang, sir? Only while Sue's with me, of course."

"Whatever."

The door opened and Helen came in. "Hi Jay. You look like you're leaving. Hang on for a minute. I want to talk to you."

"We've talked about everything important," George said.

"I have a bit of time. Sue's having a bit of a nap," Jay said.

"We need to tell Jay about Christmas," Helen said.

"He doesn't need to know anything about it," George responded, draining his glass.

"I think he does," Helen said.

"It's no big deal," George said. "We had an argument with Sue."

"You're the one who had the argument," Helen corrected, "I didn't."

"I wouldn't have, if she hadn't been drunk."

Jay looked perplexed. "Sue doesn't usually drink."

"Well, she was drunk that night," George said. "It's a good thing that her friend, Tiffany, brought her home. She was in no condition to drive."

"Did Tiff say anything about their evening?" Jay asked.

"No. She dropped her off and left," George said. "That Tiffany is one sharp looking girl. I'd like to have her as a receptionist in my office."

"Never mind Tiffany," Helen said. "We're talking about Sue."

George continued, "Sue was talking nonsense about marriage, adoption, abortion and stuff like that."

"It was as if she thought maybe she was adopted," Helen said. "We told her she wasn't."

"I told her to go to bed and sober up. We found her semiconscious a while later," George said.

"Is that the whole story?" Jay asked.

"It wasn't so much what she said. It was the way she said it. She was out of her mind about it. We naturally assumed it was because she had been drinking," Helen said.

"You might as well tell him the rest. The argument part," George said, glaring at his wife.

"She was upset that she wasn't allowed to see you, Jay," Helen said. "She said she had to talk to you. Then she and her father got into a huge argument about it."

"I told her how life has to be but she wouldn't listen."

"You told her she wasn't to have anything to do with Jay. That was harsh."

"She needed to know how we felt," George said.

"There was some more argument and she stormed off to bed. When we went to check on her an hour later, she was on the bathroom floor," Helen said.

"Naturally, we took her to the hospital," George said.

"After we found her, she wouldn't talk to anyone. All she did was ask for you. I hoped she would talk to you. Has she?" Helen asked.

"She hasn't told me anything important, if that's what you asking. She and Becky have talked a bit," Jay said.

"What did they talk about?" George asked.

"They didn't say," Jay said. "She'll tell me when she's ready, if it's any of my business. I won't pressure her."

"I want her back here," George demanded.

"Yes, sir. I know that. She will be back when she says she's ready."

"She seems to be getting back to being her old self," Helen said. "It's as if…"

"Then she should be coming home," George interrupted.

"Not that you spend any time with her when she is here," Helen said.

George ignored the comment. "We wouldn't want Jay to pay for any more nights at the hotel than necessary."

Helen looked at George. "Jay is paying for the hotel?" she asked in surprise.

"We decided that would be fair since he's using it as a holiday retreat for his friends."

"He can't afford that kind of money," Helen protested.

"He had enough money to go to California for a holiday."

"If you hadn't forced Sue to break up with him, he wouldn't have had to go on a trip he probably couldn't afford."

"You seemed happy enough when they broke up. I don't think you liked the idea of Sue going out with a half-…"

Jay interrupted. "Excuse me, sir. I should be getting back to Sue."

George glared at Jay. "Whatever."

"I wish you wouldn't use that expression," Helen said. "It makes you sound like a rude teenager."

"You mean half-breed?" George asked.

"That one, too," Helen said.

"Whatever," George said.

"Yes, that's the one."

George picked up his glass and drained the last few drops out of it.

Jay turned to Helen. "Phil is planning a dinner for New Year's Eve. Do I have your permission to take Sue?" he asked.

"I don't know why you bother to ask. You'll do whatever you want anyway," George growled.

"George. Try to be polite," Helen said. She turned to Jay, "We think that would be lovely. If you think Sue's up to it when the time comes."

"Thanks. It should be low stress and lots of fun. She'll be with people she knows. I promise we'll leave immediately if she starts to get tired."

"Whatever."

"Bye, sir."

Helen went to the door with Jay. "Don't worry about the hotel bill," she whispered. "It'll go on the Amex and he'll never notice it."

"Thanks. I'll phone you tomorrow."

The sound of giggling welcomed Jay back to the apartment. "Sue?" Jay called.

A voice called out, "We're in the kitchen, having a hen party. Come and join us."

Sue, Becky and Tiffany sat at the kitchen table. Dirty dishes, a half-eaten Salisbury House flapper pie, and three empty Diet Coke cans, gave evidence of an evening snack.

"Hi. It looks like you've had supper," Jay said.

"Help yourself to the scraps," Becky said,

"Thanks. Where's Jimmy?" Jay asked Becky.

"Cam's teaching him some computer stuff. Jimmy's keen on it. He's never been excited about learning before."

"What kind of stuff?"

"Word processing, email, the Internet. That kind of stuff. I wish we had a computer so I could learn those things, too. It's great to see him interested in something at last," Becky said.

"How's he doing with the drugs?"

"He's staying clean. Sometimes he gets depressed. I wish he were happier but I guess it's part of kicking the habit."

"You two thinking of splitting?" Jay asked.

Becky looked off into space.

"Sorry. It's none of my business. If I can help, remember I'm always here for both you guys," Jay said. "Looks like you three have been celebrating something."

Sue looked at Becky and Tiffany with a smile. "Yes. I think we were."

"Anything I should know about?"

"No," the girls said together, and doubled over in shared mirth.

Jay looked bewildered.

"It's girl talk," Tiffany said.

"How did you make out with my dad, Jay?" Sue asked.

"Not great. He doesn't seem to like me as much as he did when we first met, and he didn't like me much then."

"Was he drinking?"

"Some, I guess. He didn't seem drunk."

"If he was drinking at this time of day, he was probably drunk. Sometimes he drinks himself sober."

"Excuse me? I don't know what you mean by that," Jay said.

Becky said, "I've seen it with Jimmy a few times. He'd get so drunk he couldn't walk and could hardly talk, but he'd keep drinking. Then suddenly he'd be able to walk and talk normally, as if he were sober. The only difference was that his brain was totally turned off. He'd have no idea what he was saying or doing. It was as if he was on automatic pilot. The next morning he wouldn't remember anything of what he'd said or done."

Jay looked at Sue. "Do you think your dad's an alcoholic?"

"Yes and no. He doesn't usually drink too much. It's my fault that he's drinking now. He's worried about me."

"How can it be your fault, Sue? He's the one doing the drinking," Becky said.

"If I hadn't spun out, he wouldn't be drinking. That makes it my fault."

"You can't be responsible for how someone else reacts to a situation. You can be responsible only for your own actions. The other people are responsible for their own reactions," Becky said.

"I understand what Sue means," Jay said. "If I provoke someone into hitting me, then I'm the one responsible for what happens, not him."

"That's right, Jay," Sue said.

"But Sue wasn't provoking her dad," Becky said.

"Not intentionally, she wasn't. I'm only saying I understand why Sue feels responsible. I've been there myself," Jay said.

"It sounds like you're saying I should feel responsible for Jimmy's behavior. Well, I don't, and I'm not going to. If we have a fight, then he gets to choose whether he's going to get drunk, or hit me, or walk away, or talk it through. He's responsible for whatever choice he makes, not me."

"Chill, Becky," Tiffany said. "That's not what they mean. They're talking about how they feel. We can't change how we feel. Sue feels sorry that her dad is drinking."

"But it's not her fault. It's something beyond her control. There's no need for her to feel guilty," Becky said.

"Why else would my dad be upset?" Sue asked.

Becky opened her mouth to reply, and then closed it firmly with clenched teeth.

"Let's switch to a happier topic," Jay said.

"That suggestion happens a lot whenever my dad is involved," Sue said.

"Did you know Phil is throwing a dinner party New Year's Eve?" Jay continued.

"Great," Becky said. "Are Jimmy and I invited?"

"I'm sure you would be if Phil knew you wanted to come."

"Why wouldn't we?"

"If Steve is there, Jimmy might not want to be there. I don't think Jimmy likes Steve."

"He'll just have to get over it. No matter what Jimmy wants, we'd love to go. We can't afford to get out much these days."

"I'll put in a good word for you. I'd like to have you meet Troy and Misty. You'd get along well with them."

"Am I invited?" Sue asked.

"Of course. I checked with your mom and dad and they said you could go. That is, if you want to," Jay said.

"Yes, please," Sue said. "However, I wouldn't blame you if you were angry with me and didn't want to go with me."

"Where's that coming from?" Jay asked. "Why would I be angry at you?"

"For breaking up with you."

"But I know why you felt you had to that."

"It wasn't what I wanted to do."

"I could never be angry with you about that, Sue. And I understand that your dad was doing what he felt he had to do."

"Are you sure he'll be all right with it? I don't want to upset him even more," Sue said.

"We're doing nothing wrong. He's entitled to react in any way he wants. I'm not going to be blackmailed by the fear he'll turn to drink. We don't know how he might react."

Becky looked at Jay. "If you don't know how he'll react, I've got a great deal on the Osborne Bridge for you."

~ 9 ~

Happy New *Feng Shui* Day

Misty was in the kitchen, discussing plans for Year's Eve dinner with Phil.

"Who're you inviting?" Misty asked.

"Sue and Jay will be here for sure. And then Cam and Jamie might be here. Cam said not to count on them because the baby could arrive any time now. I hope they come because you'd like them."

"Jay's told us a bit about them. He's a gay accountant, isn't he?"

"He's an accountant, yes."

"I thought someone said he's gay."

"He and Steve dress up to do the gay bar circuit sometimes. I don't think Cam's gay. He just enjoys Steve and his gay friends."

"But Steve is gay, isn't he? Will he be here?"

"He's probably still in California."

"You didn't answer about his being gay."

"How would his being gay make any difference? He's a good friend."

"I'm sorry. I didn't mean anything by it. It's just that Troy and I don't have any, you know, like, gay friends," Misty said. "We're not sure how to behave with them."

"I thought you were from San Francisco," Phil said. "Everybody there has gay friends."

"No. San Luis Obispo. It's a little place that was founded as a mission two hundred years ago. The lifestyle there is pretty conventional."

"Just treat them like you would anyone else. Then there will be Jimmy and Becky."

"We haven't met them."

"I forgot to mention Tiffany. She's an old school chum of mine," Phil said. "I think she broke up with her boyfriend, but she might come anyway."

"Are any of the others vegetarians?" Misty asked.

"Only the two of us," Phil said. "I think Cam would be vegetarian if it weren't so much trouble."

Troy came in on the end of the conversation. "Maybe we should make regular food, and you and Misty can do something vegetarian for yourselves," he suggested. "You know, like just pick out the meat parts."

"Over my dead body," Misty said. "That would leave us with nothing but salad."

"Mine, too," Phil added. "I don't cook meat. They'll all eat vegan the same as Misty and me. Either that or they won't be eating."

"I was kidding. Vegan is cool with me," Troy said. "I can always get a hamburger at McDonald's later."

"You know I don't like to hear that kind of talk," Misty said.

"Here are some ideas to think about," Phil said. "We could have two kinds of phyllo pastry roll ups for appetizers. One vegetable-mushroom, the other Spanakopitta."

"Isn't goat cheese a main ingredient of Spanakopitta?" Misty asked.

"Usually," Phil replied. "We could try it with a tofu cheese substitute. If it doesn't turn out well, people can stick with other one."

"Have you ever tried it like that?" Troy asked.

"There's always a first time. We'll call it a spinach roll up. That way the Greeks won't sue us."

"Sounds good. What about a main course?"

"I was thinking of Tamale Pie or Sweet Potato Quesadillas and a Taco salad."

"That sounds rather Mexican. What if somebody wants something less spicy?" Troy asked.

"We could do a Tabouleh salad. It's mild," Misty said.

"Hardly a main course dish, though," Phil said.

"What about pasta with that spaghetti sauce you make with lentils?" Misty asked.

"Dude. It might be hazardous to your tablecloth," Troy said. "I'm, like, a bit of a messy eater sometimes."

"Not very fancy for a formal dinner, either," Phil said.

"What about sweet and sour gluten balls? They'd be less messy than spaghetti," Troy suggested.

"You'd have to make the wheat gluten," Phil said. "It's not something I know anything about."

"Troy made a discovery yesterday. You can buy ready prepared wheat gluten in bulk food stores. You add water and mix it gently. It sounds totally easy. Troy is such a great provider," Misty said.

"Let's do that. I get tired of tofu all the time," Phil said. "Maybe we could do Sweet Potato French Fries. They're unusual."

"I didn't know you could do Sweet Potatoes that way."

"They're the same as regular ones, except they fall apart more easily."

The three discussed ideas for modifying their favorite recipes to eliminate meat, cheese, milk, and eggs.

"I wonder if your guests know they're going to be acting as guinea pigs for your recipes," Misty mused.

"They're used to my experimenting with vegetarian recipes. Cam in particular likes trying different things. He's way more adventuresome than you'd expect an accountant to be. You should see him at the Club on a Saturday night."

By five o'clock the next day, the food was prepared and the table set. Phil went to answer the knock at the door. "You're the first ones here."

"Hi everybody. Glad we're not late," Jay said. "Troy, Misty, I want you to meet my best, and only girl, Sue."

Sue avoided eye contact as Jay introduced her to Troy and Misty.

"Pleased to meet you," she mumbled. "Good to see you again, Phil."

Jay looked around the room. "Wow. Am I in the right apartment?"

"You like it?" Phil asked.

"It looks like a different place. You have a real living room now."

"Misty did a *Feng Shui* thing for me. She says there's a Chinese proverb that says if you want to change your life, you must move twenty-seven things in your house," Phil said.

"You moved that many things?"

"At least. She says she arranged things along the earth's energy lines to create a harmonious relationship with the environment."

"What does that mean?" Jay asked.

Misty came into the living room. "Hey guys. It encourages the free flow of *chi* through the living space."

Jay grinned. "Thanks. That explains everything. Maybe you could give us a tour and explain how it all works."

"Right on," Misty said. "You remember that the hide-a-bed used to be between the kitchen and the living room space?"

"Oh yes. When it opened out it was a nuisance. I fell over it more than once when I came in late at night."

"I think it had more to do with your drinking habits than with the sofa," Phil said with a grin.

"If it was in your way when you came in, then it also blocked the natural flow of *chi* coming in through the door. With the sofa against the side wall, the life and breath of the universe is free to flow into the apartment. Then it circulates unobstructed to the bedrooms and kitchen."

"That makes sense. What's a *chi*?" Jay asked.

"The cosmic breath of the dragon is called *chi*. All things have this constantly changing living energy. *Chi* makes pathways through all physical things and thus connects them."

"So where does the dragon come from?" Jay asked.

"You don't actually have a dragon. That's just what it's called. *Chi* exists everywhere, just like the earth's magnetic field or gravity. It brings with it health, wealth and good luck for those living where it flows freely."

"The trick is to keep it flowing?"

"More or less. In a healthy person, *chi* makes pathways in the body. A blocked pathway causes pain or illness. Acupuncture is used to find the pathways and restores the flow."

Jay looked at Misty. "Maybe you could you do my room over for me?"

"You should never have someone else do your place for you. It's better to learn the process and then do it for yourself. Your own personality and your own *chi* are important factors in determining what's best for you. It helps if you practice Yoga in your home. The breathing exercises help you understand how to harmonize your body's own *chi* with the *chi* of the room."

"If I changed my room, how would I even begin? I don't own twenty-seven things, let alone moving them," Jay said.

"We can talk about what we did here and maybe you'll get some ideas about what you could try."

"All I have is a bed, a chair and a roll-top desk," Jay said.

"Most rooms are rectangular boxes. The corners trap *chi* and hold it there until it becomes stagnant."

"When I was a kid, I sometimes had to sit in the corner as punishment," Sue said.

"The stagnant *chi* makes it an unpleasant experience."

"Does that make it a bad thing to do?" Sue asked.

"Not really. However, having a time-out in a controlled space is a more spiritually healthy punishment than sitting in a pool of stagnant *chi*."

"That does sound rather disgusting," Jay said.

"Putting furniture diagonally across the corner, like we did with the hide-a-bed, is an easy solution. You might place plants or sculptures in the corner. Hanging a wind chime or crystal in the corner is also good," Misty added.

"What did you do with Phil's motorcycle?" Jay asked.

"I must admit finding it in his bedroom was a major surprise. Why is it there anyway?"

"It's the only place he has to store it during the winter," Jay explained.

"How'd he get it up here? He didn't ride it up the stairs, did he?"

"It's not as heavy as the newer ones. With one person at the front and one at the back, it rolls up easily enough. What did you do with it?"

"I left it in the corner with a blanket over it. It'll certainly counteract any stagnant *chi* in that corner."

"You might need something to counteract the smell of stagnant motor oil," Jay said. "What about my room? I don't have a motorcycle to put anywhere."

"Does the door open onto the foot of your bed?"

"Why yes, it does," Jay said.

"Move the bed to a side wall. Or even better, angle it across one corner."

"That's one move. Twenty-six to go."

"Softening any protruding sharp corners is important. Corners send out poison arrows. We call them the dragon's killing breath. They're always harmful."

"How can corners send out poison arrows?" Sue asked.

"I'll bet Benjamin Franklin could have answered that one for you," Phil said.

Misty looked bewildered.

"You know. The lightning rod. He discovered that pointed objects give off a steady stream of electrons. A pointy object on the roof will neutralize the charge in storm clouds and prevent lightning from striking."

"*Feng Shui* has been practiced in China for more than three thousand years. How could the ancient Chinese know anything about electrons?" Misty asked.

"I guess they observed the effects caused by sharp corners and didn't worry about an explanation. Sometimes I think we're too concerned with trying to explain everything instead of going on faith with what we feel," Phil said.

"Getting back to me," Jay said. "You're saying my desk corners are poisoning me?"

"Particularly if the corners point toward your bed or the door."

"I don't plan to get a sander to make them round. The desk isn't even mine. Any ideas?"

"Poison arrows travel in straight lines. If you put a cloth or a plant in front of a corner, it will diffuse the arrows and reduce their effect."

Phil looked at Jay. "We should have Misty take a look at R.B.'s room. I'll bet he doesn't have a single poison arrow anywhere in there."

"No. Only a furry one," Jay said.

Misty looked confused again.

"His dog's name is Arrow. Sorry. I'm not good with jokes. Phil says my timing is off."

Phil continued. "The first nation people have always recognized the importance of avoiding corners. Their tepees were round, and they arranged them in a circle. At their gatherings people sat or danced in a circle around the campfire or smudge pot."

"Circles are an integral part of their life and spirituality," Jay added.

"Our society meets in rectangular rooms and sits in rows facing a stage or platform with sharp edges pointing out toward the people. No wonder so many of our meetings produce anger and confrontation," Misty said.

Jay looked around the living room. "Where did the TV go, Phil?"

"It's still there. Under that flowered tablecloth. Misty explained how electronic devices such as TV's and computers draw attention to themselves, and interfere with human interaction, even when they're not turned on."

"If you hide it, your guests aren't distracted and can concentrate on talking to each other," Misty said.

At that moment, the doorbell rang. Becky and Jimmy stepped into the room.

"Hi everybody," Becky said. Jimmy waved in the general direction of the people.

Jay briefly introduced Troy and Misty.

"Come in and join the *Feng Shui* tour," Misty offered.

Becky and Jimmy looked bewildered, but obediently followed Misty to the kitchen.

"You've moved your fridge and stove," Jay commented.

"The cooking stove position is crucial. If it faces the front or back doors it will dissipate the positive *chi* entering the room," Misty explained.

"And the fridge?"

"If the fridge or sink are too close to the stove there will be a clash between the elements of fire and water," Phil said.

"And I am assuming that's a bad thing," a voice called the living room.

"Hi Cam," Phil said. "Is Jamie with you?"

"I'm right here, Phil," Jamie called. "I hope you don't mind if I sit in your favorite chair."

Jamie backed up directly in front of the chair, aimed herself carefully, and eased down gently into it. "This is good. I think I'll stay here all night," she said.

"Great. You haven't met Misty, have you, Jamie?" Phil asked.

Misty pulled a chair over and sat beside Jamie. "How's the little one coming along?"

"Getting bigger every day. I feel the size of a house."

"Do you know if it's a boy or a girl?"

"I know, but I'm not supposed to tell anyone. They want it to be a surprise."

"They?"

"Cam and our parents. Everybody wants to be surprised."

"It's due soon?"

"Due last week."

"So it could be any minute now?" Misty asked.

"I hope it's soon. This has been more trouble than I expected."

"It'll be entirely amazing to have a baby. You'll have created a new person in the world," Misty gushed.

"There are so many people in the world already but every new one is so special," Jamie said.

"I'd love to have a baby but it would be such a responsibility. I don't think I'm ready for that."

"It's been a big task so far. I'll be glad when it's over."

"Doesn't the real work begin after the baby's born?" Misty pleaded.

Jamie frowned. "Not for me. It's going to be hard to give her up. A person develops such an attachment to a baby even before it's born. I hadn't counted on that."

"You and Cam aren't keeping the baby?"

"We'd like to but that's not the plan."

"I'm sorry. I don't want to appear be snoopy. I find things about people's lives exciting. You say it's a girl?" Misty asked.

"Did I let that slip out? Don't tell anyone, please," Jamie pleaded.

"I'm good at secrets. I love knowing about people but I hardly ever gossip."

"Make yourselves comfortable. We have some appetizers, and Jay'll serve the drinks. If you don't mind, Jay," Phil said.

"Let me do the drinks, Phil. We want to hear Jay's story of his California adventures," Cam said. "You know he can't walk and chew gum at the same time, let alone serve drinks and talk."

Jay luxuriated in being the center of attention. "Where should I start?"

"Your search for your father, please," Misty asked. "I think that's totally romantic and exciting. Do you even, like, know anything about him?"

"My mother never wanted to talk about him. I think he left before I was born. I've never even seen a picture of him."

"That was when you lived up north, wasn't it?" Misty asked.

"We lived in a little shack. It wasn't too bad except in winter it could be cold."

"What did you do for heat?"

"We had to cut wood in the summer, and split it during the winter for the stove."

"Wasn't that a bit scary?" Misty asked.

"Blizzards always scared me. I was afraid the snow would cover over the whole place and we wouldn't be able to get out," Jay said.

"You and your mother lived there alone?" Jamie asked.

"I have a younger brother and sister. Someday, I'm going to have them come to visit here. They've never been anywhere."

"There are only the four of you?"

"And usually some man. As far back as I can remember there's always been a man around the house. I remember five but there could have been more."

"Tell us about how you found your real father," Misty begged.

"My mom told me his name is Nobby McNabb. I found his Social Security Number scratched into the wall of our cabin. That's where Cam, the computer wizard, came in. He used the Internet to trace him down to a few possible people in San Francisco. That's why I went there."

"Did you find him?"

"I found where he used to work and talked to a guy who worked with him last year. Steve got my dad's address from him."

"That's such an adventure," Misty said. "I'd love to be there when you see him for the first time. It would be such a totally amazing event."

Cam changed the topic. "Where are you working, Troy?"

"It's a place where they do computer graphics and special effects. They're called Frantic Films. On Arthur Street right near Old Market Square. You know where that is?"

"Sure," Jay said. "It's in the Exchange District. Where they hold the Fringe Festival every summer."

"What's a Fringe Festival?" Troy asked.

"You'll have to see it, Troy. You'd like it. They have amateur plays, music, street buskers, and all sorts of fun things. It's a smorgasbord of creativity. Your kind of thing."

"Your vocabulary is getting out of control again, Jay," Phil said, grinning broadly. "It's time for dinner."

"Would it be terribly impolite if I stayed here?" Jamie asked. "Cam could bring me a plate."

"Not at all," Phil said. "You and the little one deserve to be pampered. Why don't we make it a buffet? We can all sit around the living room and keep you company."

Jay looked at the table and then turned to Phil. "I see you still have the flowers I gave you."

"I always have them on the table. Misty says silk flowers are always good *Feng Shui* anywhere. I know they make me feel good but I thought it was because they remind me of you."

"They're exceptionally good *Feng Shui* because of that," Misty said.

"What other general things should we know about arranging our rooms?" Cam asked.

"The bathroom is important because it's strongly Yin and can unbalance the Yang of the connecting room," Misty said.

"Let's not get into the Yin Yang thing," Cam said. "Just tell me what to do."

"Remember to close the sink and bathtub drains and always put the toilet lid down."

"See, Cam. I always have to remind you to put the seat down," Jamie said.

"I think this whole *Feng Shui* thing is nothing more than a fancy way to make sure that men don't leave the toilet seat up," Cam countered.

"It's not the seat. It's the lid that needs to be down to prevent the positive *chi* from being lost down the drain."

"I can't even remember to put the lid down, so I know I'd never remember to close the drains," Cam said.

"You could keep the bathroom door closed. Maybe that would be the easiest solution for you."

The dinner was leisurely and the conversation flowed as freely as the wine. The clock showed 9:50 p.m.

"Sue and I would love to stay here to bring in the New Year with you guys, but Han Sing needs my help," Jay said. "There were people starting to gather when we left."

"I have an idea," Sue said. "When I was young, my mom used to set the clock ahead two hours. That way we could watch TV and see the big ball drop in Times Square, because New York is two time zones ahead of us."

"That's a wicked idea," Troy said. "That way our clock and New York will be the same."

Phil moved the clock ahead to 11:55. "Okay, guys. Grab a glass. I'm opening the champagne."

Jay put Auld Lang Syne on the stereo. As the clock approached midnight, they held hands and sang until the clock showed midnight. Then everyone shouted, "Happy New Year" and kissed their partner.

Phil stood alone, trying to look inconspicuous. Misty gave Troy a quick kiss and rushed over to kiss Phil. "You've been such an awesome friend to us. Thanks."

"Wow. I wasn't expecting that," Phil said. "Do we get to do this again in two hours?"

"Oh, for sure," Misty said, grinning broadly and winking at Phil.

"Bye, guys," Jay and Sue said as they went out the door. "Ciao, Phil."

Phil laughed. "You're hopeless, Jay."

~ 10 ~

WITH A LITTLE HELP FROM MY FRIENDS

 Sue and Jay stayed at The Red Dragon until well after one o'clock in the morning helping clean up after Han Sing's dinner. Several of the customers were still partying when they left. On the way back to Steve's apartment, and even after they went to bed, they carried on an animated conversation.

"That was greatest New Year's Eve ever, wasn't it?" Jay asked.

"It's the first time I've brought in the New Year twice in the same night," Sue said.

"The dinner at the Red Dragon was way better than I expected. I thought there would be a bunch of strange street people coming in for a free meal and then leaving," Jay said.

"They all seemed to have such a good time. Nobody seemed to want to go home."

"Most of them don't have a real home to go to," Jay said.

"I hadn't thought of that," Sue said.

"And imagine R.B. coming down to join us for midnight. I've never seen him out of his room before."

"What do you suppose he meant about it being his last chance for a celebration with us?" Sue asked.

"I don't want to sound morbid but he's getting old. Maybe he has a feeling about when his time will come."

"It would be nice to be that old and to know when you were fated to die. You could gather the people you want around you and go out surrounded by friends and relatives."

"Where do you suppose he would want to die? It certainly wouldn't be alone in his room," Jay mused.

"Probably he'd want to be with his family. Do you know where he comes from?"

"No. I should have spent more time talking with him. He's always been a shaman to me, more than a person."

"We'd better get some sleep," Jay said. "I promised I wouldn't let you get too tired."

"We can sleep in tomorrow morning."

"I think it's already tomorrow morning."

"Don't be so technical," Sue said, giving Jay a goodnight kiss.

A little after noon, the phone woke Jay.

"Hello."

" . . . "

"I'll see if she's free." Jay covered the mouthpiece. "It's your mom."

Jay passed the phone over to Sue.

"Hi mom."

" . . . "

"Happy New Year to you, too."

"   ."

"We haven't talked about it."

"   ."

"I don't see why not."

"   ."

"We'll be over in a little while. We haven't had breakfast yet."

"   ."

"Bye."

"What's the plan?" Jay asked, getting dressed.

"Mom wants us to come over this afternoon."

"To visit or to stay?"

"She did say it would be nice for me to start the New Year with them."

"How do you feel about it?"

"I'll have to go home sometime. Besides, Steve will be coming back soon."

"Will you be all right with your father?" Jay asked.

"It's not my father I'm worried about."

"Your mother?"

"No."

Jay went to the kitchen and returned with a glass of milk for Sue. "What then?" he asked.

"You."

"Me? How could you be worried about me? You know I'll always be here for you."

"I can't live with my parents without your support," Sue said.

"You know I can't live at your place," Jay said. "I have a feeling your dad wouldn't want to see my face every morning."

"I meant I need to have you in my life. I'm not strong enough to live without you."

"If you're saying you want me to be your boyfriend, that's great with me."

"As a minimum."

"What's the maximum?"

"That would be up to you."

"You know you're my girl. I'd do anything for you. I came back from California for you, didn't I?"

Sue gave Jay a hug. "You are good to me. As long as I have you, I can handle my parents."

"Let's go then," Jay said, throwing off the covers.

Sue got up and put a couple of slices of bread into the toaster.

"Can we get a Slurpee on the way?" she asked.

"You're my girl. You know I'd get you anything you want."

"It'll get us both in a good mood for my parents."

"Maybe we'd better get the jumbo size," Jay suggested.

Sue turned toward Jay as they reached the front door. "I have an uneasy feeling about this."

"I'm sure it'll be all right," Jay said. "I'll stick around until you feel comfortable. After all, it is your home."

Helen answered the door and ushered them into the living room. George was in his usual chair with his usual newspaper. Sue went over to sit with Helen on the sofa. Jay chose a chair facing them.

After a period of uncomfortable silence, Helen said, "Tell us about your New Year's Eve, Sue."

"It was fun. First, we went to Phil's and he did one of his super special dinners. You'd have liked it. It was all fancy ethnic food but made to be totally vegan."

"You mean vegetarian," George said.

"Vegan means no milk, cheese, eggs or meat. Misty's vegan," Sue said.

"Who's Misty?" George asked.

"You remember. I told you about Misty and Troy. Jay's friends from California," Helen said.

"Are they real people or like his other friends?" George asked.

"What do you mean by real people?" Jay asked.

"I mean do they have money? Or do they have to work to buy food?" Jay sat in confused silence.

"What else did you do?" Helen asked.

"We went to the Red Dragon for midnight," Sue said.

"You went to Jay's room?" George asked with a frown, pouring himself another drink.

"No. For your information, I've never set foot in Jay's room. We went to help Han Sing with his annual midnight dinner for his customers. And R.B. came down for it, too," Sue said.

"Sounds exciting," George said sarcastically.

"Did you make any resolutions?" Helen asked.

"Yes, but I can't tell them or they won't come true."

"You're thinking of birthday wishes, silly," Helen said. "You can tell New Year's resolutions."

"I don't want to talk about them right now, if you don't mind," Sue said.

"Now that things are back to normal, I assume you've got those two *momzers* out of the hotel," George said.

"They are checking out today," Jay said.

"I guess you'll be on your way now, too," George said.

"They just got here, George. Try to be hospitable," Helen said. "And please don't drink any more. You promised to cut down, remember?"

"I have cut down. Now that I have my daughter back, this should be a family time."

"That's what it is, George."

"Not with him here, it isn't."

"We should be grateful to Jay. The least you can do is to be nice to him."

"A *kaporeh* on that idea. The only way I'll be nice to him is if I never have to see him again."

Sue looked up. "Let's not get into an argument. This is my first day back. Let's try to be friendly."

Jay stood up. "I think it would be best if I said goodbye now."

He walked over and gave Sue a kiss. "I'll call you tomorrow."

Helen joined him at the door. "Try not to pay too much attention to George. He gets like that when he's been drinking. I'll talk to him when he's in a better frame of mind."

"I understand. I had a stepfather like that," Jay said as he went down the steps to the sidewalk. Jay walked past Sue's Mustang as he made his way toward the street. "Bye, bye, you gorgeous hunk of machinery," he said, pausing to run his hand affectionately along its fender.

"Jay. Wait," Sue called, hurrying down the steps. "I'm coming with you."

Sue went over to the Mustang. "Get in. You drive."

"We can't take your dad's car. He loaned it to me so I could get you home. Now that I've done that, I can't use it anymore."

"Oh, stop being naive. It's my car. Here are the keys. Get in and drive."

Jay held the door open for her, and then buckled up in the driver's seat. "Where are we going?"

"Anywhere away from here."

Jay and Sue drove around for half an hour, talking and trying to decide on their next move.

"I can't stay with my parents. Being there made me realize it's just not possible," Sue said.

"I won't let you go anywhere by yourself. If you aren't going to stay at home, you're going to stay with me."

"But where?"

"I'll move out of the Red Dragon and we'll get a room somewhere. I'm sure we can find a place I can afford."

"What do we do in the meantime?"

"What about staying at Steve's a little longer?"

"Will he mind?" Sue asked.

"He does have his own life, you know. I wouldn't want to impose on him too long."

"Maybe we could stay there until he gets back."

"He gets back Thursday. We need to have a plan before then," Jay said.

Jay and Sue drove back to Steve's apartment after a drive-thru McDonald's lunch.

"We've got to stop eating like this," Jay said. "Next time we cook at home or go to a place where they serve us something other than hamburgers."

Sue nodded agreement.

"We've been eating too much meat," she said.

"I need to get over to the Red Dragon to help Han Sing finish cleaning up after last night. Will you be all right here by yourself?"

"Of course, silly. Maybe I'll phone my mom. It's easier to talk to her alone. I think she understands us. Maybe I'll take a nap."

"I should be back around five," Jay said.

"That should be good. Remember you promised Tiff you'd drive her to her babysitting at six-thirty."

"Thanks for reminding me. I never think of her as a babysitter type."

"She does it only for her niece, Emma Sydney. She loves spending time with that kid."

It was five-thirty when Jay got back. "Did you talk to your mom?"

"We had a good talk. She came up with a great plan. That is, if you agree to it," Sue said.

"Does your dad have anything to do with it?"

"Don't give him a thought. Mom knows how to work around him."

"Okay. What's the plan?"

"She knows of an apartment where we could stay. It wouldn't cost us anything for rent."

"What's the catch? Nobody gives apartments away rent-free."

"My dad has some rental properties. This one isn't rented at the moment. We could move in right away."

"Your dad will be paying for it?"

"Not directly. He'll write it off as a business loss. He has a lot of ways of spending company money without it costing him anything."

"Are you sure we won't be obligated in any way? I don't want to feel in debt to him."

"It's like borrowing his car, only it's an apartment."

"We'd be living together?"

"I'd like that," Sue said.

"I would, too. Isn't it a bit strange that we'll be living together when we haven't even been seeing each other for the past month?"

"We never should have broken up."

"If you recall, it wasn't my idea. It was your dad's," Jay said.

"We should have stood up to him and stayed together through Christmas."

"I didn't want to cause you problems."

"You're so sweet. It didn't work out that way though, did it?"

"Maybe I should stand up to him now and refuse to take the apartment," Jay said.

"Why would you do that?"

"I don't like having decisions made for me by circumstances. Particularly when they're circumstances designed by your dad."

"You know you'd need to get a better paying job."

"It would be hard to leave the Red Dragon. Arrow and R.B. need me."

"They could get along without you. Are you saying you don't want to move in with me?"

"It's not that I don't want to move in with you. I don't know where I'd get a better paying job. I've never worked anywhere else."

"We don't have a choice, then, do we? You keep working at the Red Dragon and we live in Dad's apartment."

"I think we should be the ones who make the decision as to when we want to live together."

"Would you be happier staying at the Red Dragon? I'd stay in the apartment. We could go out on dates and you could come over to visit me whenever you want. That way, when we make a decision, it will be all ours."

"Would you be all right living by yourself?" Jay asked.

"Of course. I'm a big girl. Besides, you'd be as close as the phone. "

"If I had a phone. But, yes, you could always call the pay phone at the restaurant if you needed to get in touch with me."

"We'd better go pick up Tiff now. We'll talk more about this later."

Tiffany looked in the mirror on her way to the door. She checked her Smoky Azure eye shadow, patted the two blonde curls accenting the right side of her face, and smiled to check her lipstick and teeth. She stepped out of her low-rent Osborne Village apartment as Jay and Sue drove up. As always, Tiffany was a picture of carefully sculptured beauty. She moved easily on high-heeled, patent leather shoes, avoiding the cracks in the sidewalk.

"I wish I had a car. I hate imposing on my friends," Tiffany said, as she climbed into the cramped backseat of the Mustang.

"Don't give it a thought. That's what friends are for," Sue said. "Besides it gives me a chance to see little Emma Sydney again. She's such a doll."

"Are you guys going to stay awhile or are you just dropping me off?" Tiffany asked.

"I'd like to stay and visit with you, if you don't mind," Sue said.

"That would be great. We can play with Emma Sydney until she goes to bed, and then chat until her parents get back around midnight."

"Good. I never get to play with little children," Sue said.

"Do you want me to pick you up at midnight?" Jay asked.

"I'm sure they'll give us a lift home when they get back," Tiffany said.

"Cool," Jay said. "I'll drop in on Jimmy and Becky and see how they're doing. I'll see you back at the apartment."

Tiffany and Sue went into the apartment and sat on the floor to help Emma Sydney play with her toys. For the first fifteen minutes, Sue watched the action in fascinated silence. Then she took the initiative and helped Emma Sydney put cutout objects into their spaces in a picture board.

"You'll make a great little mother," Tiffany said.

Sue blushed. "I hope someday I'll get the chance to find out."

"She's not even two years old. How do you know what she wants when she gets upset?" Sue asked. "She can't tell you."

"I just undo the last thing I did. For instance, if I had just picked her up and she gets upset, then I'd set her down again."

"What if that doesn't work?"

"Then I'd distract her with her favorite toy or a story, or play a game."

All too soon for the two babysitters, it was Emma Sydney's bedtime. Tiffany picked her up and started her customary goodnight tour. She held Emma Sydney so she could flip off the kitchen light switch while Tiffany said 'goodnight kitchen.' Then off went the hall light with 'goodnight hall,' followed by the bathroom and the living room, leaving only her bedroom lit.

Then they sat on the bedroom floor together and went through photos of all the family members, saying goodnight to each person by name.

Finally, Emma Sydney turned off the bedroom light. Tiffany said 'goodnight bedroom,' put Emma Sydney in her crib, and tucked her in under her favorite blanket. In the darkened room, Tiffany recited the nightly prayer, including herself in it:

"Mommy and daddy and Tiffany love you very, very much. It's not because you're good, which you are. And it's not because you are clever, which you are. And it's not because you are beautiful, which you are. Mommy and daddy and Tiffany love you very, very much just because you're you. And we always will.

And God loves you too, and we pray He will keep you safe.

Now it's time for all the Emma Sydneys to go sleep, and since you're an Emma Sydney, it's time for you to go to sleep, too."

Tiffany tiptoed out, closing the door behind her. She turned on the living room light and said, "She'll go right to sleep now."

"Some tough job, babysitting her," Sue said.

"They're good parents. I just follow their routine."

"Should we have some popcorn?" Sue asked.

"Popcorn is a no-no when there are young children around. They might find one and choke on it."

"You've learned so much about children. I envy you."

"You'll learn when you need to," Tiffany said. "I'll teach you everything I know when the time comes."

"That won't be anytime soon."

"Becky said you've been seeing a therapist. What's it like?"

"She's very nice. We sit and talk. Sometimes she tells me things."

"What kind of things does she tell you?" Tiffany asked.

"Like that I don't get along well with my dad."

"I could have told you that."

"For my friends it's so obvious we never talk about it. Because she's a stranger we talk about things like that. It's all new to her, so I get to talk about it."

"I went to a psychiatrist once. He wanted to put me on some kind of medication."

"That was suggested to me, too," Sue said. "I told her I didn't want drugs unless it was necessary."

"If you want drugs to make you feel good, Jimmy can probably get you anything you want."

"I'd hope the legal drugs aren't as bad for you as the ones Jimmy used to use."

"Probably not, but I'm told they can be habit forming."

"The only way I'd take drugs is if it would make things easier for Jay."

"Have you asked him about it?"

"I guess I should. He's been really nice to me but sometimes I think my moods are difficult for him."

"How about some ice cream?" Tiffany asked.

"Sure. We might as well pig out while you help me decide what to do with the rest of my life," Sue replied.

"I thought you and Jay had everything worked out. You made such a great pair when you were going together."

"There were some rough spots," Sue said.

"With Jay?"

"Not Jay himself. He's a great guy."

"What then?"

"I'm not sure about getting serious with a native guy."

"He's only part native, isn't he?"

"It doesn't matter how much native blood he has. It has nothing to do with him."

"Then what?" Tiffany asked.

"It's how other people react to him because of his native heritage. And how they'll react to me, as the wife of a native."

"I didn't hear anyone talking about that when you two were going together last fall. I'd bet most of our friends never give it a thought. I know I don't."

"I'm not talking about our friends."

"Who then?"

"My parents and our relatives talk about it all the time. Particularly my dad."

"You mean they're prejudiced?" Tiffany asked.

"They'd never admit it. They're always saying they don't care if he's native but what will other people think."

"So they aren't prejudiced, it's everybody else?"

"That's what they say. Mom understands Jay. If my dad could, he'd make Jay and every other native disappear off the face of the earth."

"Is he really that way?"

"Come to think of it, he'd also like all gays to disappear, too."

"What about lesbians?"

"I doubt he even knows they exist. He's still working on trying to understand that there is such a thing as gay men."

"Any other groups he'd like to get rid of?" Tiffany asked.

"He's probably not too keen on blacks, but he doesn't see many of them so it's kind of as if they don't exist already."

"Is he going to object to your marrying Jay?"

"He made it clear to me before Christmas what kind of boyfriend I should have," Sue said.

"Let me guess. Someone exactly like himself only younger."

"That's not going to happen. I don't plan to have a husband who'll grow up to be like him."

"Did you know he offered me a job as receptionist?" Tiffany said.

"Are you taking it?"

"I should. The pay is great. A job would be a nice change from sponging off my dad. What would he be like to work for?"

"He'd be okay. It's only when he's drinking that he turns impossible. He'd be fine during business hours," Sue said.

"I wouldn't see him except at work."

"You'd have to make sure you don't talk to him after hours."

"What if he phones?" Tiffany asked.

"Caller I.D. is a great invention."

~ 11 ~

SPRECHEN SIE GERMAN?

It was a week after Phil's New Year's party. Misty was out shopping. She didn't have enough money to be buying anything, however, she enjoyed the experience of shopping in the Winnipeg stores.

Troy and Phil were chatting as they tidied up the apartment. "You have any word on when your job with Frantic Films starts?" Phil asked.

"Probably not until the end of the month. They have a project to finish before mine starts."

"That's a tough break when you're short of cash."

"I have an offer to do a gig with Channel 9 TV."

"Are you going to do it?"

"It's TV. I don't know if I can handle it."

"How much difference can there be? They both use a camera to tell a story," Phil said.

"They're doing a series of short fillers on different ethnic groups. The first one is about Hutterite Reservations. I've never even heard of them before."

"You'll find they're called Hutterite Colonies."

"Dude. You know anything about them?"

"Some."

"Hang on a minute," Troy said. He disappeared for a minute and returned with a pencil and notebook. "What can you tell me about them?"

Several pages of notes and two pots of tea later, Troy felt confident enough to begin his new assignment.

A rental van was waiting outside the TV station when Troy arrived. The television camera, tripod, lights and bags of paraphernalia had been loaded. His assistant sat in the driver's seat studying a map of Manitoba. She was a sturdy young lady with short-cropped hair, faded jeans, and a businesslike manner.

"What did you say your name was, again?" Troy asked.

"jaycee smythe."

"jaycee are your initials, right?"

"That's my name. No periods. No capitals. Smythe with a 'y' and an 'e'. And no 'Ms.'"

"Maybe I'll, like, straighten that all out later. Why do we need a map? We can just follow the road signs. A place that big can't be hard to find."

"They deliberately establish their colonies well away from the main highways and communities, ideally near a wooded area or creek. You could drive past a colony on the highway and never know they're there. They try to avoid the world's evil influences."

"You have a route?"

"If we follow the highway west to the Yellowhead Route junction, then turn left, it'll take us right past the Long Plain First Nation reserve."

"Dude. We want a Hutterite Colony, not an Indian reservation."

"Don't call me dude. Once we get that far, we'll be able to find it. Trust me. Besides, we call them reserves. And they aren't Indians. They are first nation people."

"Why do you people use different words for everything?" Troy asked.

"Maybe because we speak Canadian," jaycee said.

"What's wrong with speaking American like everyone else?"

"German would be more helpful right now."

"As if. Canadians speak English and French. I know that."

"Surprise. Hutterites speak German."

Troy set down the camera he was carrying and walked to the driver's window. "Dude. Are you serious? German? Do you speak German?"

"Not a word of it."

"We're, like, in big trouble. Dude. I only speak English."

"In your case, that's debatable. Your surfer American barely qualifies as English."

"How are we supposed to do this gig? What with their German, and like that?"

"Oh, they speak English. Most of them better than you do. Not that it's much of an accomplishment."

"German as well as English? Why don't they speak French?"

"Because they've always spoken German, I guess. Canada encourages people to preserve their heritage. That includes their language. We have a wide diversity of ethnic people. They make up our cultural mosaic."

"Yeah. As if. How can you have a unified country unless everybody speaks the same language? Like, how many languages do you have here in Winnipeg anyway?"

"Lots. St. Boniface is a French community. Also there are the Filipinos, Portuguese, Chinese, Italian, Jewish, Ukrainian, and a whole pile of others. They all try to keep their native language alive for their children."

"We have a huge Chinatown in San Francisco. The signs and everything are all, like, in Chinese. I never go there. I don't do Chinese. They have this huge Chinese New Year parade. I think it's in February. I've no idea why."

"Our Chinatown has some of my favorite restaurants. Winnipeg has a lot of great ethnic restaurants."

"You said you have people who are Jewish? Is there a special section for them somewhere?"

"There're spread out throughout the city. Their religion and family life keeps their language alive."

"Enough chat. Let's get organized. I assume you know how to work these cameras and stuff."

"Sure. I'm a videographer. I'm a pro. It seems I'm also in charge of navigation because you've never lived here, and I'm the one who does the driving because you don't have a license, and apparently you know nothing about Hutterites. Exactly what is your role in this project, anyway?"

"Dude. I'm the one who got us this gig, and I'm the one who knows something about filmmaking. I'm the one with the talent, education and artistic vision. You're the video technician. I tell you what to do and you do it. If you have a problem with that, tell me now. You can be replaced, you know."

"I don't have any problem, except that you keep calling me dude. Stop it."

Unfortunately for jaycee, Troy didn't have the time or inclination to explain that his use of the word 'dude' was not as something to call a person. The tone, not the word, was the message. Its purpose was to express surprise, pleasure, pleading, approval, or any other emotion. Having established the mood with the single word, Troy was saved the trouble of structuring the rest of the sentence.

"Load up this stuff and let's get this show on the road," Troy said.

The tires hummed along the Trans-Canada Highway. Although the fields were covered with snow and the ditches full, the two lanes of the divided highway were black and smooth. The highway was straight and flat.

Troy removed a candy from a tiny paper bag.

"Want one? They're sour somethings covered with sugar," he said.

"No thanks. They're too sour for my taste," jaycee said.

An hour's driving brought them to the first city since leaving Winnipeg.

"Do you want to go around the bypass or through the city?" jaycee asked.

"Dude. Do the city. I've forgotten what civilization looks like," Troy answered.

They drove down the main street of Portage la Prairie, with its five sets of traffic lights, and joined the divided highway again.

"That's it?" Troy asked. "How far to the next city. I blinked and missed that one."

"An hour and a quarter to Brandon. We turn off before then."

Fifteen minutes later, they turned south down a small two-lane highway. The pavement wasn't as smooth, and the corners sharper, but it was clear of snow and ice. jaycee pointed out a large building surrounded by a scattered collection of simple bungalows.

"There's the Long Plain Community Center. The road to the right leads into Long Plain," she said.

"That's the Indian reservation, right?"

"Would you believe, first nation reserve?"

"Dude. What's that tall metal thing over there? It looks like a skinny roller coaster," Troy said.

"Those are grain augers to direct the grain into different storage bins. Most colonies have one. Makes it easy for us to find them."

They made a right turn off the highway at an antique tractor displaying a sign with the name of the colony. The snow was plowed off the gravel road, well back into the ditches.

"There it is," jaycee said as they approached a cluster of buildings. "Who are we supposed to see?"

"Mr. Maendel."

"Didn't they give you a first name?"

"Yeah, but I didn't remember it. I figured we should, like, be formal and go with Mr."

"Clever. I don't suppose you realize 90% of the people on this colony have the name Maendel? They must have told you something else."

"I don't think so. Not that I remember, anyway. If they all have the same name how does anybody tell them apart?"

"That's what first names are for. Even the children address the adults by their first names. Sometimes they use nicknames when they run out of first names."

A man dressed in dark blue coveralls and a black baseball cap walked along the edge of the road.

"Excuse me," jaycee said. "We're from the TV station. Can you tell us where to go?"

Troy muttered under his breath, "Now that's a leading question if I ever heard one."

"Turn right at the next corner," the man said, pointing the way. "Three houses down. Ernest is expecting you."

The van pulled into the driveway, flanked on either side by ridges of plowed snow. jaycee parked the van carefully in the middle of the road. They got out and started to walk toward the door. The bearded man who came to the door to greet them wore a blue-checked shirt and dark pants with suspenders.

"That's the same man," Troy whispered to jaycee. "How did he get here ahead of us?"

"It looks like the same man. He has the same cap, the same full beard, and the same intense eyes. Somehow, he got to be twenty years younger, though."

"What do I say?" Troy asked. "He looks like one tough dude. Should I call him 'sir' or what?"

"Try to speak English instead of Californian," she advised sarcastically.

Troy got out of the van and started to walk toward the house. Looking back to see if jaycee was coming, he tumbled into the snow bank at the edge of the driveway. Brushing the snow off, he walked to the door. The man held out his hand. "Hello. Are you all right? You must be from the TV station."

Troy shook the man's hand. "Yeah, dude. It's cool. I'm Troy. This is my assistant, jaycee."

"Oh, way to go. Very smooth," jaycee muttered as she joined him.

"Come in. We're expecting you. My name is Ernest. This is my wife, Serena," the man said, nodding toward a robust, gently smiling woman dressed in a colorful but muted skirt, white blouse, and a black polka-dot-peppered head shawl. "And here's my daughter, Jennifer," he said, indicating a strikingly attractive young woman with bright, shiny eyes and clear skin.

"Hello," Jennifer said with a friendly, shy smile. "I'm sorry I can't stay to talk but I'm on my way to the kitchen. It's my cook-week." She held the neck of her jacket closed with one hand in anticipation of the chilly weather as she hurried out.

"You'll have tea? We have coffee, if you prefer," Serena said.

A plate of freshly baked cookies sat on the plain wooden table. A potpourri of herb stalks, leaves, and dried blossoms floated near the bottom of a Pyrex carafe on a hot plate. Four straight wooden chairs tucked under a square table waited for the guests. From where they sat, they could see into the kitchen. The counter had been skillfully crafted by colony workers, giving the space a custom-designed yet practical look. A hand-crocheted rug cushioned the floor in front of the sink and brightened the room with its vibrant shades of blue and green.

"Where's your stove?" jaycee asked.

"Most of the cooking and washing are done in the communal area. That's where Jennifer was going."

"The tea smells delightful. Such a golden color! It's homemade?" jaycee asked.

"Yes. Each family mixes its own personal tea. The gardener grows herbs like chamomile and comfrey. We have peppermint and lemon balm in our flower beds," Serena said.

"A girls' work group from one colony will go to another colony to pick linden tree blossoms or go into the woods to pick wild raspberry leaves, hyssop, and licorice. Everything is dried separately. That way, each family can create its own special blend," Ernest explained.

"It's one of the social events that brings young people from different colonies together," Serena said. She filled three mugs with tea before disappearing into another room.

The sound of a contentedly purring sewing machine drifted through the open door. Ernest sweetened his tea with a spoonful of honey and passed the jar to Troy.

Troy munched a cookie and sipped the tea. "We're here to make a film of, you know, your life here. I'd like jaycee here to take about an hour of video around the…uh…"

"Around the colony?"

"Yes."

"What would you want to see?" Ernest asked.

"Your farm operations, of course. Like, maybe the pig barn and some shots of your farm machinery. We'll need at least an hour of tape, jaycee."

"Is it going to be that long a video?" she asked.

"You should plan to have an hour of shooting for a five-minute spot. I need a lot of footage so it can be edited for maximum impact."

"Ray's the *Schweinewirt*. The pig boss. I'm the colony *Wirt*. Ray's a good man. He was my helper a few years back when I was *Schweinewirt*. He has studied pig operations all over the United States and Canada. Our equipment is as modern and efficient as you'll find anywhere. We try to be up to date in all our farm operations."

"I've heard that you set high standards for yourselves."

"Things can't be 'good enough' for us. They must be good, and that is enough," Ernest said.

"And some footage of your family life. How you live, what you do for fun, stuff like that," Troy said.

"You and I will talk about our life on the colony. The video shots will be only of the colony's work and the business aspects. Pictures cannot capture the spirit of our religious and personal life. They would be misleading when out of context. You don't want that," Ernest said.

"No pictures of the people?" Troy asked.

"Only if they are working at something. Posing for a picture shows vanity and conceit. We discourage that."

"What about other aspects of your personal lives?"

"There are few other aspects. Only different facets of our religion," Ernest said.

"What about family life?"

"The mother stays home with the children. The women don't have to take time from their other activities to prepare meals, except when they have their week of communal kitchen duty. Until her child is five years old, the mother brings home its food from the communal dining room.

From ages five to fourteen the children eat in the separate children's dining room."

"I was told the Hutterites started the first kindergarten," Troy said, checking his notes.

"Yes. Starting at age two-and-a-half, children go to the *Klanaschul* under the direction of experienced women we call *Kinderankelä*. That leaves the mothers free to work with the other women in the garden doing the hoeing, weeding and picking vegetables for canning and freezing."

"You certainly are self-sufficient, aren't you?"

"There are still a lot of things we buy. Dry goods such as shoes, fabric, and sewing materials. Grocery staples such as flour, sugar, teas and coffee. We buy toothpaste, shampoo, and medicines such as cough syrup. However, we grow our own vegetables and do all our own baking and food processing. We do a lot of our own sewing."

"You look after the people within your community, too, don't you?" Troy asked.

"Yes, except for medical and dental work, we respond to all our people's needs."

"And all the people contribute?"

"Paul's rule in the Bible says: who does not want to work, shall not eat."

"What about people who are too old or unable to work?"

"We don't require work, only the desire to work, from our communal family. We expect it from those who can, but we provide for all the people according to their needs. An old person who needs home care is the responsibility of the children, brothers, sisters, aunts, nieces and close friends who come to stay for two weeks at a time. In this way each person's turn to provide care comes around two or three times a year."

Without a knock, the door opened and a younger, thinner version of Ernest, but with a five-o'clock-shadow instead of a full beard, came in.

"This is, Ray. He will show you around the community," Ernest said.

jaycee turned toward Ray. "Why do you have such a modern-style beard?"

Ray smiled. "You should ask, instead, how long I've been married."

Troy said to Ernest, "You and I can talk while jaycee and Ray do the picture things. I'll dub in the commentary later."

Troy popped a candy into his mouth and held out the bag to Ray, then to Ernest. Ray took a nibble, puckered his lips, and exclaimed, "*Zwinkern*."

Ernest shook his head and declined Troy's offer.

"What does *Zwinkern* mean?" Troy asked.

Ray smiled. "It's an old German expression meaning to screw up your eyes. It's what my grandfather used to say when he tasted something surprising."

Ray headed toward the door and said, "Come. We can start in the barn."

"Does everyone wear black or dark clothes? Or is it a winter thing?" jaycee asked.

"No matter how hot it gets in the summer, you'll never see anyone dressed in cutoffs or sleeveless tops," Ray said as they left. "We appreciate clothes that are well-made and modest, not flashy."

Troy set his tape recorder on the table. "How about a quick history of how you came to be here. I assume that since you speak German, you must have come from Germany."

"Our way of life originated with the Anabaptist movement in the German part of Switzerland. It started in 1525 with a group of fifteen Reformed Church members who believed that the Bible, and not the Pope, was the ultimate authority in religious matters. They also agreed that true believers should not use the sword or violence to protect themselves. Before the group departed, they baptized each other. This marked the beginning of the Anabaptist movement and its tenet of adult baptism, also called believer's baptism. They wait until the person is old enough to understand that commitment to the church is the center of our life. For us, this is nineteen or older. Acceptance of these beliefs marked the beginning of the persecution of all those who shared the Anabaptist belief."

"Persecution?" Troy asked.

"In March of 1526, re-baptism was officially declared punishable by death. In 1527, Felix Mantz became the first Anabaptist martyr when he was drowned in the Limmat River in downtown Zurich. Because of this, the Anabaptists moved to other countries."

"Couldn't they have done the baptisms in secret?"

"We do not hide who and what we are."

"Cool, dude."

Ernest gave Troy a skeptical look and continued.

"The Catholics and Protestants both hated the Anabaptists for refusing to baptize their children, and for re-baptizing adults who had been baptized as children in their own churches. They were also hated for saying the country was not Christian because wars are contrary to Jesus' teaching of love for our enemies. Charles V decreed that all Anabaptists were to be regarded as dangerous heretics and exterminated. From the German-speaking countries, Anabaptists fled to Moravia, a part of what was then Czechoslovakia."

"Being Hutterite and Anabaptist is, like, the same thing?" Troy asked.

"In Moravia, the Anabaptists broke into several different groups. In 1528, Hutterites began the practice of having the community share all goods, and took their name from Jakob Hutter who was the elder from 1533 until 1536. He was publicly tortured and burned at the stake in downtown Innsbruck as a warning to those who chose to follow his teaching. Other Anabaptists became the Mennonite, Quaker, and Amish people. In 1770 our people moved to Russia to escape persecution."

"Was Russia a good country for you?"

"Yes, for a hundred years. Then czar Alexander II decreed that all instruction in school had to be carried out in Russian and that military service was compulsory for everyone. Neither requirement was acceptable to the Hutterian Brethren, so twelve hundred of them came to the Dakota Territory, which is now North and South Dakota. Only a third of those, about four hundred people, continued with the tradition of communal living and established *Bruderhöfe* or colonies. The others settled on individual farms and joined the Mennonites, who share many of our beliefs but do not practice communal ownership of property."

"Is it true all Hutterites are descended from only fifteen families?"

"It's true we have only the fifteen original surnames, except for the dozen or so individuals who have subsequently chosen to join us. Originally, there were more family surnames. However, some faded out from lack of male children."

"How many Hutterites are there all together?"

"We are presently about 40,000, living in 430 *Bruderhöfe*."

"What did you say *Bruderhöfe* meant?" Toy asked.

"We call our colony a *Bruderhof*. Literally, it means, 'brother yard'. When our yard gets too crowded, we start a new colony. Our numbers, and the number of colonies, is steadily increasing."

"You start new colonies?"

"A colony will branch out when it becomes economically necessary. Because there are quotas on the amount of grain and livestock, such as turkeys, that producers can sell, a colony eventually reaches a point where there is not enough work for the married men. This usually happens when the colony reaches somewhere between 100 and 150 people."

Troy said, "Can't you just raise more stuff? I thought Manitoba produced thousands of hogs."

"Hogs are the only agricultural product without government quotas, so it's not that simple. Besides, there is a biblical basis for maintaining a moderate size. In St. Luke's account of Jesus' feeding of the multitude, before Jesus fed the thousands, he divided them into groups of between fifty and a hundred. That's about the size of our colonies. "

"Let's get back to the history lesson. Your people were happy in the United States?"

"All was well until the First World War. We are pacifists. We do not fight in our daily life, and we don't participate in wars. The pressure of American conscription forced us to move to Canada."

"Doesn't that mean you are taking the benefits of the society but aren't willing to support it?"

"We support the society of the country where we live. Forty years ago, we lost our religious tax exemption. Since then we pay the same taxes as any large corporate farming operation. Some people criticize us for not participating in community team sports but we don't consider them important. The only important thing we don't do is that we don't join any military organizations or activities. Other than that, we support the local businesses and communities. Local blood donor clinics are always a field of suspender-supported black trousers, and polka-dotted headscarves."

The sewing machine stopped and a voice said, "It's also a chance for us to socialize with friends from other colonies. Our young people never miss a chance to meet potential marriage partners from other colonies."

Ernest continued, "Any time there is a community disaster people know they can count on us to help, without needing to be asked. Helping others is our way of life. Everyone knows his duties and obligations to his fellow man. It is not our way to ever ignore these obligations."

Troy consulted his notes. "I was told that during the flood of 1950, one of the dike builders requested, 'Send me ten more men. Or five Hutterites.' Why would he say that?"

"We bring our construction machinery with us."

The sewing machine stopped again. "Don't be modest. It's because we know how to work long and hard until the job is done."

The clang of a bell interrupted the interview. "That is the dinner bell," Ernest said.

"I suppose it's also used to call you to church?" Troy suggested.

"No. We are never summoned to church. We go voluntarily because we want to."

"But how do you remember when to go?"

"How do you remember to breathe? Religion is our life. We watch the minister's house when church time nears. When he leaves his house and walks to church, we follow. Now, you follow me to lunch."

~ 12 ~

WALKING A SPIRITUAL PATH IN PRACTICAL SHOES

Ray and jaycee joined Troy and Ernest at the dining hall entrance. Ernest led the way with the others carefully following his lead. A stainless steel cauldron held steaming, bubbling vegetable soup, which filled the room with its appetizing aroma. Stainless steel trays held dozens of baked half-chickens. On the back counter an industrial-size pasta maker waited in spotless readiness. Troy's face betrayed his amazement at the size and polish of the operation.

"We all eat at the same time. Our kitchen needs to be efficient," Ernest said, as they filled their trays. "We are lucky today. They have Hutterite French fries."

"How are they different from McDonald's?" Troy asked.

"They are cooked together with strips of onion for extra flavor."

The four joined a group of men at one of the long tables in the main dining hall. Troy looked around. "The women are all sitting on the other side of the room. Should jaycee be sitting over there instead of here?"

Ernest looked at jaycee with renewed interest while he answered, "We do not operate by rules. It is only a convention that the men and women sit separately. It has always been done that way. There is no reason to do it differently. The children eat in a separate room."

He leaned over to speak quietly into Troy's ear, "Is jaycee a woman?"

Troy smiled. "It's, like, hard to tell, isn't it? I think she is but I wouldn't bet the farm on it."

Ernest chuckled at Troy's joke, then returned his attention to his plate and the plentiful supply of freshly baked bread. A young man came into the dining room.

Ernest's gaze followed him. "That's my son. He turned fifteen last month. Now he eats with the men. It's one of our rites of passage."

"Do you have other rites?"

"When boys are two-and-a-half years old, they get to wear their first suspenders. Girls change from the *Mitz* to a head shawl at approximately age thirteen."

"What's a *Mitz*?"

"It's that attractive, peasant-style bonnet with a strap under the chin that young girls wear. Doesn't your society provide events that signify growing up?"

"Getting a driver's license is the only thing I can think of. Even that's not as significant as it used to be, now that all-terrain vehicles have become popular."

After lunch, Troy and Ernest returned to the house and resumed their interview.

"How have you managed to maintain your culture and beliefs, what with all your moving around from country to country?"

"The Bible has always been our central guide. It is the first word and the last word of our life. Our faith does not change."

"What about the services? Don't they change?" Troy asked.

"The sermons are read in church exactly as they were written 450 years ago. In German, of course. The minister may add or leave out passages, and he might ad-lib pertinent occasional comments. Sometimes the sermon is shorter, and sometimes parts are given in English."

"That's the only change after four centuries?"

"Many colonies now use hymn books instead of the traditional lining."

"Lining?"

"Having the minister say each line before we sing it."

"I see. Don't you feel a need to keep up with the changing times?"

"God does not change. The Bible does not change. Why should our church services change? Each minister has his own set of the sermons. When a new colony branches out, the one minister stays and keeps his set of volumes. The other leaves for the new colony with his own set."

"What about language? You must have had many changes in language over the centuries."

"Wherever we go, we remain German. In our homes and elsewhere in the community, we speak the Tyrolean dialect of our Austrian ancestors. Standard German is used in church. We learn the language of the country where we live. In that way, we can become part of the community."

"Isn't this difficult for the children to learn? I have trouble with one language."

"Our children speak and hear only Tyrolean in the home. It is our oral language. In *kleine Schul*, or little school, until they are five years old, they are introduced to standard German through songs and simple prayers such as table grace and the Lord's Prayer. When they start regular school, they start learning English."

"But don't they, like, forget the German?"

"What children learn in the first five years, they will never forget. Besides, they have German school, which we call *grussa Schul*, as well as English school, every day. Our church services are in German and the parents speak the Tyrolean dialect at home. We use English for business off the *Bruderhof*, not for ourselves. When we lived in Russia, we spoke Russian and German. When we moved, we would use the language of our new home when speaking to the local people, but we are always German in our own community no matter where we are."

"It sounds like a lot of school."

"What else is there? Children go to school. Adults work. That's life. You'd say we get up early and go to bed early, but it's the same for all farmers."

"I understand church is important to you. I have friends who go to church almost every week," Troy said.

"We go to church at least once every day. It's an important part of our life. Our children go to school until they are fifteen. The adults go to church all their lives."

"All the children leave school at age fifteen?"

"They usually start an informal apprenticeship at age fifteen. Many colonies believe that education beyond age fifteen can be of benefit to the colony, so individual students are allowed to continue. Some more progressive colonies are educating their own people to become teachers."

"Am I right in saying that your colony structure is patriarchal? You know, like, the man is in charge?"

"Yes. The man is the head of the household."

The sewing machine in the next room stopped abruptly. "And the woman is the neck that supports the head, and, when necessary, turns it in the right direction." The machine resumed its activity with a furious whir.

"I read that there isn't much crime on a colony," Troy continued.

"Look around. What would you want to steal? The chairs? The table?"

"I wouldn't mind having that big, fancy new truck sitting out there on the road. It was running with no one in it when we came. I could have hopped in and driven it away. You people are pacifists. You wouldn't use force to stop me, would you?"

"We believe in *Gütergemeinschaft*, the common ownership of goods, even among different colonies."

"Where did you get that idea?"

"From the Bible, of course. In Acts 4 it says that the whole group of those who believed were of one heart and soul, and no one claimed private ownership of any possessions, but they had everything in common."

"Do you actually do that? You have no personal possessions?"

"Nothing of value. Maybe a watch, a pocketknife, a Bible, and a desk or dresser. In this life, people are stewards of the land and of its material goods. It is dust to dust, nothing more."

"But that truck is yours, isn't it?"

"I drive it but it belongs equally to everyone on the colony. If you took it, someone would see you, and it would be as if you were taking his truck."

"Couldn't I just drive it off the colony?"

"You would find some machinery blocking your way before you got to the road. Then you would soon be answering to all ninety-five of us for your actions."

"I see what you mean. But there must be some theft on the colony."

"A bunch of youngsters might steal a pie from the kitchen or some pop from the communal pantry. A man might help himself to a bottle of dandelion wine for a special private occasion. Because we don't have personal possessions, we have no theft."

"What about members who do violate your way of life?"

"There is a six-man council for each *Bruderhof*. They make decisions on major policies and problems that affect the colony and its operation: the Minister, the Colony *Wirt*, the German Teacher, and the farm manager, are automatic council members. The others are elected."

"What happens to those who are guilty of breaking your rules?"

"We talk to them and explain to them the error of their ways."

"And that's it? Aren't they banished from the colony or put in jail or punished somehow?"

"If they do not see their error, we may be forced to restrict our daily interaction with them."

"You're saying you isolate them?"

"We'd start by not wishing them, 'Peace be with you' when we meet. If it were more serious, they would not be permitted to attend council. If it were even more serious, they would not eat at the table with us. They would not be banished from the *Bruderhof*, although they might choose to leave if they do not wish to follow our ways. We have a saying: you are either in the ark or you're not. There's no part way."

"What about your children and teenagers? How do you handle them? We have trouble with crime and violence involving our children."

"Our children are rarely punished. They may be unruly or foolish but they are never evil. We discourage rough play when they are little. They learn to love one another and to work together for the good of the *Bruderhof*. Children are like soft wax that can be molded and formed by words and experiences. Our children have no way to learn the thoughts or ways of crime and violence. We insulate them from the negative influences of the outside world."

As jaycee walked into the room, Troy turned off the recorder. "How did the shoot go?"

"Great. I wish I lived in their pig barn. They control the temperature to within two degrees and adjust it for different stages of the pregnancy. Their whole farm operation is super hi-tech. Computers and everything," jaycee said.

"I hope you made some notes. The temperature won't show on the tape. You'll have to add some voice-over to explain the operation."

"I suppose I'll have to explain why we're all wearing surgical masks."

"That'll be obvious. It's because of the smell."

"Obviously wrong. It's to keep from giving any of our germs to the pigs. Those animals are treated with more care and concern than we are in a hospital," jaycee said.

"What's it like to be a man living on the colony?" Troy asked.

"What would you reckon to be the perfect existence? What are the things you treasure most in your life?" Ernest countered.

"Catching a gnarly wave and riding it in. That, and kicking back with my bros on the beach. That's what I live for," Troy said.

"That may be fine for you," jaycee said, "but I'd want to have work I enjoy. And a job that gives me security, satisfaction and friendly people at work. Of course, a husband and a few kids to make me feel proud, and who don't cause me grief would be nice. I'd like to be able to retire when I'm fifty-five, knowing I'll be looked after in my old age, and live out the rest of my life surrounded by family and friends. A first-class ticket to heaven when I die would be a bonus."

"*Ja wohl.* That's life on the *Bruderhof,*" Ernest said.

On the drive back to Winnipeg, Troy asked jaycee about her experience on the colony. "What did you think of their dress and lifestyle?"

"I think they try to present a picture of themselves to the world," jaycee said.

"I like that," Troy said, pulling out his notebook and jotting it down. "What does it mean?"

"The colony wants the world to accept them as ordinary people who have chosen a different way of life from that of their neighbors. They do this by presenting themselves as a living picture of how they see themselves."

"How does their dressing in dark clothes and black baseball caps and polka-dotted head scarves do that?"

"Their clothing symbolizes simplicity and their rejection of the vanity that is mirrored in possession of worldly goods."

"So?" Troy asked.

"They live a spiritual life, in a practical world. Their religion is their life."

"Dude. That's good. We could maybe get a title for the show out of that. Anything else?"

"When they look at each other, what they see reminds them of their origins, their Christian beliefs, and the emphasis they place on preparing for life after death."

"What else did you learn?"

"They make great rhubarb, dandelion, raisin and chokecherry wines."

"Be serious. I can't use that."

"I liked the Hutterian Golden Rule."

"What's that?"

"What's mine is yours, and what's yours is mine."

Troy turned toward jaycee. "Dude. You have totally cool ideas. Would you want to help me with the commentary?"

"What does it pay?" jaycee asked. "Maybe Hutterites don't do the personal property thing but I do. And I have to eat."

"Minimum wage, at least," Troy said.

"Okay. If you quit calling me dude."

~ 13 ~

WHO'S BEEN EATING MY PORRIDGE?

Steve paused outside the Winnipeg baggage claim area to organize himself for the transition from the wet and warm of California, to the cold and sunny of Winnipeg.

"I should have come back with Jay. At least then he could have carried his own suitcase," he muttered to himself, setting the three suitcases on the floor.

He slid a black, knitted toque over his half-inch brush of bleached-blond hair and pulled it carefully down over his ears, covering the silver rings in his left ear and silver studs in his right one. His boyishly round face with its neatly trimmed, light brown five-o'clock shadow made him look younger than his twenty-eight years. Experience had taught him to remove his diamond nose stud when traveling.

Turning up his collar, he shoved his hands into his fur-lined gloves, tucked one suitcase under his arm, picked up the other two, and ventured out onto the street. A dark blue Mustang sat at the curb in the no-parking zone with its motor running and its heater struggling to keep the side windows clear of frost.

As Steve walked beside the car, its window rolled down and a voice called out, "Hey, Steve. Hop in, I'm going your way."

"Hi, Mustang Boy. Every time I see a Mustang I always think of you, and here you are," Steve said, climbing into the car.

"Why does a Mustang make you think of me?" Jay asked.

"I know how much you used to like driving Sue's car when you two were going together."

"It may not be a Lexus like yours, and it's not even a convertible but it'll get me where I want to go," Jay said.

"I was halfway afraid Phil might come to pick me up," Steve said.

"On his motorcycle? He'd have to be crazy to ride a motorcycle in the winter. You'd be crazy to ride with him. The streets are solid ice."

"He's done crazier things than that. Thanks for coming to pick me up. I could have taken a taxi but this is nice."

"It was the least I could do."

"You mean for helping you get back from California and bringing your stuff? Forget it."

"That and other things."

Steve looked over at Jay. Jay concentrated on the road.

"How's Sue?" Steve asked.

"She's fine, except she tires easily."

"Did they find out what was wrong with her?"

"Some kind of emotional trauma," Jay answered.

"Is she getting over it?"

"I think so. However, emotional pain hurts. And Tylenol doesn't help."

"I know what you mean. I've been there. Often. Do you know what happened to her?" Steve asked.

"Nobody seems to know or doesn't want to say. I don't pry."

"Sounds like a good idea. Is she still in the hospital?"

"She's out but doesn't want to stay at home."

"So where is she?"

"Surprise. We're staying at your place. I hope you don't mind," Jay said with a hopeful grin.

"I'm happy to help."

"I know I should have asked you first but I didn't have much choice."

"You're both welcome anytime. You know that," Steve said.

"Thanks. We didn't know what else to do. She didn't want to go home."

"My spare room is usually empty. Sue has problems at home, does she?"

"Her dad is heavy into the booze. He's a different guy from when I knew him before. He seems to be down on everything."

"You included?"

"Big time. I used to think he liked me a little but he's barely civil to me now."

"Any clues why?" Steve asked.

"Maybe he's angry that I'm back in Sue's life."

"That would be my guess but maybe there's more to it than that."

"Like what?"

"Maybe he realizes his little girl if going to leave the nest someday soon."

"I never know how to deal with him," Jay said.

"Don't ask me for advice. I'm the guy whose dad pays him to stay away, remember?"

"Too bad I'm not gay. Maybe I could get some kind of deal like that."

"Be careful what you wish for. You might get your wish and regret it," Steve said.

"I'll think about that later. Right now, I'm more concerned about getting Sue established."

"What's stopping you?"

"Her dad's planning on setting her up in an apartment. If I move in with her, then I'll be taking charity from her dad. He'd own me."

"Only if you let him. People accept favors all the time. It's the motivation that makes the difference. That, and your reaction to the situation. You need to talk it over with him."

"Maybe later. After things have settled into a routine."

Jay parked in front of Steve's apartment. "Let me carry your suitcase."

"Some of it's your stuff, anyway," Steve said.

"Hi Sue. We're here," Jay called as he and Steve entered the apartment.

"Hi guys," Sue called from the kitchen. "I made some coffee and we have a few Oreos left."

"We'll be there in a minute," Jay said.

Jay accompanied Steve as he made a fast inspection tour around his apartment. "It's so clean and tidy. Usually my friends leave the place looking like a refugee camp," Steve said.

"It's important to leave things the way you find them. Phil taught me how to keep things neat and tidy."

"I hope you've learned a few things from me as well."

"Oh, yes. You're a very special person to me. I owe you a lot."

"Thanks. It means a lot to me that you can accept me, what with knowing I'm gay and all," Steve said.

"It used to be an issue. But gay or straight, it makes no difference to me now. I like you as a person. Your sex life is none of my business, and it doesn't bother me at all," Jay said. After a moment's silence he added, "Especially if I don't think about it."

Jay and Steve joined Sue in the kitchen. "How was San Francisco?" Sue asked. "I've always dreamed of going there."

"Unbelievable. I can hardly wait to go back again," Steve said.

"It was a real eye-opener for me," Jay added. "I hope we can spend some time there when I go to see my father, Sue. We could explore the city together. Those hilly streets are so amazing. And the view from across the Golden Gate Bridge is absolutely breathtaking. You'd love it."

"That would be nice. I've never been anywhere outside Manitoba," Sue said.

"I'd have thought your parents would have traveled all over the world," Jay said.

"They've traveled overseas and everything but they always left me here because I had to go to school. My grandparents would look after me for weeks at a time. I hated it."

"Didn't you like your grandparents?"

"Oh, I liked them all right. It was the idea of being left out that I didn't like."

"I'll make it up to you," Jay said.

"Before you two start getting all mushy, there's something I want to give you, Jay," Steve said.

"What?"

"Your father's address."

"You mean the one in San Francisco?"

"No. I mean the address where he moved. I went to Nob Hill and got your dad's letter from the guy he used to work with," Steve said.

"You went to all that trouble for me?" Jay asked.

"It seemed to be the right thing to do at the time."

"You left when you were so close to finding your dad? Just to help me?" Sue asked.

"Of course. You're the most important thing in my life," Jay said, going over to kiss Sue.

"Okay, you lovebirds," Steve said. "Enough of that stuff."

"Can I have the letter, please?" Jay asked, practically jumping up and down with excitement.

"It's there in your suitcase with your parka," Steve said. "I'm going to visit Cam and Jamie when I get unpacked. The baby's not here yet, is it?"

"I don't think so, at least it wasn't when I saw them New Year's Eve," Jay said.

They went into Steve's bedroom. Steve carefully unpacked his suit-case, hanging each item carefully in the closet or folding it neatly into a dresser drawer. Jay checked through his suitcase looking for the letter.

"It was good of you to get my things from the hotel," Jay said.

"You didn't leave me much choice, taking off the way you did."

"You could have left them. It wasn't your problem."

"It was my problem because I'm your friend. Your problems are my problems," Steve said.

"If I get the chance I hope I can be as good a friend as you are."

"I think you've proven yourself with Sue already."

"Thanks. I'm trying to," Jay said.

"There's something I should tell you. I didn't want to mention it in front of Sue."

"Something serious?"

"Not serious. It's just that I have a friend coming to visit for a few days."

"That means you'll be needing the spare bedroom?"

"Not necessarily."

"You'd want us out of here, anyway," Jay said.

"It's up to you. There's lots of room. However, I don't know how Sue would react to having the four of us living here together."

"I'm not sure how I'd react, either. It's a bit different seeing people living together."

"It won't be until early next week, anyway. Don't get me wrong, you're welcome to stay. I just didn't want you to be uncomfortable with the situation."

"No problem. We're looking at an apartment tomorrow. We'll be out of here in a day or so."

"I hope you don't feel I'm pushing you out."

"Not at all. You've been totally understanding about our moving in like we did. We really appreciate it."

Jay moved off to the living room to read his father's letter:

La Queresadore Ranch
1231 Alamore Pintata Road
Solvang CA 93427

Hi Buddy—

I bet you didn't think you'd ever hear from me again after I left San Francisco. For the first couple of days the hitchhiking was bad. I didn't get a single ride. I was beginning to think I should turn around and go back to my old job. We did have fun working together, didn't we, even if the pay wasn't all that much.

Then I lucked out getting a ride with a salesman going to L.A. He was stopping at all the small towns along the way so he took me right to Solvang. Everyone here is really nice. I'm living in their house trailer and there's lots of room. You could stay here if you come to visit.

They have guests all the time so they are looking for another worker—maybe you could come and get their faucets to quit leaking. You really should pack up and move here—the pay is good and they treat me like family. The phone number is 402 555 6215. The weather here is great—it's a perfect place to live. They say there are rattlesnakes but I haven't seen any. The annual tarantula migration apparently goes across their driveway but that's only in November, and it doesn't last all that long. Tom says tarantulas are friendly things—they just get bad press.

I'm using my proper name now—Winston—so if you phone, ask for Winston.

Your old buddy,
Nobby

Jay sat reading and rereading the letter until his eyes became too moist to see the words. "Now I know where my middle name came from. He really must be my dad," he said to himself.

After breakfast, Jay and Sue packed their things into the car and drove down Portage Avenue to the apartment block. The recent coat of paint didn't succeed in hiding the age of the rambling two-story complex.

"Which entrance do we use?" Jay asked.

"I don't suppose it matters. Mom said the apartment was at the west end. There should be parking at the back."

Sue unlocked the door. Jay scooped her up in his arms and carried her into the apartment.

"What are you doing?" Sue laughed.

"It's your first apartment. I felt we needed to do something to mark the occasion, and I didn't have time to chill a bottle of champagne to christen it."

"That's for ships, silly," Sue said.

They looked at the empty rooms. The cracked walls needed paint. The windows were permanently stuck shut from too much paint. A suspicious looking hole in the baseboard hinted that they might not be the only ones who would be living there.

Jay looked at the hole. "Do you want to hear a joke?" he asked Sue.

"Sure."

"You know that it's the early bird that gets the worm?"

"Yes."

"But it's the second mouse that gets the cheese," Jay said.

"Clever," Sue said.

"Sometimes I wish I were the second mouse with you dad."

"He'd just keep resetting the trap."

"The room will look better when it has some furniture in it," Jay suggested tentatively.

"I'll need everything. A kitchen table and chairs. Sofa and chairs. A bedroom set. Television."

"Don't forget a stereo. It's going to cost a lot."

"You still have the Amex card, don't you?" Sue asked.

"We can't use it for furniture unless we ask first. Do your folks have any old stuff they can let you use to get started?" Jay asked.

"I wouldn't want to go through the hassle of asking my dad."

"Maybe we could ask your mom."

"That could work," Sue said.

"Maybe you could leave the second bedroom empty for now."

"Some pictures might help," Sue said. Jay and Sue looked at each other. "Not like the ones Steve has," they said together and laughed.

"We need Misty here. This place could use some *Feng Shui*," Jay said.

"You're right. It needs all the help it can get."

"Are you sure you want to stay here?" Jay asked. "You don't have to, you know."

"It'll be fine. I can learn to dodge the poison arrows."

"Some big puffy furniture would absorb them. It'll be a challenge."

"I'm not going to live with my parents. If we can't afford to pay for a place on your wages, maybe I can get a job. This will do fine until we can afford somewhere better."

"I'd have thought your dad would have wanted you to be in a fancier place than this. He's usually so concerned about appearances."

"You have a lot to learn about him. He's hoping I won't like it, and will move back home. Getting his own way is important to him."

"I guess he doesn't know you very well, does he?"

"He's been too involved with his work to notice I've grown up. And lately, booze takes up all his spare time."

"You're worried about him, aren't you?" Jay asked.

"I feel responsible for the stress I put on him," Sue said.

"You aren't doing anything that should cause him stress. If he's stressed, it's because of how he chooses to react. That makes it his problem, not ours."

"You're right, of course. But I still feel guilty," Sue said.

"I know. Words don't change feelings. Emotions never listen to logic."

"Let's go furniture shopping. We'll just go ahead and use the card. I find it's always easier to get forgiven than to get permission."

"You're a lot like your mom in some ways, aren't you? What style are you thinking of going with?"

Sue's brow furrowed. "It's hard to imagine a style for this apartment. Maybe we should go with the garage-sale look."

"Or you could go with new stuff now. Then it would fit into our new place when we get it."

"Ah. You said, our place. That's sweet of you. Let's go with second-hand stuff. My dad won't be able to complain about the cost, and we won't have to worry about sticking with a motif."

"I know the perfect place. Let's do a tour of Value Village stores."

"I've heard of them but I've never been to one. Aren't they like junk stores?"

"Jimmy and I spend a lot of time shopping there. They have great stuff. It's old but some of it's barely used."

"We could say we're going for a retro look."

"Besides, we'd be helping a charity. They get the goods donated, and give the money to a good cause, like diabetes research."

"Would it be tax deductible? My dad only donates to charities that give tax receipts."

"I doubt it. Doesn't your dad ever do anything without having an angle to benefit himself?"

"Not that he'd ever admit."

"If we find some things we like, then I'll see if I can borrow a truck tomorrow," Jay said.

"Where do you want to go for lunch?"

"Let's go back to Steve's place and start packing up our stuff. We can grab a bite there."

"Good idea. Steve's been great about our staying there. We should get out of his way while he's still happy with us."

Jay and Sue spent the afternoon touring furniture and secondhand stores. It was nearly dinnertime when they returned to Steve's apartment.

Steve was engrossed in vacuuming the living room. Jay walked up behind him and tapped him on the shoulder. Steve jumped and said something undecipherable, but clearly profane.

"Sorry, man," Jay said. "I didn't mean to scare you."

"Forget it. I scare easily. It comes with the territory."

"What territory?" Sue asked.

"Being gay. A lot of people consider gays fair game for hassling. We learn to scare easily when we're young."

"I'm sorry," Jay said. "I'll try to remember next time."

"Do you have plans for dinner?" Steve asked.

"Nothing specific. However, we do plan to eat," Jay answered.

"Good. Let's go to The Panic Restaurant on Broadway. Maybe they still do vertical food."

Jay looked at the ceiling. "Oh, great. Here we go again. Is it only you or do all guys like you want to go to places I've never heard of?"

Steve smiled. "It's all guys like me. Travel agents like to eat in fancy places. I assume that's what you meant."

"Smart guy. I deserved that. Can Sue and I afford vertical food? It sounds expensive, whatever it is."

"You could use the credit card," Sue suggested.

"That wouldn't be fair. I don't want to abuse your mom's generosity."

"My treat," Steve said. "I'm an incurable romantic. You two make such a cute couple. For a pair of straights, that is. I'd love to treat you to a fancy dinner."

"Thanks, you're a sweetheart. By the way, we'll be moving out tomorrow," Sue said.

"You know you're welcome to stay if you want. Where are you going?"

"We'll drive by the apartment on our way to dinner so you can see it," Jay said.

"Great. Let's go," Steve said.

After a brief stop at the apartment block, they arrived at the restaurant.

"Nothing on this menu makes any sense," Jay said. "Especially the prices."

"Leave it up to me," Steve said. "I love playing the host."

The waiter came by and flipped a napkin onto each of their laps.

"And what will you be having this evening?" he asked.

"We'll have three orders of vertical food," Steve said.

"We don't do that much anymore but I'm sure we can accommodate you. What would you like?"

"Surprise us. Tell Lenny it's for Steve and his friends. He'll make something impressive for us."

"Very good, sir. And to drink?"

"A bottle of *Dom Pérignon*. Well chilled."

"An excellent choice," the waiter said, with a little bow as he headed to the kitchen.

Steve leaned over the table and said in a conspiratorial whisper, "I shouldn't admit it but this is one of my favorite ways to feel important. Whenever I'm down on myself, I come to an expensive restaurant like this, where the waiter knows how to be properly obsequious. It's great for my ego."

"Not great for the pocket book, though," Sue said.

"What's money for if not to get what you want?" Steve asked.

Sue lapsed into a thoughtful silence.

"Did I say something wrong?" Steve asked.

Jay jumped into the conversation. "What do you think about the apartment?"

"I assume you're paying for it. Sue's dad would have gone a bit more upscale."

"It's his building. He isn't collecting rent from us. Besides, I'll be staying at the Red Dragon."

Steve lapsed into silence.

Jay looked confused. "A penny for your thoughts, Steve."

"I'd rather not say. It's none of my business," Steve said.

The mounting tension around the table was broken by Lenny, the chef, who came in with a tray of little savory tarts as appetizers.

Steve briefly introduced Sue and Jay, and then asked, "What do you recommend for my special friends?"

"Perhaps a cold pepper, tomato, and cucumber soup to begin. Then a salad, and to finish we have a tray of pastries. The main dish will be a surprise, just for you," Lenny said, giving Steve a sly wink.

"That sounds great to me," Jay said.

Lenny returned to the kitchen, leaving the group to their lack of conversation.

"Come on guys," Jay said. "Let's get things out in the open. At this rate, I'll be talking to myself all through dinner."

Steve took a deep breath. "Don't you think he's being manipulative? He sounds like my dad when he was trying to shape me to fit into his straight world."

"We've thought about that. If it begins to pinch, we can always move out," Jay said.

The waiter brought in a cauliflower mousseline with very long, curly, thin, deep-fried potato strips sticking out of it as decorations.

"Easier said than done. Once you get used to a better way of life, it's hard to give it up."

"I'm considering it to be generosity, at least until I have evidence to prove otherwise," Jay said.

The waiter arrived at the table with the soup, each served in an empty eggshell with sesame seeds stuck around the edges. The eggshell was held upright by a tiny ceramic flowerpot. He placed a colorful salad made from little squares of vegetables sitting on a bed of lettuce in the center of the table.

Jay surveyed the soup in its eggshell container.

"How is this going to work?" he asked.

Sue picked up a short drinking straw from her plate.

"Maybe we pretend it's a Slurpee?" she asked.

She took a gentle sip of the soup through the straw.

"Delicious," she declared.

"Do they do everything in miniature here?" Jay asked.

"When you have several courses, each one has to be small. That forces you to pace yourself," Steve said.

"When you said money gets you what you want, it made me wonder about my dad's motives," Sue said. "Do you think he's trying to put us into an awkward situation so I'll end up going home?"

"It's always dangerous to assign motives," Steve said. "It's usually not that simple. I'd say he's only making sure that it isn't any more attractive than necessary for you to be with Jay."

"Aren't you really saying that he's trying to make it difficult for us so Sue will go home?" Jay asked.

"You may be right. It's a matter of degree."

The waiter arrived with the main course. It consisted of layers of tiny corn pancakes and goat cheese stacked up over a black lentil salad. Isolated sprigs of rosemary seemed to grow out of the pancake stack.

"This is fabulous," Sue said. "Mine looks like a little Eiffel tower."

"Mine's more like the Leaning Tower of Pisa," Jay said, nudging the tall sprig of rosemary with his fork in order to straighten it. "Is there a rule about how to eat these things?"

"Don't let it intimidate you. The person who pays the bill gets to set the rules," Steve said. "And, I might add, gets to break them."

"That's what we are afraid of with Sue's dad," Jay said.

~ 14 ~

IT TAKES ALL KINDS

"This is the last of the furniture," Steve said, tilting an armchair so it would fit through the door. The chair had the typical 70's orange and reddish brown upholstery with wooden arm accents.

"Now all we have to do to spread things around a bit so it looks like we've done something," Jimmy said.

"Tiffany will be coming over with Sue, later. They'll probably want to arrange the furniture. We might as well leave things as they are for now," Jay said.

"I can't believe all the stuff you got for so little money," said Steve. "I spent more than that just on my new sectional alone. And here you are with four rooms of furniture."

"You should hang out with us more often, Steve," Jay said. "Think how much money you'd save. I do want to thank you guys for all the help you've been. I'd never have been able to do it without you."

Jay went to the fridge. "What can I get you? I've got beer for the working men and martinis for the..."

He stopped abruptly, looked sheepishly around, and added, "There's just no right way to finish that sentence, is there?"

Steve leapt to Jay's assistance. "It's okay. I know your heart's in the right place, even if your foot's in your mouth. You're trying too hard to cater to the gay guy. Actually, I'd like a beer. Like any other real man."

Jay set bottles of beer on the kitchen table and everyone gathered around to relax.

Jimmy passed a beer to Steve. "I don't know how you can expect us to consider you to be a real man, when you and your friends use 'hi girlfriend' as a greeting."

"Take it easy there, Jimmy," Jay said. "Let's not get into an argument. We're all friends here."

"That's okay, Jay," said Steve. "You make a good point, Jimmy. However, I think you're being far too black-and-white."

"What do you mean?" Jimmy asked.

"Like a lot of straight people, you're looking at a stereotype not the person. Gay people are as complex as straight people. Sometimes I feel like a beer. Sometimes I like a martini."

"Well, I always have beer. You'll never find me drinking something like Long Island Iced Tea or a martini."

"And I suppose you always go to the same kind of movie?" asked Steve.

"Of course. If it doesn't have lots of action in it, I can't be bothered watching it."

"You're saying you never go to a movie that has an interesting romantic story?"

"Only if I'm with Becky. She doesn't like action movies. I have to humor her occasionally."

"I take back my statement about gay people being as complex as straight people. They're more complex than straight people. Have you ever heard the term two-spirited?" Steve asked.

"I have," Jay said. "R.B. sometimes uses the term when he is referring to a medicine man or a shaman. He says being two-spirited in their culture is considered to be a special gift which brings with it special powers."

"What kind of powers could that be?" asked Jimmy.

"It gives them the power to understand the thoughts and emotions of both men and women," Jay said. "That gives them unusual power."

"I'd like to learn that kind of power," Jimmy said. "Most of the time I don't understand Becky at all. Or any other girl, as far as that goes."

"It's not the sort of thing you learn. You have to be born with it. Unfortunately, people born that way often find it to be more of a curse than a blessing," Steve said.

"Why would that be?" Jimmy asked.

"Because in our society people label them as gay, with all the negative things that go along with that term."

"You lost me somewhere along the way," Jimmy said. "I don't think I know what we're talking about anymore."

Steve deliberately switched the conversation. "How have Troy and Misty been making out with the Winnipeg winter?"

"I haven't talked to them since they got here," said Jay. "Phil said Troy doesn't start work with Frantic Films until next month. He's been getting some work with the local TV studio to fill in."

"Is that with APTN?" Jimmy asked.

"I don't even know what that is," Jay said.

"It's the Aboriginal People's Television Network," Jimmy said.

"I didn't know we had such a thing. How do you know about it?"

"It's on Portage Avenue. I walk by it every day. I've watched it a couple of times. It's got stuff from the Arctic and everywhere."

"Thanks for mentioning it," Jay said. "I'll check it out. However, I don't think that's where Troy is working."

"I was talking to Phil a few days ago," Cam said. "He sounded happy to have them there with him."

"It should be good for him to have somebody living with him. Do you think he's ever going to go back to work?" Jay asked.

"As soon as he gets his own life on an even keel, he will," Cam said. "He just needs more time."

Jimmy pulled out a package of cigarettes. "You mind if I smoke?"

Jay's brow furrowed. "I thought you were going to quit."

"I said as soon as you take me to Montreal, I'd quit."

"That might be a long time. We don't have any spare cash. Sue's looking for work and so am I."

"You'd leave the Red Dragon?" Jimmy asked.

"Han Sing doesn't need me. Anybody can do what I do. Besides, I want more than that from life."

"So you would leave?"

"I'd miss Arrow if I left. I don't think R.B. is going to be able to look after him much longer. They're both getting old."

"You certainly have become attached to that dog, haven't you?" Jimmy said, putting a cigarette to his lips.

"If you don't mind, we'd rather you didn't smoke in the apartment. It's not good for Jamie and the baby to be around smoke. She's coming over this evening to see our place, if she feels up to it."

"So what should I do?"

"Probably it would be best for your own health if you didn't smoke. I guess if you must have a cigarette, you'll have to go outside."

"It's not such a big deal. I'm cutting back anyway, you know."

The door opened and Tiffany held it open for Sue. "Wait until you see what we bought," Sue said, as she set a big box on the table.

"It looks like dishes," Jay said.

"Good guess, Jay. We needed something to eat off. It's a twenty-piece setting, and it was only twenty-five dollars."

"That's a reasonable price," Steve said. "At twenty-five dollars a piece that's only five hundred dollars."

"No, no, Steve. It was twenty-five dollars for the setting," Sue said.

"Well that's even better. A hundred dollars for a setting for four. Now that's really cheap."

"It was twenty-five dollars for the whole box of dishes. All twenty pieces."

"Well, that's just plain ridiculous. I'd pay twenty-five dollars for one plate. Where would you get a deal like this?" Steve asked.

"Canadian Tire," Sue said. "Tiffany saw their sale flyer in the newspaper."

"You buy dishes at a tire store?" Steve asked. "I've seen those stores around but I've never been in one because I get my tires from the car dealer."

"It's a funny name for a store which sells tons of great stuff other than car supplies. And at cheap prices, too."

"It doesn't sound like my kind of place," Steve said. "My friends would die laughing if I told them I bought dishes at a tire store."

"Did you have fun, Sue?" Jay asked

"It was great. Not something I'd want to do every day but I wouldn't have missed it for the world. I couldn't have done it without Tiffany's help. She knows everything about finding bargains."

"Shopping is always fun, especially with someone else's money. I just wish it weren't so cold," Tiffany said. "No matter how much I bundle up, I'm still freezing."

"That short skirt doesn't look like bundling up to me," Steve said.

Tiffany stuck out her tongue at him. "One has to look decent in public."

"You know I'm kidding," Steve said. "You always look great."

"I always think I'll get used to the cold," Jay said. "But every winter it comes as a surprise how cold it can get."

"Do you plan to put the furniture around the apartment?" asked Tiffany. "Or are you going to leave it all in the middle of the room?"

Jay and Jimmy exchanged knowing looks. "I guess now that we have our decorating experts with us, we might as well finish doing this," Jay said.

"Let's put the sofa over there," Tiffany said, pointing to a place against the wall.

Twenty minutes later, the furniture had been placed, moved and then moved again. Jay, Sue and Jimmy did all the moving. Steve and Tiffany gave advice and suggestions.

"Now that looks totally excellent," Jay said.

"You're not saying that just to make us stop, are you?" asked Tiffany.

"What would make you think that?"

"It's the fourth time you've said everything looks perfect."

"Well, this time I mean it," Jay said.

"I almost forgot to tell you. I applied for a job," Sue said.

"At Canadian Tire?" Steve asked.

"I'd be afraid to work there. It's much too big a store, and I have no experience. I'd have to learn about all their different stock and code numbers and cash registers and that sort of thing."

"So where is it?"

"We stopped for an Orange Julius in the mall. They were advertising a job so I applied."

"That doesn't necessarily mean you'll get it."

"The manager said I could come in for an interview tomorrow. He said if everything checks out, I could be starting work this week. I'll be a trainee."

"I think it's great," Jay said. "Did he say what sort of hours you could expect to be working?"

"He didn't say. Probably it'll be the hours nobody else wants. I'll be low girl on the totem pole."

"You'll be all right with that?"

"I think so. I'm not like my dad."

"I'm glad of that," Jay said.

"Speaking of fathers," Steve said, "have you found anything more about your errant father."

"I wrote him a letter last night," Jay said.

"What did you say?"

"Not much. Just said I was his son and that I wanted to meet him."

"You gave him your phone number, I guess."

"I gave him the phone number here," Jay said.

"Does that mean you live here now?" Steve asked.

"I wouldn't say that."

"At least not yet," Sue said.

"By the way, has your friend arrived yet?" Jay asked Steve.

"Flew in yesterday."

"What's your friend's name?"

"Taylor."

Jay and Jimmy looked at each other, contemplating how to be subtle. Steve smiled at their uneasiness, and answered their unspoken question. "He's male. Although, you might not think so."

"Because?"

"He wears women's clothes," Steve said.

"You're saying he's a transvestite?" Jay asked.

"I guess you could say that. However, he's thinking about changing."

"He's planning to quit wearing women's clothes?" Jimmy asked.

"No. He's planning to change his sex."

Jimmy's brow furrowed with concentration as he tried to understand the situation. "You mean he's going to become homosexual?"

"No. He's quite happy being heterosexual. A person doesn't change his sexual preference."

"Most of the people I know don't usually change their sex either," Jimmy retorted.

"He's trying to get his gender and sex to match," Steve explained.

"I thought gender and sex were the same thing," Jimmy said. "My gender is male and my sex is male. It's all very simple. I like it that way."

"Gender is what's between your ears. Sex is what's between your…"

"I don't have anything between my ears," Jimmy interrupted.

He paused for a moment. "Sexual, that is," he added.

"Gender is how you think of yourself. Sex is physical. For Taylor, he knows inside his mind he's female but on the outside he's physically male," Steve explained.

"Couldn't he just wear men's clothes. Then he'd be a man who looks like a man and likes women," Jimmy said. "That sounds normal to me."

"In appearance and actions, yes. But he'd still feel the way he does now."

"How's that?"

"Like a woman trapped in a male body."

Jay tried to clarify the discussion. "If he has a sex-change operation, then he'll be a woman in a woman's body, and everything would be the way it should be. Right?"

"Right," Steve said.

Jimmy continued struggling with the concept. "If he likes girls now, then after he's had the operation will he still like girls?"

"Of course. His mind won't be changed."

"Won't that make him a lesbian?"

"Is that a problem?" Steve asked.

"But then he'll be less normal than he is now," Jimmy said.

"Which is better, to be a lesbian trapped in a male body, or to be a normal lesbian?" Steve asked.

"There's no such thing as a normal lesbian," Jimmy said.

"Aren't there any other choices?" Jay asked.

"Not for him. For most people, their sex and gender are the same. For others, it requires medical intervention to make then match."

Jimmy gave Steve an annoyed look. "Why does talking to you always leave me more confused than when I started? Why can't you and your friends just be like everybody else?"

"For the same reason you can't be like us," Steve said. "I think it's time I went home. Can I give anybody a ride?"

Tiffany and Jimmy both accepted the offer. Jimmy declared the proviso that they had to talk about nothing other than the weather or sports on the way.

Jay and Sue sat on their newly acquired sofa after supper. "What do you think we should do tonight, Jay?"

"Let's go see Cam and Jamie. I'm so excited about their baby," Jay said.

"I wish you wouldn't talk about the baby. It worries me," Sue said.

"Why is that?"

"I'm afraid something will happen before it's born. It's bad luck to talk about it."

"Their pediatrician says everything is going well. They've had ultrasound, and everything."

"Then why isn't the baby here? It must be overdue by now."

"Nature has a way of doing things her own way. We know how to control a few things, but the important things in life are beyond our control."

"I'm still worried."

"When we get married, I want to have at least two. A boy and a girl."

"What if I can't have a baby? What then?"

"Of course you'll be able to have babies."

"But what if I couldn't? Suppose there's something wrong with me so I couldn't have a baby. Would you still want to marry me?"

"We could adopt. I'd rather have a little person who's half me and half you, but if we had to I'd want to adopt a baby."

"You didn't answer my question," Sue persisted.

"Yes. I'd marry you. Do you want me to propose right now?" Jay dropped down on one knee in a mock proposal.

"Don't try to be funny."

"Sorry."

"You know marriage is nothing to joke about," Sue said.

"I wasn't joking. I'd marry you right now, but we should wait until I get established. Then we won't have to feel in debt to anyone."

"Enough talk. Let's go see how the baby's coming."

~ 15 ~

LIFE'S NOT JUST A BOWL OF CHERRIES

Jamie opened the door and ushered the two friends into her apartment. "Come in."

"Hi Jamie. Any baby news?" Jay asked.

"I'm going to the hospital tomorrow morning. The doctor says it's time to get on with this business."

"They're going to induce labor?" Jay asked.

"Is there a problem?" Sue asked.

"She thinks it's time, and goodness knows I'm ready to move on with my life. She doesn't think there's any problem. Can I get you something to drink? Or some munchies?"

"Oh, no. Thanks. We just finished supper," Jay said. "Where's Cam?"

"He's at one of his monthly coffee house meetings."

"Accountants have coffee house meetings?" Jay asked, as they all made themselves comfortable in the living room.

"It's the *Bahá'í* devotional gathering," Jamie said. "I usually go with him but I haven't felt up to going to any group things lately."

Sue gave Jay a quizzical look. "I don't know what you mean," she asked Jamie.

"I mean that I get tired easily. That, and I don't like to get too far away from a bathroom."

"We meant we don't know anything about *Bahá'í.*"

Jay excused himself to phone Steve from the kitchen.

"It's the faith we're working on," Jamie said.

"Your religion?" Sue asked.

"It isn't a religion the way you probably think of religions. It's more a way of life and a way of looking at the world. It's an expression of our faith in the evolution of humankind."

"I don't believe in evolution. The Biblical story of creation is more important to me than Darwin's theory of evolution," Sue said.

"I didn't mean Darwin's theory of evolution. We can't be bothered concerning ourselves with that sort of argument. For us, scientific facts and religion are simply two different ways of looking at the same thing. There is a fundamental oneness between them. They have to be in agreement with each other because they are both the same thing."

"Doesn't the theory of evolution contradict the Bible's description of creation?"

"If there appears to be disagreement it's from our interpretation, not in the facts. In science a theory is an attempt to explain something. A theory can never be right or wrong; it can only be a better or poorer explanation. In a word, creation is what God did. Evolution is only one theory to explain how He did it."

"What about the Bible's description of it taking six days to create the world?" Sue asked.

"We don't interpret specific Biblical writings literally. What with translations and the changes in society, the specific English words in our Bible probably don't have the same meaning as the original Hebrew. Isn't it possible that what is translated as a 'day' in the Bible might have originally been used as a general indication of a period of time? It could as easily refer to an eon instead of a twenty-four hour day."

"I'm sorry. I interrupted what you started to say about the evolution of humankind," Sue said.

"I meant that the spiritual development of the human race is continually evolving. Each particular religion represents a stage in this evolution. God has intervened in the past through Divine Messengers such as Abraham, Moses, Buddha, Jesus, and Mohammed, to provide the link between God the creator, and man his creation."

"Where does *Bahá'í* fit into this?"

"The *Bahá'í* Faith represents the current stage in the evolution of the world's religions, and *Bahá'u'lláh* is the most recent manifestation or Messenger of God. Through him the *Bahá'í* Faith was revealed to the world in Persia during the 19th century."

"Don't different religions worship different gods?"

"The *Bahá'í* believe in unity. There is one God who is the same for all religions. That's the fundamental oneness in all the world's religions. Then, there is the oneness of all mankind. There are diverse people but they are all of one race—mankind. The search of religion is to realize that unity."

"How can you say that all the world's religions are the same?"

"The churches or temples may be different; the trappings, rituals, and speakers may be different; but it is the same spirit of God being channeled through them."

Cam walked in. "Hi, Sue. Glad to see Jamie is entertaining you. Is Jay here?"

"Hi Cam," Jay called from the kitchen. "I'll be right there."

"We wanted to see the soon-to-be mother," Sue said.

Jay said goodbye to Steve on the phone. He returned to the living room and glanced around. "Do you have a room for the baby?"

Cam and Jamie exchanged looks. Cam said, "We haven't made it public yet but we'll have to soon. I guess we might as well start with you. Jamie and I aren't keeping the baby."

"You're not keeping it? Why wouldn't you keep it?" Jay asked.

"How could anyone give away a baby?" Sue asked with a look of horror.

"We couldn't raise a child. We're roommates, not a couple."

"There are lots of one parent families. Don't you want to keep it, Jamie?" Sue asked.

"We never planned to keep it. I'm doing this as a favor for my brother and his partner, Kris," Jamie said.

"How is your having a baby a favor to them?" Jay asked.

"They wanted a family," Cam said.

"Couldn't they adopt?"

"Maybe. However, they wanted to feel that the baby was part of them. They wanted to have a genetic connection with the baby."

"I can relate to that," Jay said. "Until I get to know my biological father I won't feel I fully know myself."

"It'll be so great for your brother to see a reflection of himself in the baby as it grows up," Sue said.

"It'll be charming for Kris, too," Jamie said.

"She'll be able to see her partner in the baby," Jay said.

"He'll like that," Jamie added.

"You did say 'he,' didn't you?" Jay asked.

"Yes."

"You mean they're…"

"Yes. Gay as hedgehogs. But they both wanted to have a family," Cam said. "They talked all the time about adopting kids. Then Kris suggested that maybe they could find a girl who would be a surrogate mother for them."

"When they told us about their idea I knew it had to be me," Jamie said. "This way the baby will have our family genes."

"That was brave of you," Sue said.

"And from there it was a short jump to the idea that it would be perfect if it had Kris' genes as well."

Jay thought for a moment. "I don't mean to be nosy or gross but how will it have Kris' genes?"

"He's the sperm donor," Cam said. "I'm sorry for misleading you when we first met by implying I was the father. We didn't know how to explain this to people. We're still not sure how to explain it to people."

"It's perfect," Sue gushed. "The baby will be almost their own biological child."

"But what about you, Jamie. Can you handle giving up your baby after nine months?" Jay asked.

"I thought it would be easy. Now that it's getting close I'm feeling nervous about it. I'm going to feel so empty. No pun intended."

"I'll be here for you. It'll be all right," Cam said.

"You've been unbelievably good to me during these past months. Like a real husband," Jamie said. "I'm sure some of my mood swings weren't easy for you."

"It's been an awesome trip, believe me."

"We've been talking about the *Bahá'í* Faith. Now that you're here, maybe you can explain it better than I can. I'm overdue for a bathroom break."

"If I'd known you wanted to hear about *Bahá'í*, I could have had some of our friends come over to help explain it. What more do you want to know?" Cam asked.

"I'd never heard of *Bahá'í* before now. Is it some sort of sect or cult?" Sue asked.

"It's a well-established religion. Worldwide, it's the second most widespread religion after Christianity. There are more than six million people in the *Bahá'í* community."

"Then why haven't we heard of it?" Sue asked.

"The Faith forbids them to recruit members. Parents allow their children to make their own decision concerning the Faith, based on their experiences within the family unit and the informal teaching of their parents."

"Then how do they get new members?"

"They hold small study groups in their homes. Like we are doing here right now only with more people."

"Sort of like a cocktail party," Sue said.

"Exactly. Except the conversation has more meaningful content and they don't serve cocktails. In Montreal during the early 1930's, they started calling these meetings 'firesides.' Now, firesides occur all around the world in more than two hundred and thirty countries. They include more than two thousand ethnic groups," Cam said.

"I don't understand how it got spread so widely if they don't preach or recruit."

"They believe that service to others is the purpose of both individual life and social arrangements. Many of them, and their children, go to underdeveloped parts of the world to do what they call 'pioneering.' They're willing to reorganize their lives for the sole purpose of introducing the Faith to a new region, either locally or internationally."

"Does that mean religion becomes their whole life?" Sue asked.

"It means that their whole life is their religion. Religion and life are one and the same thing."

"Doesn't that mean they spend all their time in worship?"

"Not at all. It's a religious obligation for them to pray and meditate every day and to participate in a period of fasting once a year."

"And that's all?"

"It's also an expectation that they must be wholly engaged in the world at large. When they pioneer they are not acting as missionaries. They live the life of the people around them. Their lives don't appear any different from that of their friends and neighbors."

"I still don't understand. What do they get out of this?" Jay asked.

"For them, good deeds and service to humanity are the most important elements of spiritual training and personal development. *Bahá'í* is as much a faith as it is a religion. There aren't the rituals and clergy of traditional religions. Each individual is responsible for his or her own spiritual growth. Each person reaches the highest level of his own human happiness."

"It sounds a lot like the New Age philosophy," Sue said.

"I think there are some fundamental similarities between the New Age philosophy and the *Bahá'í* Faith," Cam said.

"Like what?"

"New Age and the *Bahá'í* Faith both believe in direct spiritual development by each individual, rather than relying on the dogma of an organized religion. In addition, they both believe that nothing is important unless it is done for the benefit of others. They also believe in the unity and oneness of all people."

"Then why did you choose the *Bahá'í* Faith instead of following the New Age philosophy?"

"I think they both start with the same philosophy and head in the same direction—finding answers to life's major questions. However, New Age is an unorganized philosophy. The *Bahá'í* Faith has a formal structure and administrative order. There are specific laws in the *Bahá'í* Faith to which the believers adhere. Besides, New Age makes use of tools which I find more distracting than useful."

"Such as?" Sue asked.

"Things like candles, incense, chanting and drums to help a person meditate."

"That sounds harmless enough. I sometimes like music and incense when I want to relax," Sue said. "My therapist agrees with me that they can be helpful."

"But you don't rely on them for your spiritual development, do you?"

"Sometimes I do when I'm meditating."

"They also use tarot cards, runes, pendulum, bodywork and toning to help them guide their lives."

"I wouldn't put much trust in those things," Sue said.

"And then there's the whole aliens from space thing."

"They believe in UFO's and stuff?"

"Some of them do. I met this New Age person and she kept talking about the Galactic Federation's twelve mother ships surrounding our solar system," Cam said.

"What have you got against Star Wars?" Jay asked. "I love those movies."

"This isn't Star Wars. This is part of their belief system. She talked about alien spirits inhabiting human bodies."

"How does that work?" Sue asked.

"She said some children are born with an alien soul. They call them Star-seed. In other cases the alien soul enters later in life. These are called Walk-ins."

"That's more than I want to think about," Jay said.

Jamie came back into the room carrying a plate of cookies.

"Are you and Cam planning to become *Bahá'í*?" Sue asked.

"We'd like to someday," Jamie said. "We like the way the *Bahá'í* Faith stresses the similarity between people and their beliefs instead of emphasizing the differences that separate them."

"Why don't you join, then?"

"We'll have to get our lifestyles in order first."

"Why is that?"

"Our lifestyles would have to reflect our Faith. It's not like some religions that seem to be mostly an hour on Sundays. Being *Bahá'í* is twenty-four hours a day, every day. We'd have to live the life."

"Don't you do that now? You seem like such good people already."

"Unity is the basis of the *Bahá'í* community. There must be unity between the diverse peoples of the world and unity within oneself. However, unity within the family is the most fundamental."

"You mean your *Bahá'í* friends disapprove of your being room-mates?"

"They would never be so harsh as to judge any person that way. It's more that we wouldn't feel we were presenting an appropriate image of the *Bahá'í* Faith to the world, particularly when Jamie is pregnant."

"Is it the living together thing?"

"A *Bahá'í* is expected to refrain from sexual intimacy before marriage, and to be faithful in marriage. We know there isn't anything sexual between us, but our lifestyle doesn't show an appropriate respect for marriage and the sanctity of the family."

"You two do seem to be advertising some of the wrong things."

"I think what we are doing is right. People can think what they want but I'm actually a virgin. However, we won't accept the Faith until our lifestyle reflects our beliefs more accurately than it does now."

"Will Cam have to give up his bar friends?"

"That will be easy for you, won't it, Cam?" Jamie asked.

"The bar has been more of a social club than anything else for me. I'm finding the same kind of companionship and support from my *Bahá'í* friends as I did from my bar friends," Cam said.

"You say you're not members but I thought you were attending a service?"

"Not a formal service. We don't attend their formal services, which they call Feasts," Cam said.

"That sounds like a banquet."

"It's a feast for the soul. The Feast has three parts. A devotional time during which members read selections from *Bahá'í* writings, because there is no clergy. Then there is a sort of business meeting when the members are consulted concerning the day-to-day operation and policies. The last part is a social event, usually with a simple buffet meal," Cam explained.

"That sounds like more of a major event than the usual church service. They wouldn't do these every week, would they?"

"Only on the first day of each *Bahá'í* month."

"*Bahá'í* months are different from ours?" Jay asked.

"Their calendar has nine months with nineteen days in each month. Somewhere there are catch-up days to make up the other four days."

"What kind of meetings do you and Jamie go to?"

"We attend the Holy Day Celebrations and devotional gatherings. Anyone is welcome to these."

"Do they have churches?"

"They meet in what they call a 'Center.' It can be anywhere convenient. Usually it's in a home or a rented hall. Some larger communities have their own center. Here in Winnipeg they have a building on McMillan Avenue."

"What about a big building? Like a cathedral or something?"

"There are a few *Bahá'í* temples, each on a different continent. Each is planned to be available for use by all the religions."

"Excuse me, but I'm going to make a pot of herbal tea. Anyone want something different?" Jamie interrupted. She looked around for a reaction, and getting none, disappeared into the kitchen.

"If there is no clergy or ritual, what are the services like?" Sue asked.

"Most of the service is taken from the *Bahá'í* writings. At the discretion of the local community, readings and prayers from the world's religions may be used. Sometimes there will be *a capella* singing or instrumental music, depending on the talents of the group," Cam said.

"I'm still not clear how this whole thing works. Don't religions need to have a clergy to direct the people through a set of rituals?" Jay said, taking over the conversation.

"It's a gathering where people of all religious faiths can meet to worship God without dogma or restrictions."

"That doesn't tell me how it happens."

"Each *Bahá'í* accepts individual responsibility to follow the *Bahá'í* laws. Even though Jamie and I are only seekers of the Faith, we are preparing ourselves by following the laws."

"Such as?"

"Daily private prayers are required."

"Prayers never work for me," Jay said. "I used to pray for things but my prayers were never answered."

"There are three compulsory prayers designated in the writings of *Bahá'u'lláh*. We are to choose from among those three."

"You don't pray for specific things or people?"

"The *Bahá'í* believe that God intervenes in human affairs through His Messengers, not on individual request."

"I don't think I'd be mature enough to follow a set of rules without having direction from a minister or a priest or something."

"You know how a baby goes through a series of successive developmental steps to reach the adult stage. In the same way, humankind has gradually evolved through separate religions toward its collective maturity. You have all the collective maturity of the ages within you. All you have to do is to turn your mind inward to find it."

"Will following their laws and prayers do this?" Jay asked.

"They think so, and it seems to work for me. The *Bahá'í* Faith represents the current stage of this process of evolution in religion."

"What do you see for the future? Will everyone become *Bahá'í*?" Sue asked.

"Not likely. The *Bahá'í* Faith is currently the latest stage in the unification of humankind. It will not be the last stage."

Jay stood up. "Sorry to cut our discussion short but we have to go. Steve set up an appointment for me to see about writing the G.E.D."

"The what?" Jamie asked.

"The General Education Development program," Jay said. "Steve says I should try for it. It'll give me the equivalent of a Grade 12 graduation. Then if I decide to go to university I'll have the entrance requirements."

"Let me know if I can help. You're welcome to use my computer anytime you want. We all know you're one smart cookie," Cam said.

"It's mostly that I seem to remember everything I read," Jay said.

"And he reads everything he can get his hands on," Sue added.

"Thanks for the encouragement. I'll need all the help I can get," Jay said.

"We should continue this discussion another day," Sue said. "Maybe you could get us invited to a fireside sometime."

Jamie smiled. "I'd like that. We'll let you know when there's going to be one."

~ 16 ~

CIRCULAR JUSTICE

February in Manitoba is a slow month. The clear sunny sky masks the bone-chilling, finger-numbing, ear-freezing cold. At the typical temperature of minus 30 degrees, even a light wind will cause exposed skin to freeze in less than a minute. For those who don't have to go out to work, cabin fever becomes a reality. Tempers flare and then depression sets in to await the arrival of spring.

Jay was spending most of his time at Sue's apartment and taking the bus to work every day. Sue's Mustang didn't like cold weather. If left for more than two hours without being plugged in, it would stubbornly refuse to start. Jay tried taking it to work but the Red Dragon didn't have any electric outlets to plug the car in and Jay soon tired of going out every couple of hours to warm it up. Bus service was every five minutes and the ride only twenty minutes. Besides, as Sue pointed out, the bus was more environmentally friendly.

Jamie's baby had been born on the fourth of January. Kris flew in from Toronto to take the big, healthy baby boy home to meet his other daddy, Harold. Jamie was left with only Cam to give her comfort in filling the void left by the baby's absence.

Sue was happy working at Orange Julius afternoons and weekends. She said it was good to be out meeting people instead of moping around feeling sorry for herself. She said that her twice-weekly therapy sessions had been good for her. However, she was planning to discontinue them soon.

Jay and Sue set aside Sunday afternoons for visiting with their friends. They usually discussed every minute detail of their lives and played a few hands of Hearts over tea and cookies. Phil had learned long ago that winter storms could negate overnight a week's planning for a dinner party, so he went into hibernation to wait for the end of winter.

One Sunday afternoon in early February, Jay responded to the doorbell. "Hi, Jimmy. Isn't Becky with you?"

"She said it's too cold to go out."

"Everything's all right, isn't it? She's not mad at us or anything, is she?"

"Nothing to worry about. She just wants spring to come."

"Don't we all? Let me hang up your coat."

"Hi Jimmy," Sue called from the living room. "Is it still cold out there?"

"Not bad. It's up to minus 25. It doesn't seem so cold because the sunshine is glorious and there's no wind."

"Did I tell you about my new job?" asked Jimmy. "I'm working at that little coffee counter in Broadway Drugs."

"And here I thought you were giving up on drugs," Jay said jokingly.

"Very funny," Jimmy said.

"I knew you'd find something eventually, if you kept trying," Jay said.

"It's not great but at least I'm bringing in some money to help pay for the groceries. Besides, it gives me a chance to meet a lot of important people who come in on their coffee breaks."

"What are your hours? We'll drop in and have coffee with you some-time next week," Sue said.

"It is only part-time. I'm there noon and supper times, and for coffee breaks. That's when they're busiest. I'm hoping maybe to be full-time soon. How are you doing at Orange Julius, Sue?"

"It's fun. I think I'm fitting in well, considering it's my first job."

"You're a super girl. There must be lots of better jobs than that for you."

"It's low stress, and that's important right now. When I leave work, I don't have any worries to take home with me."

"How's your job, Jay?"

"I'm thinking of changing jobs. There's been a guy dropping in at the Red Dragon. He's asked me if I'd like to work in his store."

"What kind of job does he have for you?" Jimmy asked.

"It's as assistant manager of a clothing shop in Osborne Village."

"Do you know anything about being an assistant manager?"

"Not a thing. I told him I don't have any experience. He said they'd train me on the job."

"Do you know anything about clothes?" Jimmy asked.

"I can always ask Steve. Clothes are his life. That, and silver jewelry."

"Why would he want to give you a job?"

"Maybe he just likes the look of me."

"Trust me. You wouldn't be getting offers based on your looks," Jimmy said with a big smile. "Why don't you give it a try? You haven't anything to lose."

"What if it I don't like it?"

"Han Sing would take you back if it didn't work out."

"What makes you think he'd take me back?"

"He probably won't hire anyone to replace you."

"You mean I wouldn't leave a vacancy? Thanks for the compliment," Jay said, making a wry face. "Enough about me. What have you been doing for excitement?"

"Do you know my friend, Peter?"

"I've never met him but isn't he the guy that got into a big car accident?" Jay asked.

"Yeah, that's the guy. He was involved in a fatal car accident. And he'd been drinking."

"He must be in jail by now."

"He's doing a community sentence."

"What does that mean?" Sue asked.

"He's living at home doing community service things."

"How does he get away with that?"

"It's not all that easy. It has to be decided through a sentencing circle. I went to his last week."

"I've never heard of a sentencing circle," Sue said. "How does it work?"

"It's done on the reserve. This one was in their community hall. It was set up with two circles of chairs. The inner circle was for Peter, his lawyers, family members and people from the community. The outer one was for spectators."

"Is there significance in having circles?" Sue asked.

"A circle has no beginning and no end. Everyone is equal. No one is better or more powerful than any other person. In the center there was a smoldering pan of sweetgrass."

"It was sort of a public trial, then?" Sue asked.

"It wasn't a trial, because he had already pleaded guilty. I was expecting there to be more details about the accident, but even the RCMP officer spoke only about his feelings when he saw the accident and how he was upset about it for days afterwards. Everyone spoke from the heart, not the head."

"Did everyone speak?"

"Only those in the inner circle had a chance to speak. The outer circle was completely silent. The elder, holding a white eagle feather, spoke first and explained to the group what would happen. Then he took a different eagle feather and passed it to the person on his left. A person can speak only if holding a feather. If a person chose not to speak, the feather passed on to the next person. The feather moved from person to person in a clockwise direction."

"If someone wants to reply to a speaker, what do they do? Walk over and take the feather?" Sue asked.

"No way. There's no discussion. Each person has a chance to have his or her say, but there is no back and forth discussion between people. The feather moves from person to person around the circle without reversing direction until it completes the circle. People have to be patient, and show their respect by listening."

"If there's no discussion of the crime and no discussion between the participants, what do the people say?"

"They express their feelings about the crime and about what it would be like to have Peter living in the community. Peter told them what he would try to do to make up for the past."

"How does a person redeem himself for a fatal accident?" Sue asked.

"It began when he pleaded guilty in order to avoid putting the victims through the pain of court proceedings."

"A good point. But there must be more," Sue said.

"He promised to make presentations to schools and the community. His story might prevent others from making the same mistakes he did. For example, he said he would use his experience to show how drinking had caused his problems."

"He'll live at home and have a normal life? That sounds a bit soft," Sue said.

"It won't be a normal life. He'll have a strict curfew, enforced by the community."

"What if he breaks curfew?"

"He would be reported to the authorities and spend the rest of his sentence in jail."

"Is this enough punishment, considering the people he hurt?" Sue asked.

"They try for rehabilitation, not punishment. Besides, this gives a chance for healing to take place in the victims and their families."

"I don't see how that would that happen," Sue said.

"One person pointed out that having Peter confined to his home would serve as a message to all the community members, particularly the younger ones. Every time they drive by his house the parents will remind their children of what happened to him and why. Peter will also talk to the people who were hurt by the accident. If he went to jail, people would forget all about him."

"Did this take as long as a regular trial?"

"It took most of a day."

"They must have had a lunch break, eh?" Jay asked.

"There was coffee and donuts on tables near the door. People in the outer circle helped themselves, being careful to walk around the outer edge of the circle, of course."

"People in the inner circle were served individually at various times. Maybe they had some sort of secret signal when they wanted something because I didn't see any interruptions."

"This sounds more like a spiritual experience than a sentencing," Jay said.

"It was. One man kept the pan of sweetgrass going. He was the only one who stepped inside the circle."

"Is this option open for anyone?" Sue asked.

"Only if the sentence is less than two years. The sentencing circle is to decide if there is enough community support to rehabilitate the person."

"Why haven't I heard about this before?" Sue asked.

Jay answered, "I know of a few people who have been given conditional sentences for minor crimes. The person does community service instead of sitting in jail. For the first nation people it has special significance because it gives them a chance to deal with their offenders in a traditional manner. The white man's courts and jails haven't worked well for native people."

"They're getting better. Jails allow smudges, sweatlodges and meetings with elders to give the native people some spiritual guidance," Jimmy said.

Sue looked at Jimmy. "You're not native. How do you know so much about this?"

"I was in the Headingly jail for a while, remember? Over half the people in jail are first nation people. That's a lot, when they make up only about ten percent of the population. While I was there, Calvin Pompana, a respected native elder, would come and hold weekly spiritual gatherings, complete with smudging and drums and everything."

"I don't see why this has to be different for native people. Can't they do this through our regular courts?" Sue asked.

"Native tradition doesn't involve outsiders, such as a judge or jury. It relies on people who have personal knowledge of the situation and the people," Jay said.

"They also expect the criminal to be honest and open in explaining his conduct and the situation," Jimmy added.

"Our regular court system encourages dishonesty and deceit. From the first question, 'how do you plead?' the defendant has no incentive to tell the truth. He is expected to plead not guilty. The prosecutor's role is to get a conviction, not to find the truth. It's an adversarial system, with each side dedicated to winning," Jay said, "not in finding the truth."

"The sentencing circle could happen only if Peter pleaded guilty and accepted his responsibility for the accident," Jimmy said.

"We say justice is blind," Sue said. "Native justice has its eyes wide open. I think I like that."

"By the way, I saw your old Rolex in the pawnshop window," Jimmy said. "Someday, I'd like to get that watch back."

"I plan to get it back for you as soon as I save up some money. That might be quite awhile at the rate I'm going," Jay said.

"What watch?" Sue said, snuggling up beside Jay.

"When I needed money to go to San Francisco, good old Jimmy, here, loaned me this Rolex his grandfather had given him."

"Not loaned," Jimmy interjected. "I gave it to you."

"Anyway, I pawned it to get the money. Without Jimmy and his watch I wouldn't have been able to go to California."

"It looks so lonely, sitting there in the window begging to be worn," Jimmy said. "Let's have a race and see who can raise the money to get it back."

"When I get a better job, I'll be able to get the watch back for you. Maybe I'll have shorter hours and have more time to study for my G.E.D., too."

"How's the studying going, anyway?" Jimmy asked.

"It's going okay. Cam showed me on the Internet where I could get lessons and tests to help me study. Unfortunately, they're American."

"So what are you doing?"

"I'm studying mostly on my own. I go to classes once a week. It seems easy enough. I get a chance to write it in June," Jay said.

"And then what?" Jimmy asked. "University?"

"I'd love that."

"Can you afford it?"

"I'll save up from my wages until school starts. I can work part-time to cover expenses while I'm at school. Maybe I can get a student loan."

"Are you okay with that, Sue?" Jimmy asked.

"Of course. He's my man. I'll be proud to have a college man for a boyfriend."

"I hope that's me you're referring to," Jay said.

"Unless some other college man comes along first," Sue teased.

"At my age I should be halfway through university, not preparing to get in."

"Don't be in too much of a rush. Remember that in life the journey is often its own reward," Jimmy said.

"And sometimes the only reward," Sue added.

"How did you get so smart all of a sudden, Jimmy?" Jay asked.

"Toilet paper."

"What?"

"Toilet paper. Becky gave me a roll of toilet paper will all these sayings on it. I memorize one a day. It's helping me to focus my scattered brain and remember things."

"Jay has to go to university to learn things. Jimmy just has to go to the bathroom," Sue said.

VIVE LA VIE FRANÇAISE

Business had been slow at the Red Dragon during February, so Han Sing hadn't minded when Jay left to take a new job in an Osborne Village clothing store. The Crypt, a subculture streetware clothing and shoe shop, also provides body piercing and other accoutrements for young people who are much more avant-garde than Jay could ever be, even in his wildest dreams.

March came in like a lamb, bathing the frozen city in warm sunshine. The longer days gradually won over the cold, and started an early spring thaw, clearing the streets of the snow and ice left by the snowplows. Then, March went out like a lion with a sudden blizzard that dropped four inches of snow and created three foot drifts. However, snow doesn't last long under the hot April sun, and within a week the snow was almost all gone.

One warm day in April, Jimmy went into the Crypt where Jay was working.

"Hey, man," Jay said. "I haven't seen you in here before."

"I've never had the nerve to come in before. Places like this scare me."

"Look around. It's just clothes and shoes and stuff."

"It's the stuff part that worries me."

"Don't you like the name? I think it's rather appropriate for the merchandise."

"Somehow you don't fit the image," Jimmy said. "Do you even know what Industrial Clothes are?"

"I guess the clothes have to match the type of music you listen to."

"That makes sense," Jimmy said sarcastically.

"Anyway, I work behind the scenes. You know, bookkeeping and ordering. That sort of thing. It's the salespeople who have to fit the image," Jay said, nodding toward the seventeen-year-old behind the counter with color-streaked hair, pierced eyebrow and a vacant stare.

"I see what you mean," Jimmy said.

"We also do body piercing," Jay said.

"I'll pass on that for now," Jimmy said with an involuntary shudder.

"What's new in your life?" Jay asked. "I haven't seen you for weeks."

"A lot. I'm starting to pull my life together."

"I see you finally got a haircut. Styled, even. And those clothes are great. Not totally cool like we sell, but still cool. And expensive."

"Things have been looking up for me lately."

"You have a new job?" Jay asked.

"Still the same one."

"Where's all the money coming from?"

"I've got some good business connections."

Jay looked at Jimmy suspiciously. "You aren't hustling, are you?"

"No way. You know I couldn't do that with a guy," Jimmy said.

"You're a gigolo?"

"I wish. Even with this gorgeous hair, I don't have much success with the ladies. Not even for free."

"Well, it's your life. But be careful what you're getting into."

"The reason I came," Jimmy said, "is that I'm going to Montreal."

"Wow," Jay exclaimed. "You're not moving there, are you?"

"Just a quick trip. And guess what. You're coming with me."

"I am?"

"Yes."

"Just the two us?"

"Becky is coming with me, and we'd love to have you and Sue come, too."

"I'm sure she'd be delighted. I'll ask her tonight," Jay said. "What about money? Sue and I run rather low by the time payday rolls around."

"The plane tickets and money for expenses are all looked after," Jimmy said. "We'd have to go right away because it's a business trip."

"Is it legal?"

"Of course it's legal. I told you I'm trying to turn over a new leaf. No more breaking the law."

"This is exciting," Jay said. "Do you want to go out for a cup of coffee?"

"Thanks, but I get all the coffee I want at work."

"You happy with your job?"

"It's okay. I usually only work at coffee breaks and noon hour when the office workers are out, so I don't get in a lot of hours."

"What about the rest of the time?"

"Mostly it's free time for me. I like that. I met this businessman who gets me to deliver papers for him. He's always in the middle of some big buying and selling deal downtown. He says it's easier and faster to use me as his private courier. He's the reason I have the haircut."

"You need a haircut to deliver packages?"

"He's concerned about appearances. His courier has to look respectable."

"Is that where the new clothes came from?"

"You got it. He says image is important in business deals. You have to look successful to be successful."

"You're sure this is legit?"

"For sure. I looked in a package to make sure there wasn't anything in there except papers."

"Good. A person can't be too careful about what they're delivering. I learned that the hard way when I got sucked into delivering drugs."

"He's bossy and pushy. But he's also generous. He says as long as I do exactly what he wants we'll get along fine. That suits me, as long as he keeps on being generous."

"Well, watch yourself. You have to be careful of strangers. Sometimes they're not exactly what they appear to be."

"So. Are you coming with us?"

"I'll talk to Sue about it tonight."

"Great. Sorry I couldn't give you more warning but we'll have to leave this Friday. He said he's got the airline tickets and if we don't use them they'll be wasted. We'll be away for a week."

"Does this mean you'll keep your promise to give up smoking?"

"No way. The deal was I'd quit if you took me to Montreal. This doesn't count because I'm taking you."

"That sounds like hairsplitting to me," Jay said. "But I'll accept it this time."

Jay walked into the apartment. "Hi, Sue. I've got exciting news."

"I do, too," Sue said.

"Ladies first."

"My dad phoned to say my favorite grandmother is coming to visit."

"That should be fun," Jay said.

"He says I'll be in charge of taking her around to visit all the relatives. She's eighty-five. It may be the last chance she gets to see everyone. At her age you never know."

"Are there a lot of relatives?" Jay asked.

"They're all over. Selkirk, Elie, Portage and even way up north in Flin Flon. I'll get to drive all around the countryside."

"Flin Flon is getting near where I live. That would be such fun for us to travel up there together. You could meet my family. They'd be so surprised."

"I'd love to meet your family."

"When's your grandmother coming?" Jay asked.

"She's flying in on Monday and will be staying all week."

"Oh," Jay said.

"You don't seem to be happy about this."

"Jimmy said he and Becky are going to Montreal for a week and if we want, they'll take us with them."

"That would be great. When do we go?" Sue asked.

"He says we'd have to leave this Friday."

"What a horrible coincidence. My grandmother will be here then."

"I know. What are we going to do?"

"My dad says I have to be here to drive her around. He was very specific about that."

"Can't your mother drive her around?"

"Mom's nervous about driving on the highway. And you know she doesn't ever drive at night. There's no way I can leave her to look after Grandma."

"Then I can't go."

"But you and Jimmy have always had this thing about going to Montreal. It's the perfect opportunity for you."

"There'll be other times. I should be here with you. I wouldn't enjoy Montreal without you."

"How sweet of you. But admit it, you'd have fun even without me."

"It'd be fun, I guess. But I'd miss you terribly."

"I'll be off with Grandma most of the time anyway. It doesn't make sense for you to stay here alone when you could be in Montreal."

"If I stayed here, I could go up north with you. It's been almost a year since I've seen my family. Well, more like nine months, I guess. It seems like a lifetime."

"It would be nice to have you along. We could share the driving."

"There'll be lots more chances to go to Montreal. I'll phone Jimmy and tell him we can't go." Jay dialed the phone:

"Hi Becky, is Jimmy there?"

" . . . "

"Hi Jimmy."

" . . . "

"Yes we did. I'm sorry, but Sue's grandmother is coming to visit. We won't be able to go with you."

" . . . "

"Can't you find someone else to go with you?"

" . . . "

"Don't be silly. Of course you can go without us."

" . . . "

"You're not making any sense. Why couldn't you go without me?"

" . . . "

"Of course I don't want to be responsible for you and Becky missing out on the trip."

" . . . "

"I'll talk to you later."

Jay hung up the telephone. He looked at Sue with a frown and said, "Jimmy's upset. He says they can't go if we don't go."

"Why would they need us? Maybe Jimmy doesn't have many friends but Becky knows lots of people who would be delighted to go with them."

"He says he won't go without me. It sounded as if he meant it."

"Then you have to go. He's your friend. You can't let him down like that."

"You're my girlfriend. I can't let you down. You mean more to me than Jimmy does."

"Let's not get into a competition here. Let's try to think about what would be best for everyone concerned."

"How about we think about what you and I would like best," Jay said.

"No, Jay. We need to think about other people, not just ourselves. Whose need is the greatest?"

"Whose need for what? I feel like I'm being pulled apart here."

"Do you honestly think Becky and Jimmy won't go without you?" Sue asked.

"I'm afraid so. He was totally upset when I said I couldn't go."

"We have a choice. If you stay here, then Jimmy and Becky don't get to go to Montreal. If you go with them, then I have to get along without you for a week."

"Well, if you put it like that, the decision is easy," Jay said.

"You're going to Montreal then?"

"No. I thought it was obvious I would stay with you."

"We have our whole lives to be together. This may be the only chance Jimmy and Becky ever get to go to Montreal. Neither of them is likely to ever get enough money together for a trip like this on their own. It's their chance of a lifetime," Sue said.

"I'm not keeping Jimmy from going. If he weren't such a wimp he'd go without me."

"For whatever reason, if you don't go with him, then he won't go."

"Good grief. How did I get to be responsible for him?"

"Aren't we all responsible for each other? I thought that was what our little gang was all about. We look after each other," Sue said.

"Are you sure you wouldn't mind if I went? I'd actually like to go."

"Look at it this way. We'll be doing something nice for Becky and Jimmy."

"If you're sure about this, I'll phone Jimmy tomorrow and tell him I'm going."

"Why not phone him now?"

"It'll do him good to sweat a little. Then he'll realize what a big favor I'm doing him."

"Sometimes you have a mean streak," Sue said.

Jay paused for a moment. "You're right. That wouldn't be showing proper respect for Jimmy. Sometimes, I think I'm not a very nice person. I don't know what comes over me every so often."

"It's not very often," Sue said.

"I'll have to watch out for it, and try to show more respect. I'll phone Jimmy tonight."

"Do we have enough money to pay your share of a trip like that?"

"That's what's amazing about it. He says he has the tickets, the hotel is paid for, and he even has cash for expenses."

"Why didn't you tell me that in the first place?" Sue asked.

"I didn't want our decision to be made on the basis of money."

"In that case, there's no question about it. You have to go."

Jay, Becky, and Jimmy were up before the alarm went off and skipped breakfast in their eagerness to be at the airport much earlier than necessary. "Are you sure this ticket thing is going to work?" Jimmy asked, looking around the terminal.

"It should be easy. All you have to do is give the ticket agent your confirmation number and a piece of picture identification and they'll give you your boarding pass," Jay said. "Steve told me all about it. He's a travel agent. He should know about that sort of thing."

"But I always thought you needed to have a ticket to fly on an airplane."

"This is the new hi-tech way to go. Think of all the paper it saves. Computers are great."

"I'm too excited to think about saving trees right now. This will be the first time I've ever been on an airplane. In fact, this will be the first time I've been out of Winnipeg," Jimmy said.

"Unless you count the time you spend in Headingly," Becky said.

"Headingly is practically a suburb of Winnipeg. Besides, jail-time doesn't count. It's a separate world. That part of my life is over with. I'll never go to jail again."

"Relax. There's nothing to worry about," Becky said, taking Jimmy's arm and escorting him to the ticket window. In a matter of minutes they were through the boarding gate. Three quarters of an hour later they were on their way to Montreal.

Two hours later, they hailed a cab outside Dorval Airport. "Place To Pee hotel, please," Jay said to the driver. He turned to Jimmy. "Steve taught me how to say that. It's easy to remember that way."

"*Le Hôtel Gouverneur Place Dupuis, monsieur?*"

"Sure," Jay said with a shrug.

The cab sped along at 115 km/hr along *Autoroute de la Côte Liesse*, and around the interchange to the *Autoroute Décarie*. It barely kept up with the flow of traffic, which was blissfully ignoring the posted speed of 70 km/hr.

Jay checked the street signs as they turned onto *Rue Sherbooke*. "Watch this," he said to Jimmy. Leaning forward, he said to the driver, "Could you go down *Sainte Catherine*, please?"

"Steve told me it's the most interesting route," Jay added to his friends.

The cab traveled on for several more blocks and then made a right turn at the traffic light, honking its horn to force a path through the stream of pedestrians who, also having a green light, crossed with little regard for the oncoming traffic.

"I was expecting big department stores and malls," Becky said. "There are tall office buildings but I don't see any big stores."

They crossed *Boulevard de Maisonneuve*, then turned left on *rue Ste-Catherine*, with the cabbie again using his horn to slice a path through the pedestrians.

The streets were packed with traffic. The sidewalks teemed with pedestrians. Jay commented about the tall office buildings and specialty boutiques. He noticed in silence the neon-lighted strip clubs scattered along the street.

"I guess Montreal doesn't go in for malls," he said. "I thought it was famous for shopping."

They continued past the *Place des Arts*, a modern center for the performing arts, and past the *Université de Montréal* which is the French language university. There are two other universities in the city. McGill University is an English language university. Concordia is a 25,000 student, two-campus, facility where the language of instruction is English, but students may write any papers or exams in French. Thus, Montreal has English, French, and bilingual universities.

Soon the cab stopped at the *Hôtel Place Dupuis*. The driver turned to his passengers. *"Voici votre hôtel. Trente-cinq dollars, s'il vous plaît."*

Jimmy looked at Becky. Becky shrugged her shoulders. "Excuse me. We don't speak French," Jimmy said.

"Pas de problème. Forty dollars," the cab driver said.

Jimmy handed the driver two twenties. The driver kept his hand extended. Becky leaned over and whispered in Jimmy's ear, "Tip."

Jimmy added another five to the twenties as they left the car.

"This is so cool," Jimmy said. "It makes me feel important. I wish there were more people for me to tip."

"Don't worry," Becky said. "From the look of the hotel, you should have no difficulty finding a few more people to make happy."

The hotel was obviously luxurious and expensive in spite of being located in the middle of a rundown area of Montreal. Connected to the hotel, a shopping area provided guests with access to essential goods such as clothing, jewelry, perfume and souvenirs.

Jimmy wandered around the lobby, his jaw hanging slightly open, and his eyes darting from side to side as he made his way to the desk. "This place is immense. All the homeless people in Winnipeg could fit in here."

"And they could find shelter under these trees," Becky added.

"*Oui, monsieur?*" the clerk said to Jimmy.

"You speak English?" Jimmy asked.

"Of course. May I help you?"

"I'm supposed to tell you the access number is 4236."

The clerk punched the number into the computer. "I'm sorry, sir. We have nothing under that registration number."

Jimmy frowned in concentration. "Could you try 4326?"

"Ah, yes. Here we are. G. P. Enterprises. Two rooms."

"We get two rooms?"

"One moment, please…ah…here it is. The reservation shows two different parties. One is already taken. You'll be in 1712."

"You don't have our names?" Jay asked.

"No, sir. The company simply reserved the two rooms. If you would all sign your names here, please. The bellhop will show you to your room." He tapped the bell.

"Do I get to tip him?" Jimmy whispered to Becky.

"No. He's paid to look after reservations."

The bellboy loaded the bags onto a trolley and ferried them up to the 17th floor. He carried the baggage into the room, opened one of the windows half an inch, looked into the bathroom and then stood casually at the door.

Jimmy whispered into Becky's ear, "What about him?"

"Yes," she replied. "But only a couple of bucks. We didn't have much luggage."

Jimmy took a toonie from his pocket and dropped the two-dollar coin into the boy's expectant hand, causing him to vanish out the door.

"Are you sure that's enough? I don't want him to be mad at me."

"You don't even know him. Why would you possibly care if he's angry with you?" Becky asked.

"I don't have any friends other than you guys. Not real friends, anyway. A person without friends can't afford to make enemies."

"You have imaginary friends?" Jay asked.

"I have cyber friends through email and chat rooms on the Internet. It's totally cool but I don't think of them as real friends."

"Why not?" asked Becky.

"On the Internet people can say they're anything they want."

"You mean you lie to people on the Internet?"

"I know a lot of people do. I don't lie. Well, maybe a little on my looks."

"Like your being six feet tall, blond, blue-eyed with a buff bod?" Becky asked.

"How did you know I say that?" Jimmy asked.

"I didn't. It was just a guess but now I know."

"That was a sneaky trick."

"How do you know other people lie?" Jay asked.

"Their stories change. They forget what they said in earlier sessions."

"Does that mean if a person has a good memory, you wouldn't know if they're lying?"

"I guess not until you met them in person."

"You guys can chat all you want about computers. I'm going to freshen up, and then let's hit the streets," Becky said.

~ 18 ~

LA VIE EN ROSE

 They stepped out of the hotel and onto *rue Ste-Catherine*, savoring the warmth of the late April sun. Magnolia trees were bursting into bloom all over the city, filling the nose with their fresh aroma and the eye with their lush pink blossoms.

"Wow! Look at all the flags," said Jimmy. "I'll bet those are the flags of Quebec."

"I wouldn't bet on it," said Becky. "The Quebec flag is *fleur-de-lis* on a blue background. Those are rainbow flags."

"I've seen flags like those before," said Jay. "In San Francisco the streets were lined with flags like these on every lamp post."

"Everywhere in San Francisco?" asked Becky.

"In the area where Steve and I stayed, they were," said Jay.

"Let me guess. That would be the Castro area, wouldn't it?"

Jay thought for a minute. "Are you suggesting this is the gay area of Montreal?"

"Well, it doesn't look like the shopping center of the city," said Becky. "And there seem to be a lot of stylishly dressed young people hanging out everywhere."

"I don't care what area it is," said Jimmy. "That hotel is marvelous and I love this city. It makes me feel so happy to be alive."

"My guess is the city center is back the way we came. Let's walk that direction and see what we find," suggested Becky.

"Keep your eyes open for a store called *Priape*," Jay said. "Steve asked me to pick up something for him there."

"Are you sure this is the right street for it?" Becky asked.

"He gave me a map that shows *Priape* and the hotel on the same street."

"I don't suppose you have the map with you."

"It's back in the hotel. We can get it later if we need to," Jay said.

They walked along the street, looking in the windows of mom-and-pop stores, tiny eating establishments, and convenience stores.

Jimmy looked in a window. "Forty-nine cents for a slice of pizza. I wish we had places like this in Winnipeg. It's cheaper than Mcdonald's."

"Steve said we should go to a place called *Pizzédélic*," Jay said.

"Knowing Steve, I'll bet it's more than forty-nine cents a slice."

"He says it's inexpensive, but his idea of expense and ours are different by at least a factor of ten. It's not pizza as we know it. They make them with exotic toppings like feta cheese, snails, and artichokes on a square pizza crust."

"That would be in the English section of Montreal, I bet," Becky said.

"Why would you think that?" Jay asked.

"It shows the gap between the English and French philosophy in Quebec."

"What's the connection between forty-nine cent pizza and *Pizzédélic*?" Jay asked.

"A family establishment giving good value is typically traditional French. *Pizzédélic* represents the English love of novelty to create profit. They ignore the French people's respect for tradition."

"I read in the paper before we left that the separatists have been throwing bricks through McDonald's windows again," Jay said.

"Why would they do that? They obviously like cheap food," Jimmy said.

"Probably chains like Mcdonald's represent the English influence. They're impersonal and profit oriented," Becky said.

"Now there's a fancy store," said Jimmy, pointing in the window. "They seem to sell leather goods...and chains, and...oh my goodness...I have no idea what some of this stuff is."

"That's the store you're looking for, Jay," said Becky.

"It's *Priape*, all right," said Jay. "I might have known Steve would send me to some place like this. Hang on guys. We're going in."

They wandered through the store, trying to look casual among the array of clothes, belts, masks, whips, and skimpy underwear, all made from soft black leather. Beside a section of videos, a flight of stairs led down to a lower level. Becky looked questioningly at Jay.

"Why not? What've we got to lose?" Jay said, leading the way, "except our reputations."

"And our self-respect. I'll meet you guys outside," Jimmy said. "This isn't my kind of scene."

"Stout heart never won fair lady," Jay said.

"What?" Becky asked.

"No. That's wrong. It's fair heart never won stout lady," Jay said. "Oh. Never mind. I can't think straight in a place like this."

"Why can't he buy things himself?" Becky asked.

"He said Winnipeg doesn't have them in stock. It would take time to order it, and you know Steve. He's not the world's most patient guy."

"It would be as fast to order them through the Internet," Jimmy said.

"He likes to have people do things for him. I think it's his way of feeling that people care about him. Whatever the reason, it's the least I can do after his help in San Francisco. I hope they speak English."

They wandered aimlessly among the display cases and racks of clothing until Jay spotted a case containing trays of silver hoops, bars, clamps, and assorted body jewelry. He was peering intently through the glass trying to make some sense of the assorted paraphernalia, when the clerk came over.

"*Bonjour. Est-ce que je peux vous aider?*" the clerk asked.

"Do you speak English?" Jay asked.

"*Je regrette. Je ne parle que français.*"

Jay took a deep breath. Speaking slowly, clearly, and a bit too loudly, he said, "I'm looking for little bars with a ball on each end. They are used with body piercing."

The clerk pointed to the tray of rings and looked at Jay questioningly.

"No. It's for…"

Jay gestured vaguely toward his chest.

"*Mais oui,*" the man said. With that, he pulled up his T-shirt to display his nipple ring. "*Comme çi?*"

"That's it. Yes," Jay said, nodding his head and wishing the man would pull down his T-shirt.

"*Quelle taille?*"

"They need to be like little barbells."

"*Pardonnez-moi?*"

Jay picked up a pencil from the counter and drew a sketchy picture.

The clerk nodded. "*Quelles dimensions?*" he asked.

"Silver?" Jay suggested.

"*Quelle taille?*" the clerk asked again.

"He said they have to be 10-gauge."

"*Combien?*"

Jay wrote '10' on the paper.

"*Dix? Nous n'avons que six.*"

Jay's brow furrowed with confusion. He wrote '10-gauge.' The clerk shrugged his shoulders. Jay tried adding dimension arrows to indicate diameter.

The clerk smiled and nodded. "*Un ou deux?*"

"I don't understand."

The clerk placed two of the 10-gauge ones on the counter.

Jay looked at them carefully, pretending to know what he was examining. After a few seconds, he picked them up gently between finger and thumb, one at a time, as if afraid they might bite him. He handed them both to the clerk.

"*Quatre-vingts dollars plus l'impôt,*" the clerk said pointing to the cash register display.

Jay pocketed the change from the hundred-dollar bill Steve had given him.

Back on the sidewalk, they joined Jimmy. "Did you get what you wanted?" he asked.

"Shut up and find me a bar," Jay said. "I need a drink."

"Let's go back to the hotel. We can have drinks and dinner and put everything on the hotel bill."

"Are you sure we're supposed to be doing that?" Becky asked.

"He said if I played ball with him, he'd look after our expenses."

"What did he mean by playing ball?"

"Doing what he asked, I guess," Jimmy said.

"And what's that?"

"He gave me an envelope I'm supposed to deliver to the hotel manager personally."

"And that's all?" Becky asked.

"He said for me not to think too much."

"That part should be easy for you."

The dining room was a sea of white tablecloths topped with polished silverware, napkins shaped like tiny peacocks, crystal goblets begging to be filled with imported French wine, and a huge vase of fresh flowers.

Most of the chairs were empty. Near the window, a girl sat with her back to the door. The *maitre d'* escorted Jay, Jimmy, and Becky to a table also near the window.

"You can order anything you want from the menu," Jimmy said.

"We shouldn't be too extravagant," Becky said. "It's not nice to be greedy."

"We just charge it to the room and it'll all be paid for," Jimmy said.

"Are you sure he doesn't care?" Becky asked.

"He said to charge whatever we want."

"I'm a bit concerned about all this money you seem to have, Jimmy," Jay said. "He must be wanting something more from you."

"Don't worry about it. I'm supposed to deliver the envelope. That's it."

"I hate to ask this but you did remember to bring the envelope, didn't you?" Becky asked.

Jimmy pretended to look hurt.

"My memory's getting better all the time. Your toilet paper is working miracles for me," he said.

"Did it remind you to deliver the envelope?"

"I'll do it tomorrow," Jimmy said.

After the waiter took their order, they looked around the room.

"Doesn't that girl look familiar?" Becky asked.

"I know I've seen her before," Jimmy said. "Isn't she the person who did a séance with us? What was her name?" Jimmy asked.

"If I didn't know better, I'd say it's Tanya," Becky said.

"What would she be doing here in Montreal?" Jimmy asked.

"I'm sure it's Tanya," Jay said, leaning over and waving his hand to catch the girl's attention.

The girl's gaze moved in their general direction and then focused. Her face brightened in surprise as she recognized them.

"Come and join us," Becky called.

"Hi guys. What are you doing here? Goodness, gracious. I never expected to see you people here," Tanya said.

"We didn't expect to see you here either," Becky said.

"I've been here since yesterday."

"We got here last night," Jay said.

"You look amazing, Jimmy," Tanya said. "What have you done with yourself?"

"I'm totally off drugs now. And I've quit smoking."

"Good for you. I see you've also learned how to dress yourself."

"He has a system," Becky said. "He goes into a store and finds a cute salesgirl. Then he lets her dress him the way she likes."

"This time last week I thought I'd be spending the rest of my life in Manitoba," Jimmy said.

"This trip came as a surprise to me, too," Tanya said.

"Did you win a contest of some kind?" Becky asked.

"I was watching a fashion show at the Portage Plaza Mall when this fellow singled me out from the crowd and asked me if I'd like to model their line of clothes here in Montreal. What could I say? Here I am. What are you guys doing here, anyway?"

"Jimmy got tickets and rooms for all of us through a businessman he works for. It sounds a bit strange but it seems to be working," Becky said.

"This is all too weird. We don't see each other for months, and then suddenly here we all are in Montreal," said Tanya. "It must be synchronicity."

"What's that mean?" Jimmy asked.

"It's like fate. Things happening at the same time for some cosmic reason," Tanya explained. Turning her attention to Jay, she said, "It's good to see you again."

"You did say that if it was written in the stars that we should meet again, then it would happen," Jay said.

"And it has. Are there only the three of you here?"

"Yes. Is that a subtle way of asking about Sue?" Jay asked.

"I didn't want to pry into your private life."

"There's nothing to hide. We've been back together since New Year's."

"She's a lucky girl. I wanted to visit her in the hospital when I heard she was ill but it didn't seem like such a good idea. She didn't like me much even before she met you. Then there was that thing about her thinking we were dating. She's all right, then?"

"Oh, yes. She had some kind of major trauma but she's getting over it."

"I'm glad she's going to be okay. Is she at home?"

"As a matter of fact we're sort of living together," Jay said.

"How do two people sort of live together?" Tanya asked.

"Sometimes I stay at her apartment and sometimes I stay at the Red Dragon."

"Where do you keep your razor?"

"What do you mean by that?"

"Your razor. Where do you keep it? Her place or yours?" Tanya asked again.

"Her place."

"Then you're living together."

"I think it only proves she and my razor are living together."

"Why isn't she here?"

"She had to stay home to look after her grandmother," Jay said.

"She's a good girl. Her family has always been important to her," Tanya said.

"I assume you're staying in the hotel here?"

"Room 1714."

"What an awesome coincidence. We're in 1712," Jay said.

"This really must be synchronicity. I have a good feeling about this little holiday. The karma feels so right," Tanya said.

"Have you checked out the night life yet?"

"Of course."

"So, what's it like?"

"Great. I met this guy, Mel, in a coffee shop downtown. He's lived in Montreal all his life so he knows his way around. Besides, he has a car."

"Are you seeing him tonight?" Jay asked.

"I'd rather hang with you guys, if you don't mind."

"That would be great," Becky said. "We could use a guide."

"I let the stars lead me. You can't miss. All the clubs here are hot."

"Come on, then," Jimmy said. "Let's do the town. I'm paying."

"Until you're flat broke, anyway," Becky muttered to herself.

"Maybe we should ask at the desk for some directions. At least they speak English," Jay suggested.

The desk clerk was polite and eager to help. "There's a *Métro* station right under the hotel. The *Métro* will take you anywhere you want to go in the city."

"How will we know where to get off? We haven't any idea where we want to go."

"Simply get off at any station. There's a whole underground city of modern buildings, stores, and theaters connected by underground promenades and the *Métro*."

"Can you give us some suggestions?" Jay asked.

"*Place Ville-Marie* has lots of shops and a lovely sculptured fountain. I would suggest *St-Denis* for theaters, and maybe *St-Laurent* for restaurants. However, follow your impulses and explore. It's safe and fun anywhere in Underground *Montréal*"

It was well into the small morning hours when the foursome found their way back to the hotel.

"I have no idea where we've been or how we got back," said Jimmy. "But it certainly was exciting. And so easy."

"That subway system is amazing," said Becky, as they got off the elevator at the 17th floor, chattering nonstop in their enthusiasm.

"Did you hear that fellow say they had to prop up a whole cathedral to excavate under it for the subway station?"

"I can't believe they'd do that. You'd think it would have been easier to tear it down and rebuild it," Jay said.

"They care about maintaining their roots to the past," Becky said.

"I guess a cathedral is a pretty big root."

"What about that other station," Jimmy added, "with its two underground levels and escalators and everything. Every one of those stations was like a whole shopping mall."

"Do you realize we've spent the whole night underground?" Jay asked.

They arrived at their rooms. "Here's my room," Tanya said, stopping in front of 1714.

"And here we are, right next door," Jimmy said. "See you in the morning."

Jimmy, Becky, and Jay went into their room. "What's this extra door for?" asked Jimmy.

"I'll bet we're connected to the room next door," said Becky.

Jimmy knocked on the connecting door. "Let's unlock our door, and see if Tanya will open her side."

A voice responded through the door, "Hello?"

"Hi. It's Jimmy. Unlock the door."

Tanya opened the door. She stepped into the room and looked around. "This is nice." She sat on the foot of one bed. "I'm going to be lonely all by myself next door. Maybe we could all share one room."

"Or one of us could go to your room and keep you company," Becky suggested.

"What a great idea," said Tanya. "I choose Jay."

"That would give the two of you some privacy," said Jay. "You do have an extra bed, don't you, Tanya?"

"Sure. Same as you guys. Two double beds."

Jay went to the bathroom to pick up his toiletry bag. He noticed his razor sitting on the sink. Jay looked at it for a moment, started to reach for it, and then left without it.

"G'night guys," Tanya said, taking Jay by the arm and leading him to her room. The door closed and locked behind them.

"Let's see what's on television. I'm sure they must have something in English," Tanya said.

"How about some snackies from the mini bar," Jay said, opening the door. "Oh, look. They have little miniature bottles of booze."

"Let's have some champagne to celebrate being in Montreal. It would be the French thing to do, wouldn't it?" Tanya suggested.

"Why not? It'll be charged to the room."

Jay and Tanya curled up on the bed. The late-night movie droned on in the background.

"This is nice," Tanya said. "I always knew we would somehow, some-time, get together again. Ever since that night at the Fringe Festival."

"That was months ago. I remember you wanted to call me Truro," Jay said.

"Winnipeg has so many good things in the summer."

"Like Folklorama, with all those ethnic groups putting on their tradi-tional entertainment and food events."

"It makes one realize how many different cultural roots we have," Tanya said.

"They say the one in Winnipeg is the biggest show of its kind in Canada."

"You do remember the séance we had at Tiffany's place, don't you?"

"I've always wondered if that was for real. Are you honestly a psy-chic?" Jay asked.

"Heavens, no. I like helping people get in touch with themselves. It has nothing to do with the supernatural."

"Where did you learn to do that stuff, then?"

"I got started with New Age things because I liked their music."

"Did someone teach you?"

"The bookstores are full of New Age things. I pick out the ideas I like."

"However you learned it, what you did at that séance helped Steve and me to understand each other better."

"That was where somebody got the idea you and I were seeing each other," Tanya said, "and then went and told Sue."

"Oh, yes. I heard about that a few times," Jay said.

"Are you and Sue okay with things now?" Tanya asked.

"We've been getting along great. Her dad's a different story."

"What are you planning to do about that?"

"There's not much I can do except try to stay out of his way."

"You and Sue are serious, aren't you?"

"I am, and I think she is, too."

"Are you thinking marriage?"

"I want to be part of a family some day. All my life, I was always on the outside of my own family, somehow."

"Why was that?"

"Maybe because my sister and brother knew their father. I didn't."

"You went looking for him in California, didn't you?" Tanya asked.

"I got an address for him and wrote him but I haven't heard back yet."

"Does the idea of meeting him scare you?"

"It doesn't scare me. However, it does make me a bit nervous. What if he doesn't want anything to do with me? What if he doesn't like me?"

"You don't need to worry. Everybody likes you."

"I wish. Time we went to sleep. I'll hop over to the other bed."

"You don't need to move unless you want to."

"I meant to phone Sue tonight. Remind me in the morning."

"Okay, Truro."

~ 19 ~

THERE'S MANY A SLIP

Jay and Tanya went back for their second refill at the hotel's Sunday brunch buffet.

"This is a totally awesome spread," Jay said. "It would be so great to stay long enough to try one of everything."

"Mel said this hotel is famous for its Sunday brunch. He knows all about Montreal," Tanya said.

"You like this Mel guy?"

"He's all right, but he's no Truro."

"Stop that. I belong to Sue."

"I don't want to own you, just borrow you," Tanya teased.

"Now, stop that. What are we going to do today? We should do something French."

"Mel said Montreal has a world famous bagel store."

"That sounds more Jewish than French."

"Probably Mel is Jewish. Things like that don't mean much to me. I go by the inner person, not the outer appearances."

"How do we find this bagel place?"

"Mel would take us there, if you don't mind having him along."

"Can Jimmy and Becky come, too? I'd feel uncomfortable with only the three of us."

"You check with them and I'll phone Mel."

Tanya headed for the pay phone and Jay went up to the room. "Hey, guys, open the door," Jay said knocking on the door.

Jimmy, clad in a hotel bathrobe, opened the door. "Come in. Is Tanya with you?"

"She'll be up right away. She's making plans for the day. Have you had breakfast, yet?"

"We had room service send it up. They have the greatest orange juice here. They call it Mimosa. I wish we could get that brand of orange in Winnipeg."

"Do you have any plans or do you want to join us?"

"I thought we'd done well to plan breakfast," Becky said coming into the room. "What did you have in mind?"

"It sounds a bit strange but Tanya wants to go to a bagel store."

"What could be so special about bagels? We can get bagels anywhere," Becky said.

"She says the shop is world famous. She's phoning Mel right now to see if he will act as our guide."

"Who's Mel?" asked Jimmy.

"A guy she met here. He's lived here all his life and knows where to go and how to get there."

Tanya came into the room. "Mel thinks it would be great for all of us to go to the bagel place. He says it's an interesting area of Montreal. Can you guys get some clothes on and be ready in half an hour? He's coming to pick us up."

"He has a car?" Jimmy asked.

"Trust Tanya to find a guy with the car," Jay said.

"Don't get smart with me," Tanya said, mussing up Jay's hair. "Come on, I need help to get ready," she said tugging Jay to the door.

Although Mel had dressed in casual pants and an open-necked shirt, he still gave the impression of being a serious professional, older than his 23 years. Perhaps a salesman, a stockbroker or a lawyer. His sculptured black beard and moustache dominated his features. He had an easy smile and hazel eyes that sparkled at the slightest provocation.

Mel drove down *rue Ste-Catherine* with the speed and forcefulness of a typical Montreal driver, pulling his baseball cap down over his eyes to shade them.

"You have to watch out for the taxi drivers. They tend to ignore red lights," he said, coasting through the tail end of a yellow light. "It's one of those things they do."

"So what's this place we're going to?" Becky asked. "Why is it famous?"

"It's been in operation forever and still uses the old-fashioned traditional methods, like a lot of things in the province of Quebec. They knead the dough by hand and use a wood-burning oven. The bagels are always fresh, 24 hours a day."

"Are there enough tourists to be open 24 hours a day?"

"It's probably not by coincidence that they're right beside a major Jewish section of Montreal. We'll take a drive through there."

"Don't bother. We have lots of Jewish areas in Winnipeg," Jay said. "The neighborhood where Sue's dad lives is becoming largely Jewish but it doesn't look any different from any other section of Winnipeg."

"Trust me. This is different," Mel said, driving down *Avenue du Parc* and then turning left on *St-Viateur*. "These are Hasidic Jews."

"How's that different?"

"Have a look and then you tell me."

"There's one in a black top hat, long suit jacket, and black leggings," Jimmy said.

"They all look like that," Becky said. "Nothing but Abe Lincolns everywhere."

"Why do they dress like that?" Jay asked.

"They're Orthodox Jews. The outfit is their way of showing their pride in their mystical heritage. Even the children look like miniature Lincolns," Mel explained.

"Look at the long curly wisps of hair hanging down the side of their faces," Jimmy said.

"They're called earlocks. Hairdressers sometimes call them tendrils or side curls. A lot of men have full beards."

"Why would they have earlocks?" Becky asked.

"I know that one," Jay said. "It says in the Bible that you should not cut the corners of your hair. Their earlocks are corners, I guess."

"Very impressive, Jay. We refer to the Torah but the quotation's the same. You know a lot about the Bible. It's not a common quotation," Mel said.

"I had a stepfather who quoted the Bible a lot. He particularly liked to quote from Revelations. Spare the rod and spoil the child was a favorite."

Mel returned down *Rue St-Viateur* and crossed *Avenue du Parc*.

"There aren't any on this side of the street. Across the street there's nobody else. Is there some sort of law that keeps them over there?" Jimmy asked.

"They have no need to be over here, unless it's to buy bagels. It's that simple," Mel said. "They prefer to live in a close-knit community because that makes it easier to avoid the distractions presented by other people's lives."

"It's as if there's an invisible banner of faith around their area," Becky said. "I felt like an intruder when we were there."

"There's the place we're looking for," Mel said, pointing to a tiny building near the corner on the left.

"Are you sure?" Jimmy asked.

"It's called the *St-Viateur* Bagel Shop, and that's the street we're on."

"I don't see any neon sign. If it's so famous wouldn't there be signs everywhere?"

"That's not the traditional Francophone way," Mel said. "They don't brag with advertising."

"Except places like the 'Club Super Sex' downtown," Jimmy said.

Becky gave Jimmy a sharp look. "You aren't supposed to be looking at things like that."

"It was kind of hard to miss," Jimmy retorted.

"That's the English influence," Mel said. "It's things like that make the *Quebeçois* want to secede from the rest of Canada."

"Can you explain why Quebec wants to leave Canada?" Jay asked. "It's something I've never been able to understand."

"You need to have lived here to understand it," Mel said. "The license plate says it all. *Je me souviens*. I remember."

"I don't understand that at all," Jay said.

"Francophones try to live history the way it was."

"What does that mean?"

"You see that old building across the street?"

"The one they're scraping the paint off?"

"Yes. They're uncovering the original brass of the embossed frieze work."

"It looks like an awful lot of hard work. Is it worth it?"

"We like to live things the way they used to be. We have reverence for our history. Not the way the English have written it, but as we know it was."

"I still don't get it," Jay said.

"Where you come from, they'd tear that building down to build a new one. They'd call it progress. We'd call it wasteful, and an insult to our heritage."

"We like things to be new and modern."

"Maybe that's the problem. The rest of Canada doesn't understand the French way of thinking," Mel said.

"How about an example?" Jay asked.

"You remember the last referendum when people for all over Canada came to Quebec to convince us to vote against secession? Do you remember what their T-shirts said?"

"Sure. They said, 'Quebec, we love you', right across the front."

"Exactly."

"What's wrong with that?" Jay asked.

"It would have meant more to us if they had said, '*Québec, nous t'aimons*'. The message on the shirts was made for themselves, not for us."

Inside the Bagel Shop, hundred-pound bags of sesame seeds and flour lined one wall. The interior looked as if it hadn't been renovated more than once in the past hundred years. Bagels slid in a steady stream down a chute beside the tiny counter and low-tech cash register.

"Claustrophobia time," Jay said under his breath.

Mel bought a bag of assorted bagels, and they went back to the car.

"I'll take another quick tour through the Hasidic area," he said. "You'll notice how similar the houses all are. They don't try to be better than their neighbours."

"What about women?" Jimmy asked. "I don't see any on the street. Why is that?"

"Most socializing takes place in the synagogues, schools and in each other's houses," Mel explained.

"What would the women dress like?" Jimmy asked.

"They wear head coverings, like scarves or wigs. And modest, full-length dresses, of course."

"It sounds like a boring life," Jimmy said.

"The Hasidic way of life is gentle, beautiful and joyful," Mel said.

"They don't look all that joyful," Becky said.

"Sometimes they get harassed on the streets because of their appearance. They've learned to avoid eye contact with people they don't know.

Many put on a stern face in public for self-protection. It's not easy being an obvious minority group."

"There are only a few men on the sidewalks," Jay observed.

"It's not the custom to hang out on the street the way some other people do. They go onto the streets to get somewhere. On holy days, they spend hours around the festive table singing traditional songs, telling stories, and visiting with family and friends. But the world doesn't see this joyful celebrating, because it takes place in the privacy of their homes."

"Don't they have something to do with the *Kabbalah*?" Tanya asked. "I sometimes use it for numerology. That's how I came up with the name Truro for Jay."

"People are often astonished that Hasidic Jews would believe in things like reincarnation, prophetic dreams, miracles, angels and spiritual healing."

"Those are typical New Age ideas," Tanya said.

"What can I tell you? For you, maybe it's New Age but for them it's ancient history."

"How can they be so old-fashioned in appearance and be New Age in their thinking?" Jimmy asked.

"Looks can be deceiving," Mel said. "You know what they say, never judge a book by its cover."

"This is fascinating," Tanya said. "Do you happen to know how I can find out more?"

"There's a lot of information on the Internet. They even have complete courses in the Hasidic philosophy and way of life that you can download free."

"Great. Now all I need is a computer and somebody who knows how to work it," Tanya said.

"I can do that standing on my head," Jimmy said. "I'll show you how to do it when we get back to Winnipeg."

"Where would I find a computer?"

"Libraries have free Internet connections. You don't even need a library card," Jimmy said.

Jay turned to Mel. "You seem to know an awful lot about this."

"I should. I'm a closet Hasidic Jew."

"You're a what?" Jay asked, almost dropping his bagel in surprise.

"I'm an Hasidic Jew, and always have been. I just don't dress that way."

"Can you do that?"

"Why not? It's a faith and a way of life, not a monastery. Individuals are free to do whatever makes them feel comfortable."

"What about the earlocks?" Tanya asked.

Mel took off his baseball cap to reveal a *yarmulke*, with the ends of his earlocks tucked neatly underneath it. "I have the long coat and vest and hat for religious occasions and attending synagogue. People at work know I'm Jewish but they don't suspect I'm Hasidic."

"Why do you hide it?"

"Some people think our lifestyle is fanatical. Others are turned off by the formality of the clothes. In my work I have to meet the public, so I try to be as generic as possible."

"Do you think you'll ever come out of the closet at work?" Jay asked.

"I'd like to but I have to wait until society is ready for it. I can't afford to be ostracized by my clients."

"Don't you feel you're deceiving your clients?"

"My clients pay for the work I do, not how I look. I'm just as good a lawyer no matter what I look like. Except in court, maybe. Jury members tend to react as much to appearances as to the words."

"What about betraying your faith?"

"I'm as good a Jew with or without the black top hat. If I am betraying anything, it's myself I'm betraying. Sometimes I feel I am not being true to myself when I hide who I am. It makes me feel guilty sometimes, but I have to consider my career."

"What's it like to be Jewish?" Tanya asked.

"To begin with, it's more than a religion. It's a total community and family thing. Even if I didn't believe in God, I would still be a Jew. My way of life and my morals would still be those of a Jew."

"Can you give an example of how Jewish morals are different from ours?" Becky asked.

"For one, we don't believe in charity. There's no Yiddish word for it."

"You don't contribute to helping the poor?" Becky asked.

"Just the opposite. It's a moral and religious obligation to act justly and compassionately as a part of our life. In fact, helping our fellow man is our most important obligation. We're forbidden by our religion to turn away or ignore any of our people who ask for help."

"What about people who don't ask? Like, people who live far away?" Tanya asked.

"We have little boxes, called *pushkes*, on a window sill in the kitchen. They're provided by the organizations we wish to support. Every Friday night, just before lighting the Sabbath candles, a few coins are put into each *pushke*. This is our duty, not a noble act of charity."

"Are you saying you shouldn't feel good about giving to the poor?"

"It's fine to feel good about it, but the poor and needy must be saved from embarrassment. It must be done as fulfilling an obligation and not as a favor bestowed."

"Doing things anonymously is good, then?" Becky asked.

"Let me tell you the legend of the Thirty-six Saints. As the story goes, at any given time there are six special men in the world. We call them *tzaddickim*. No one knows who they are and even they themselves do not know they are a *tzaddick*. It's only through the selfless works of these thirty-six unidentified saints that the world continues to exist, according to the legend. The *Talmud* encourages the doing of good without recognition or reward."

"You said it is your duty to act justly to your fellow man. How do you do that?" Tanya asked.

"In all our dealings, including financial, we must never allow ourselves to benefit from another's misfortune," Mel said.

"So if a person goes bankrupt you can't buy his goods at a reduced price and make a profit on them?"

"Only through an open and honest business deal. We're forbidden to take advantage of him and his bad luck."

"That sounds like it's covered by the Golden Rule," Jimmy suggested.

"We say that what is hateful to you, do not to your fellow man," Mel said.

"Does your toilet paper have Golden Rules, too?" Jay asked.

Jimmy just smiled, although you could tell his mind was working hard to try to come up with a good retort.

"Hasidic Jews live their life apart from the rest of the world. It is the only way we can maintain our religion, beliefs and lifestyle," Mel said. "We have to maintain our separate existence in order to survive."

Seven of the bagels had disappeared by the time the group got back to the hotel. "I should phone Sue," Jay said. "Is it all right if I charge it to the room?"

"Go for it," Jimmy replied. "Charge away."

Jay tried phoning Sue's apartment but there was no answer. He dialed Sue's parents and got Helen:

"Hi. Is Sue there?"

"   . . .   "

"I thought she might be away with her grandmother."

"   . . .   "

"That's too bad. Sue could have come with us, if we'd known."

"   . . .   "

"Can I talk to her?"

"   . . .   "

"Why would she be mad at me?"

" . . . "

"Well, yes. Tanya is here."

" . . . "

"Can I talk to Sue?"

" . . . "

"Hi Sue."

" . . . "

"Well, yes. Tanya is here but . . . "

" . . . "

"Please. Don't cry."

" . . . "

"Of course I love you."

" . . . "

"No. I didn't plan this whole thing as a way to get together with Tanya."

" . . . "

"How can you have proof?"

" . . . "

"There must be some mistake. That's impossible."

" . . . "

"I'm coming home right away. We can straighten this whole thing out."

" . . . "

"I don't care what anyone says. It's not true."

" . . . "

"Please, believe me. I didn't plan this as a way to be with Tanya."

Jay hung up the phone and turned to his friends. "Sue's upset. She thinks Tanya and I planned this trip as an excuse to be together."

"How would she even know I'm here?" Tanya asked.

"Her dad probably has someone following me. It's a habit of his."

"Why does he do that?"

"You'd have to ask him. I guess he likes to know everything. Sue said he has proof."

"What kind of proof?"

"Something written, I think. Like letters."

"We've never written letters to each other, have we?" Tanya asked.

"No. Sue's totally mistaken about this."

"Maybe somebody's trying to mess with you and Sue," Becky said.

"Who'd want to do that?" Jimmy asked.

"There's something strange about this whole thing," Becky said.

"Hang on a minute," Jay said. "Didn't the desk clerk say both these rooms were paid for by the same company?"

"You're right. He did," Becky said.

"I think it's about time we got some straight answers here," Jay said. "Jimmy, do you have anything to say that would be helpful?"

"No."

"You're lying," Becky said.

"Why are you always accusing me of lying?" Jimmy whined.

"Because your first reaction is always to try and save face."

"That's because I've had a bad life and I don't want to admit anything about my past."

"And your second reaction is to avoid the question by changing the topic," Becky continued. "Now start talking. And no lies."

"We need to know," Tanya added.

Jimmy looked down at the table. "It's like I told you. This fellow told me that if I would come to Montreal and bring two or three friends with me he'd pay all my expenses. That's it."

"What about you, Tanya? What's the deal on you're getting here with your expenses paid?" said Becky.

"It's like I said. This person, whom I've never seen before in my life, told me he was representing a firm that models clothes. He said his company would pay my expenses for ten days if I'd come here and model for them. He gave me a plane ticket, reserved my hotel room, and gave me some spending money."

"When and where are you supposed to be modeling these clothes?" asked Becky.

"He said that someone would contact me at the hotel. I have to wait until they tell me what they want me to do."

"Has anyone tried to contact you yet?" Becky asked.

"Not that I know of."

"There's got to be some connection here," said Jay. "The desk clerk said it was G. P. Enterprises or something like that. Do any of you recognize that name?"

"Jimmy. I think you know who's behind all this. Who was it gave you the tickets?" Becky asked.

"I promised I wouldn't tell," Jimmy said, looking down at the table to avoid eye contact.

Jay looked around the table. Everyone looked blank. Jay's eyes rested for a moment on Jimmy's right wrist.

"Don't I recognize that watch?" he asked.

Jimmy looked up with a guilty look on his face. "Maybe."

"How did you get it out of the pawn shop?" asked Jay. "I was going to get it for you."

"It was given to me."

"Nobody gives a watch like that without expecting something in return."

"I gave it to you without expecting anything back," Jimmy said.

"That was different. We're friends. Whoever gave it to you had a reason."

"I didn't do anything wrong. It wasn't anything illegal."

"Then tell us what you did do," Becky said.

"He said he'd get my watch back for me if I made sure Jay went on this trip," Jimmy said.

"You mean this whole thing was a set up to get me here?" Jay asked.

"I guess so. I hadn't thought of it that way."

"Do you expect us to believe you don't know who this person was?"

"I'd never seen him before," Jimmy said.

"How did you meet him, then?"

"I promised I wouldn't tell."

Jimmy looked up at the intense faces around the table and his resolve crumbled. "Sue's dad told me that this fellow had a job for me."

"That would mean Sue's dad was behind getting me here, too," Tanya said.

"Why would he do that?" Jimmy asked.

Jay and Becky exchanged looks.

"You mean he's gone to all this work just to make trouble for Sue and me? What kind of a person does that?" Jay asked.

"A father who loves his daughter way too much might," Becky said.

"I'm sorry, Jay. I'd never have come here if I had known it was going to cause trouble between you and Sue. I hope you know that," Tanya said.

"It's not your fault, Tanya. We've all been used as pawns in a malicious chess game," Jay said.

"I'm so ashamed for being so stupid," Jimmy said.

"I'm going to phone the airline and get my ticket changed to the next flight home," Jay said, dialing the airline:

"I need to change the date of my return ticket from Montreal to Winnipeg."

"   . . .   "

"It's an electronic ticket. Confirmation number 384T64J."

"   . . .   "

"Are you sure?"

"   . . .   "

"What can I do?"

"   . . .   "

"Thanks."

Jay hung up the receiver and sat staring blankly at the phone.

"What's the problem?" Becky asked.

"They say it was a one-way ticket. I have no way to get back to Winnipeg."

"What a horrible mistake," Jimmy said.

"Or what a horribly dirty trick," Tanya said.

"I have no money and no ticket. What do I do now?"

"I'm going to phone room service," Jimmy said. "We're going to run up the biggest bill that guy's ever seen. That'll serve him right."

"Hang on Jimmy. That'll backfire on you. He'll take it out on you somehow when you get back. We need to play this hand out as calmly as we can," Becky said. "You need to be patient."

"But this whole mess is my fault," Jimmy said. "I've got to make it up to you guys somehow."

"It's not your fault, Jimmy. Your only sin is being gullible and way too trusting," Jay said. "You meant no harm. The three of you should enjoy the rest of your holiday. This is my problem to sort out."

"We should check our tickets. Maybe all the tickets are one-way," Becky said.

"Good idea," they agreed.

"Let me do it," Jay said. "I'll check mine again at the same time."

A short phone call established that Jay was the only one without a return ticket.

"Why don't you take my ticket?" Jimmy said. "I'll stay here. After all, it was my fault."

"Stop saying that. It wasn't your fault. What would you do in Montreal if you stayed here?" Jay said.

"You know me. I can survive anywhere," Jimmy said. "Besides, I really love this city. I'd like to live here."

"If anyone is staying here, it should be me," Tanya said. "My parents will send me money for a ticket. I'll get a huge lecture but I'm used to that. I'm sure Mel would entertain me for a few more days."

"You can't use someone else's ticket, anyway," Becky said. "You have to show a picture I.D."

"He can use my I.D.," Jimmy said.

"I don't look at all like you, Jimmy," Jay said.

"Jimmy doesn't look much like his I.D. picture anymore, either," Becky said. "It might work."

"Maybe Jimmy could get the boarding pass, and then give it to Jay at the boarding gate," Tanya suggested.

"I'm not leaving you here, Jimmy," Jay said. "You're finally getting your life together, and I won't let you put yourself in jeopardy over this. I know you'd survive, at least physically. It's what you might have to do to survive that worries me. There must be a better solution."

Jimmy looked up suddenly. With a big smile, he said, "It's so cool."

"Then tell us, already," Becky said.

"We pawn the Rolex."

"You wouldn't mind?" Jay asked.

"It was a bribe, anyway. I wouldn't feel right getting it back that way. Here, Jay. It's yours. Again."

"You're the greatest, Jimmy. I'll get it back for you somehow. I promise."

"Don't worry about it. It's the least I can do for getting you into this mess."

"You had no way of knowing it was a setup."

"Why am I always getting into trouble?" Jimmy asked plaintively.

"You're too trusting. You need to learn that if something sounds too good to be true, it isn't," Becky said.

"I'm off to the pawn shop. If I hurry, I might get a flight out tonight," Jay said.

"Let me come with you," Jimmy said. "I want to help."

"Thanks. I need all the help I can get."

"I hope they speak English in pawn shops."

"I'm sure they do. It seems they speak English whenever it's useful for them," Jay said.

~ 20 ~

EAGLE *VS* HAWK

A fifteen-minute cab ride got Jay from the Winnipeg airport to the Parkington's house. Helen answered his knock.

"This is a surprise," she said.

"Could I talk to Sue?" Jay asked.

"She doesn't want to talk to you."

"I know she's angry with me and I need to know why."

"George says you are no longer welcome in our house."

"There's something strange going on here," Jay said. "The only way to get to the bottom of this is for you to let me in so we can talk about it."

"I guess it's all right for you to talk to me. George won't be home for a little while."

"May I come in, then?"

"Certainly. I'm sorry. This whole thing has me terribly upset. I've forgotten my manners. Please. Come in."

215

Jay and Helen sat awkwardly on the edge of two chairs in the living room. "May I get you something to drink?"

"No, thank-you," Jay said.

"I don't know where to start."

"Maybe with your husband's mother," Jay said. "I thought she was coming to visit you. Sue couldn't come to Montreal with me because of her grandmother was coming here."

"That was the strangest thing. First, I didn't know she was coming to visit. Then I found out she was coming to visit, and then suddenly she wasn't coming to visit. It all seemed to happen so fast."

"I understood from Sue that it was all arranged. Sue would be driving her grandmother around to visit relatives."

"Where would she get that idea?"

"Maybe from your husband?" Jay asked.

"He didn't tell me anything about that. But then, he doesn't include me in all his plans."

"It must have been a misunderstanding," Jay said.

"Your arrangements with Tanya weren't any misunderstanding," Helen said, looking at Jay with disapproval.

"I didn't make any arrangements with Tanya."

"Then how do explain the letters."

"What letters? I never write letters," Jay said.

"We have a copy of email between you and Tanya."

"I've never sent an email in my life. I wouldn't even know how to go about it."

"Let me show it to you."

Helen went into the kitchen, returning with two pieces of paper. "See. It has conversations back and forth between the two of you. Planning to meet in Montreal."

Jay scrutinized the pages carefully. "This doesn't make any sense at all. I didn't write any of this. May I speak with Sue?"

"That wouldn't be wise," Helen said.

"May I take these with me? I'd like to show them to Cam and see if he can explain what's going on here. He's an expert in computer things."

"Certainly. Now, you'd better go before George gets here."

"I'll be back when I have some answers. Then I may have a few questions of my own," Jay said, going to the door.

"Do you need a ride?" Helen asked.

"I'll just call a cab, thanks," Jay said. "Do you mind if I use your phone?"

"You can borrow my car if you want."

"I don't think that would be a good idea. I don't want to cause any more trouble."

"Go ahead," Helen said. "George won't notice."

Jay took the keys from Helen and headed down the street. He found himself accelerating faster from the traffic lights and changing lanes rather more abruptly than usual as he enjoyed the spirit and handling of the car. Immediately, he felt guilty and reverted to his more sedate style of driving. "What a waste to keep a machine like this in the city," he said to himself. "It should have the freedom to run on the wide-open county roads. Or on a racetrack."

He parked Helen's BMW and went up to Cam's apartment.

"Hi, Cam," said Jay.

"What brings you here?" asked Cam.

"I need a favor."

"What's the deal?"

"I'm sorry I don't have time to tell you the whole story right now. What I need is for you to explain email to me."

"Sure. Come on in and I'll show you how to send an email," said Cam.

"That's not exactly what I had in mind," Jay said, handing Cam the sheets of paper. "Sue got these email printouts. She thinks they prove I planned a meeting with Tanya in Montreal."

Cam looked over at the pages carefully. "These do appear to show email between you and Tanya."

"That's impossible."

"You're saying you didn't send this email?"

"No way. I've never sent email in my life. How can this be possible?"

"Obviously, the email was sent. However, the names and messages on email can be fictitious."

"How's that possible? The printed word doesn't lie," Jay said.

"The simplest way would be for someone to set up two accounts, one in your name and one in Tanya's name. Then that person would write email back and forth between the two accounts, print them out, and there you are. Email that looks as if it is between you and Tanya."

"Is it that easy to set up an account?"

"Sure. There are a dozen companies that will give you free Internet email accounts."

"I need to prove I didn't write this email."

"I'm afraid we can't prove you didn't write them. However, this doesn't prove you did write them, either."

"This is all very interesting but it isn't solving my problem. How do I convince Sue and her parents that I didn't write this email?"

"I don't have an answer for that. There is no way to find out who actually sent them unless you have access to the computer they came from. The printout doesn't tell us that."

"This has to be a deliberate setup, doesn't it?"

"If you didn't write them, someone else had to. Would Sue's dad do that sort of thing?" Cam asked.

"He might if he knew how. However, he doesn't strike me as very hi-tech person."

"Maybe some private eye earned a bonus by providing proof?" Cam said.

"That's possible but I don't know how we'd prove something like that."

"I'm afraid I can't be much help with that," Cam said.

"Would you be willing to explain all this to the Parkingtons if they don't understand me? Or don't believe me."

"I can tell them what I've told you. Maybe they'll believe you."

"It's the only hope I have at the moment."

After a brief stop at his apartment, Jay hustled back to the Parkington's residence. He carefully parked the BMW exactly where he had found it.

Jay Helen held the door for Jay. "Come on in. I tried to talk to George but he doesn't seem to want to be any help. He keeps saying there's nothing he can do about what you've done."

"Let me try talking to him. I brought my eagle feather with me."

"That's the good luck charm you found in California, isn't it?" Helen asked.

"It's more than a good luck charm. The eagle is my spiritual guide. This feather makes it more real to me, and puts me in touch with the eagle spirit."

"Do you want me to be there when you talk to George?"

"It's up to you."

"In that case, I think I'll leave the two of you alone. Wait here and I'll tell George you're here."

A couple of minutes later, Helen called to Jay, "Come on into the study, please."

Mr. Parkington sat behind a polished oak desk, backed by a wall of books and a fireplace, his arms firmly folded across his chest. A soft-leather chair waited in front of the desk. Jay looked in awe at the rows of leather and gold bound books.

"I'll leave you two alone, now," Helen said, scurrying from the room.

"Don't just stand there with your mouth hanging open," George said. "Sit."

"Thank-you, sir," Jay said, dragging his eyes away from the wall of books.

"I hadn't expected to see you again. I'll give you five minutes to explain your atrocious behavior toward Sue. After that, I hope I never have to see you again."

Jay sat in a chair facing the desk. He leaned forward and placed the eagle feather in the center of the desk. "I didn't come here to explain my behavior. I have done nothing that needs explaining."

George's eyes moved back and forth uneasily between Jay and the feather. "Running off to Montreal to be with another girl certainly requires some explaining."

"It would require some explaining, if it were true. I think you know it's not true."

"I've no idea what you are talking about. It's obvious you and Tanya planned this whole thing together."

"Presumably, you are referring to the email. Cam said he could explain to you how the email has been falsified. They have nothing to do with me. I've never sent an email in my life."

"I don't much care what any your friends say. I trust the information I get from my investigator."

"What did he say?"

"He gave them to me. They show they were sent by Jay McNabb. That's you."

"That proves they weren't sent by me."

"Why do you say that?"

"Because I wouldn't have used the name McNabb."

"Why wouldn't you? That is your name. The same as your father's," George said, adding for emphasis, "He lives in Ohio."

"Why do you say my father lives in Ohio?" Jay asked.

"Because he does."

"I thought he was living in California."

"He lives in Ohio. His name's the same as yours. He's Jay McNabb, and you're Jay Winston McNabb junior."

"You have two out of four right," Jay said.

"What do you mean by that?"

"I may be Jay Winston. However, I'm not McNabb and I'm certainly not junior."

"What do you mean by that?"

"Although my biological father's name is McNabb, neither my mother nor I have ever used that name. Besides, I think his name's Nobby, not Jay."

"Is Nobby a real name?" George asked.

"Probably not," Jay said. "I'm fairly sure you have the wrong McNabb. There are quite a lot of them around, you know."

George furrowed his brow. "Why can't those guys get anything right?"

"Wouldn't it have been easier if you had just asked me?"

"I don't want you seeing Sue again."

"I'm sorry you feel that way. However, Sue is the one who should decide that," Jay said.

"She's so mad at you right now she doesn't ever want to talk to you again. I think that makes her decision clear enough."

"She might react differently if she knew the facts about the trip," Jay said.

"She knows everything she needs to know," George said.

Jay clenched his teeth. He looked at the eagle feather and then at George.

"Thank-you for the trip to Montreal," he said. "The hotel accommodation was most generous of you."

"I don't know what you are talking about."

"I think you do," Jay challenged.

"What makes you think that?"

"G. P. Enterprises was most generous."

"What does that have to do with me?"

"I think you know who the G. P. stands for."

"What if I do?" George asked. "That doesn't prove anything."

"Unfortunately, there was an error with my ticket. It was only one-way."

"That's too bad. I don't know why you're telling me this," George said. "Now I think you should leave. Your time is up."

"I'm not going anywhere without Sue."

George picked up the phone from his desk. "I can call the police and have you removed. You are trespassing."

"I'll just come back," Jay said.

"I can have you arrested for breaking and entering."

"Only if I break in. It's legal for me to enter if someone opens the door for me," Jay said.

"Whatever," George said under his breath as he hung up the phone. He glared at Jay.

"I can sit here as long as you can," George said.

"Tanya seemed to enjoy her trip a lot. I think she'd like to stay there a few more days, if she could," Jay said.

"I've never even met the girl. It doesn't matter to me what she does."

"I understand that G. P. Enterprises paid her way, too."

"What's that got to do with me? I don't control what some company does," George said.

"I think you do," Jay said.

"You haven't a shred of evidence about any of this. Why don't you just go home?"

"Jimmy was happy to get his Rolex watch back, too."

"You mean he took it with him to Montreal? I didn't think he was that stupid," George blurted out.

"So, you admit you were behind his going to Montreal?" Jay asked.

"I admit nothing," George said.

Jay placed the pawn ticket on the desk beside the feather. "The watch is still in Montreal. Jimmy pawned it so I could get a ticket home. I think he deserves to have his watch back."

George leaned back in his chair and looked thoughtfully at the ceiling, clenching and unclenching his jaw. Then he looked back at Jay.

"You're going to keep on seeing Sue, aren't you?" he asked.

"Yes. I am."

"I don't suppose there's anything I can do to change your mind," George said softly. "It would be worth a lot to me."

"There's absolutely nothing you can do," Jay said.

"They say everyone has his price."

"I'm not everyone," Jay said.

George stood up and began pacing around the room, breathing slowly and deeply as if practicing yoga breathing.

Finally he said, "How about a drink? I don't have any Long Island Iced Tea but you might like a shot of Amarula. Long Island Iced Tea isn't a man's drink, anyway."

Without waiting for an answer, George dropped a couple of ice cubes into a glass, picked up a brown bottle with a golden cord around the neck, and poured three ounces of the liquid over the ice.

"Thank-you, sir. That would be nice. At least your investigator got my favorite drink right. You shouldn't be too hard on him. Even most of my friends don't know my last name, and I'm always talking about McNabb as my father."

"Maybe I misjudged you," George said, handing Jay the glass. "You've got more *chutzpah* than I gave you credit for."

"Thank-you. For the drink and for the compliment. Assuming *chutzpah* means what I think it does."

Jay took a sip of his drink. It was sweet, creamy and not at all agreeable to his taste. He resisted the impulse to spit it out.

"Good, isn't it?" George asked. "It's Helen's favorite drink. Imported from South Africa, you know."

Jay swallowed with difficulty. "Yes, sir. I'm sure it is."

He set his glass on the coffee table, being careful to use a coaster.

"I have your father's Ohio address. It cost me a pile of money. Do you want it?"

"Yes, please. I wrote my dad in California but I didn't get a reply. Maybe he's moved again."

"You should phone," George said. "Always take the direct approach."

"Good idea. It might save me the trouble of paying for a private investigator," Jay said with a tentative smile.

George walked to the study door and shouted, "Sue. Come down here. Right now."

Sue walked silently into the study with her head bowed.

"Jay and I have been talking about the situation in Montreal. It seems there has been some confusion. I think you owe Jay an apology for what you were thinking."

Jay looked astonished. "You don't owe me any apology, Sue," he said earnestly. "There's no way you could have thought anything else from the information you had. If any apologies are necessary, I think they should be coming from…"

Sue interrupted, "I do owe you an apology, Jay. I should have trusted you. I'm sorry."

"We will forget all about Montreal," George said, looking directly at Jay. "There is nothing to be gained by talking about it any more."

"You're right, sir," Jay said. Then turning to Sue he asked, "Are you ready to come home?"

"Yes," Sue answered quietly.

"Could I get you a Slurpee or something on the way?"

Sue smiled.

Jay picked up his eagle feather and the pawn ticket, walked over to George, and handed him the ticket. "Thank-you, sir," he said, looking George straight in the eye.

George gave a barely perceptible nod of acceptance.

"I'll come upstairs with you to help you get your things together," Jay said.

"Thanks," Sue said.

"Are you all right with me now?" he asked, as they packed her suitcase.

"I think so. It was all so confusing. Particularly with my starting a new job and everything."

"You left the Orange Julius?"

"I got a new job the day after you left for Montreal," Sue said.

"What's the job?"

"I'm a sales clerk at Molly's Dress Boutique. The hours are regular and the pay is double that at Orange Julius."

"That's great. How did you find it?"

"Pure luck. One of Dad's friends owns the store."

"Why doesn't that surprise me?" Jay asked.

"Why do you say that?"

"I have a feeling your dad is trying to control our lives."

"In what way?"

"I'll bet either he or one of his friends also owns the store I'm working in, too."

"He's only being helpful. We should be grateful to have him looking out for us like he does," Sue said.

"It would be nicer if he'd talk things over with us before he does things," Jay said. "Or at least tell us what he's doing after he's done it."

"It's not his way."

"I love you, and if your father comes along as part of a package deal, then I'll have to learn to cope with it, won't I?"

"Can you do that?"

"I'll try. However, I can't make any promises."

"I have faith in you," Sue said. "And I'll try not to be part of the problem."

"You could never be a problem for me," Jay said. "As long as I have you by my side I'm certain I can cope with your father."

~ 21 ~

THE BEST LAID PLANS

Spring is a beautiful time in Manitoba. The dreary months of snow and winter are gone, to be replaced by green grass, early spring flowers, pleasant temperatures and warm, invigorating sunshine. The streets have been swept clean of the salt and sand used to control the ice during the winter. Robins appear by magic on the slowly greening lawns, as if they had never been away, only hiding.

June came and went without notice as Sue and Jay settled into a daily routine for their lives. Sue enjoyed being busy with her afternoon and evening at the Orange Julius. Jay easily learned the day-to-day operation of The Crypt. Except for ordering stock, that is. The styles kept changing and made no sense to him. Fortunately for Jay, the manager was very helpful, and Steve was delighted to drop in every few days to give his usually impractical advice. During the evenings Jay studied for his G.E.D. exams.

One day in early July, Troy and Misty had just left Jay and Sue after their dinner of vegetarian pizza and Diet Coke.

"That pizza was great. I could become vegetarian," Sue said, as they cleaned up the kitchen.

"Do you have the feeling that Misty is less concerned than she used to be about being vegan?" Jay asked. "She didn't even ask about what might be in the pizza."

"I think she's getting more concerned with animal rights, and less concerned with what she eats."

"It's pretty tough to be a vegetarian in Manitoba in the winter," Jay said. "Now that there's more fresh produce in the stores, I wouldn't mind cutting down on the amount of meat we eat."

"It would be cheaper that way, too," Sue said.

"By the way, I forgot to tell you. My G.E.D. results came today," Jay said.

"And?"

"I passed. Now I can apply to go to University."

"I'm so proud of you. What were your marks?" Sue asked.

"I passed. That's all that matters."

"I want to know your marks."

"They're here if you want to look," Jay said, pulling a paper out of his pocket and putting it on the table.

Sue looked at it. "All A's. Why wouldn't you tell me? You should be proud of yourself."

"It's not my nature. We are taught that all people are equal with no one any better than any other."

"But you did so well."

"I did what I needed to do. Life is not a competition between people."

"Try explaining that to my dad. I should tell you he thinks you should go to the University of Winnipeg."

"Any particular reason?"

"You know my dad. He always has a reason for everything he does."

"Usually he's the only one who understands the reason for what he is doing. Did he say why?"

"Mom said he's arranged for you to be admitted as a mature student."

"I didn't think I'd qualify."

"You know him. He has a way of getting around regulations. People like to make him happy."

"What did he do? Offer to build a library?"

"Now don't be like that. He's only trying to be helpful."

"I think he's more concerned with his reputation than with helping. He's determined to make me look respectable."

"It'd be more convenient for you to go to the university near where we live instead of having to drive way out the edge of the city every day, wouldn't it?"

"It's mostly that I hate having him trying to control my life," Jay said.

"If you go to the University of Manitoba just to spite him, then that's letting him control you."

"In a negative sort of way, I guess. However, if I do go to the University of Winnipeg I'll get there on my own merits."

"Would you do me a big favor?" Sue asked.

"What's that?"

"Let him think he got you in. It would make him happy."

"For you, I'll humor him. But if he pushes the issue, I'll have to tell the truth," Jay said.

"I wouldn't want you to lie. Then again, I'd rather not have him annoyed at us."

"Speaking of his being annoyed, we should talk to him about our getting married."

"You haven't proposed yet," Sue said.

"I will. I'm waiting for a special, romantic moment."

"Then we should be talking to him about marriage."

"Am I supposed to ask him for your hand?"

"He'd like it if you did."

"I was hoping it was an outdated tradition. What if he refuses?"

"Then we elope," Sue said.

A knock on the door announced Troy's return to the apartment. Jay opened the door. "Forget something?"

"Yeah. My cell phone," Troy said, picking it up off the sofa. "In the film business things move fast. If you're not available, they'll find someone else."

"Let's ask Troy about proposals," Sue suggested.

Unknown to Jay, Troy had been working in his spare time on expanding his three-minute Hutterian TV spot into a full-length documentary on their lifestyle.

"We were wondering whether or not a guy should ask the girl's father for permission to get married."

"Be glad you're not a Hutterite," Troy said.

"What do you mean?" Jay asked.

"If you were, you'd first have to ask for permission from Sue's dad just for you and your male relatives to meet with him so that you could ask him for his permission to get married."

"That would be a problem. I don't have any male relatives handy."

"Assuming you did, and he agreed to the meeting, there would be an engagement party where both families celebrate together. After supper, everyone asks everyone else for permission for the marriage to take place."

"Everyone?"

"It seems that way. The minister of the groom's colony brings a written request to the bride's minister. Then the groom's father asks the bride's father for permission for the marriage. If they approve, then the groom asks both the bride's mother and father for their permission. It ends with the bride being asked if she accepts, and then they have toasts and speeches."

"That sounds more like the whole wedding."

"It's somewhat like our wedding rehearsal party. The actual wedding takes place the Sunday following the engagement."

"That soon? I was thinking more like six months or a year of being engaged," Sue said.

"Thanks for the irrelevant information, Troy," Jay said. "It does give me an idea, though. When I go to ask him, maybe I should take all my friends with me for moral support."

"I'd better run," Troy said, picking up his phone. "Misty will wonder what happened to me. Call me if you need any more advice."

"In your dreams, man," Jay said as he showed Troy out.

Jay often returned to the Red Dragon to visit with R.B. and Arrow. They both seemed to have aged considerably over the winter.

On one of his visits, Han Sing said, "Join me for a cup of coffee, Jay. We need to talk."

"It's about R.B., isn't it?" Jay asked.

"Yes. He says it's time for him to be with his people."

"Back to the home of his ancestors?"

"He has family and friends living on the White Earth reservation in Minnesota. He says the government moved all the small Ojibwe reservations into that single big one."

"Why would they do that?"

"It's an example of the white man's wisdom. They wanted all the Ojibwe people in one place so they would learn the habits of civilized life. It's like we did with our residential schools," Han Sing said.

"Isn't that where the Shooting Star Casino is?"

"Like I said, they learn civilized life."

"Do you have any idea how we can get him there?" Jay asked.

"I suppose we could put him on a bus, but someone would have to go with him."

"Then what about Arrow? They don't allow dogs on Greyhound buses."

"I don't think Arrow would survive on the reservation, anyway. He needs care."

"I can probably find someone to take R.B.," Jay said. "But I don't know what to do about poor old Arrow."

"The kindest thing would be to take him to the vet and have him put to sleep," Han Sing said.

"I'll go up and have a talk with them. It's important to know what they want."

"Good luck talking to Arrow," Han Sing said. "I don't speak his language."

Jay came back down half an hour later. "We had a good talk. I'm going to take R.B. to Minnesota."

"And what about Arrow?"

"I'll look after Arrow," Jay said.

"That would probably be for the best," Han Sing said.

"I feel it's my duty to look after him."

"He's had a long, full life. You'll be doing him a favor."

"What do you mean?"

"It's the kind thing to do."

"I don't mean I'm going to have him put down," Jay said, "if that's what you mean."

"He's old and can't look after himself."

"He isn't in pain. He deserves to live out his life in his own way. I have to try to do what I can to help him fulfill his destiny."

"What does a dog that age have for a destiny?" Han Sing asked.

"People could say the same about you. However, a lot of people had a happier New Year's because of you. I'm taking him home with me. No one should try to control another's destiny."

"Sue will be delighted with that idea," Han Sing said sarcastically.

"She's never been one for pets. But then, old Arrow isn't exactly what you'd call a pet."

"You're right about that. If I had to choose between you and Arrow, I'd choose you. That's not much recommendation for Arrow," Han Sing said jokingly.

Han Sing and Jay talked about Jay's new job and his plans for the future with Sue. Jay ignored Han Sing's hints and questions about marriage. On his way home, Jay stopped in to talk to Phil.

"What did you want to talk to me about?" Phil asked.

"I need some advice. Something has to be done about getting R.B. back to his reservation in Minnesota."

"That doesn't sound like a difficult task."

"It is if you don't have a vehicle."

"What about Sue's Mustang?"

"It would be crowded with the three of us. Not to mention Arrow and the luggage."

"I hope you don't expect me to take him there on my motorcycle."

"That would make a startling picture, wouldn't it? You roaring along with your bushy red beard and black vinyl biker look, while skinny old R.B. hangs on behind you for dear life, with his long white hair streaming straight out behind him. They'd never let you across the border."

Phil laughed. "I'd probably rent a sidecar for the occasion. He'd probably enjoy the experience of riding in the open air with the wind blowing in his face."

"Maybe for the first hour. However, we're looking at a four-hour drive. That's a long trip for an old guy."

"You're right. Not everybody enjoys the wind in the face experience as much as I do. He might. I've gotten to know him well since you introduced us. He's told me stories about things he did when he was younger that would make your hair stand on end."

"I should have taken the time to get to know him better. I was always too concerned about my own problems. Either that or I was looking after Arrow."

"I've spent a lot of time with him. He's been my soul patcher."

"What's a soul patcher?"

"Someone who patches up me up when I am feeling down. He heals those deep wounds of mine that have been plaguing me for so long."

"How's he do that?"

"As a shaman he carries with him all the pain and suffering of his ancestors. It's as if he's experienced them all himself. He is the ultimate wounded healer."

"But what does he do?"

"The same as he does for you, I imagine," Phil said. "He listens to me and I know he understands what I'm feeling. He makes me feel safe and secure more than anyone else has ever been able to do."

"I know he's helped Sue. I'm not sure how, but he puts her mind at ease so she can heal herself," Jay said.

"You'll find him to be fascinating company on the trip. He has a wealth of funny stories," Phil said.

"It's sad to think of him going home to die."

"Where did you get that idea?" Phil asked.

"I just assumed it, I guess."

"Well, think again. His people want him to come back to educate people about their ceremonies and traditions."

"He's a great old guy. He'll be a good person to foster first nation spirituality."

"It's more than that. There's a problem with people promoting native activities for profit."

"Is that a bad thing?" Jay asked. "At least they're promoting native spirituality."

"The problem is that the people don't get spiritually involved. They only go through the motions of the ceremonies."

"In what way?"

"For example, some New Age people carry a little bottle of spray with them. They spray it around a person or area and say they are smudging."

"That's definitely easier than making a fire," Jay said.

"It may smell nice but it has nothing to do with the spirituality of smudging."

"It doesn't seem to have much connection with native culture and heritage, either."

"These people trivialize native spirituality. There's no emotional involvement, and then people wonder why it doesn't meet their expectations."

"Who's doing this and why?"

"New Agers and white Wannabe Medicine Men. Even a few native people themselves have been promoting first nation ceremonies such as drumming and sweatlodges, and the use of things like the Talking Stick and Sacred Pipe. They set up training sessions and charge people to learn the techniques. It's become a big business."

"Is there much money in it?"

"There is when you charge several hundred dollars a head for a few hours in a sweatlodge or hold twenty-minute group pay-for-a-vision sessions."

"Isn't it contrary to the native philosophy to charge for those things?" Jay asked.

"It's contrary to all serious religions to pay for ceremonies. Donations are one thing; having a fee schedule is something else. The true shaman or medicine man doesn't charge."

"Charging for rituals and ceremonies is wrong, but is it the only problem?"

"The lack of a spiritual leader is a bigger problem. It misleads the people who pay for a ceremony," Phil said. "They pay for a sweatlodge, but without the input of an elder during and after the sweat it is nothing more than a high-priced sauna."

"But what can a person like R.B. do?"

"He feels he must be there to do what he can. People will listen to his voice and recognize the truth in what he says. The Plastic Shaman may come to see that these are sacred teachings, not a way to make money."

"Why have I never heard of a Plastic Shaman?"

"It started as a California thing. Doesn't everything?"

"I wonder why that is."

"I think it has something to do with the distortion of electromagnetic fields because of the earthquakes," Phil said. "They confuse the flow of *chi*."

"Could be, I guess," Jay said without actually thinking about it and missing Phil's attempt at humor. "Then the ideas spread to the rest of us, right?"

"That's why it's important for all the first nation people."

"Getting back to me, I have one other small problem," Jay said.

"You usually do," Phil said with a smile. "That's why I love you. You make my life interesting."

"If Sue and I were going to make this into a bit of a holiday, we'd be gone for the weekend. What would happen with Arrow while we're away? I don't fancy including him in our holiday. He's not exactly the sort of pet a motel would be delighted to have."

"Well. That's easy. He can stay with me while you're away."

"Thanks, Phil. I was hoping you'd say that," Jay said with a grin. "You always were a sucker for strays. Would it be all right if I dropped him off this Friday?"

"Anytime you want. Maybe bring him over Wednesday or Thursday. That would give us a little time to get used to each other before the weekend. He might find my usual weekend visitors a bit confusing."

"I know I did when I first came here," Jay said. "You're sure it'll be all right? Maybe you should check with Troy and Misty first?"

"They won't mind. I can always put him in my room so he doesn't bother them, if I have to."

"I'll bring him around next Wednesday, then, if everything else works out."

Jay and Sue were spending a lazy spring Sunday morning tidying up the breakfast dishes.

"Let's pick up Jimmy and Becky and go to the park," Jay said.

"What brought that on?" Sue asked.

"It's too nice a day to be inside. If we went to Assiniboine Park, we could go to the zoo and the Conservatory and things like that."

"Maybe we could take a picnic lunch," Sue suggested. "I'll phone Becky and see what she thinks."

Becky and Sue made the arrangements for food and getting to the park.

"That was surprisingly easy," Sue said. "It's almost as if she was expecting me to call."

"Maybe it's one of those synchronicity things," Jay said.

"That's as good an explanation as any, I guess."

After a leisurely lunch on the grass in the park, Jimmy said, "Now what should we do?"

"Let's have a treasure hunt," Jay suggested.

"You can't just decide to have a treasure hunt," Sue said. "It needs preparation."

"Trust me," Jay said. "You start off with Jimmy and Becky, and it'll all work like magic. You'll see."

"What about you? Aren't you going to take part in it?"

"I'll catch up with you. I need to…ah…go to the washroom. You guys go ahead. I'll clean up here."

"Okay. But hurry."

"Here's the first clue," Jimmy said, handing Sue a folded piece of blue paper.

Sue read the message: "To get your next clue use your brain. Go chug along to the choo choo _____."

"Train," Sue said. "That's easy."

They walked across the lawn to the children's steam train ride. Looking around the miniature station, Sue noticed a similar blue note pinned to the station wall. This message read: "Now join the creatures at the zoo. Ask at the entrance for your clue."

The girl in the wicket was examining her nails in boredom. They walked up to her, and Sue asked, "Do you have a message for us?"

The girl looked up with interest at the prospect of a break in her routine. She recognized Becky and gave her a smile and a surreptitious wink.

"Good luck," she said as she handed Sue a blue note.

"Thanks," Sue said. The note read: "This garden's Mol is not small and furry. Look for a big one. No need to hurry."

"I don't get it," Sue said.

"I bet it's the Leo Mol garden. You know, where they have all those metal statues of his," Becky said.

With a little guiding from Jimmy, they passed the decorative pool, went around the pavilion and found the large bronze statue representing a bull carrying a girl on its horns.

"Now what?" Sue asked.

"I guess we have to look around for a clue," Becky said.

They looked in the grass around the front of the statue, and checked the bushes on either side. Sue finally looked cautiously behind the statue. She gave a little scream and jumped back.

There was Jay, down on one knee, holding a ring box extended to Sue.

"Will you marry me?" Jay asked.

After a moment to collect her composure, Sue took the box and opened it. "It's gorgeous," she exclaimed, putting the ring on her finger.

"Do I take that as a yes?"

She gave Jay a big hug and kiss. "For sure."

Jay slipped the ring on her finger. "Now it's your move. You get to choose the date."

"I'll have to think about that," Sue said, twisting up her face as she pretended to think. "How's the twenty-first of June sound?"

"How long have you had that date picked?" Jay asked.

Sue smiled. "Not long. I choose a date every year, just to be prepared."

"That's almost a year away," Jay said.

"We can always elope if you're in a hurry," Sue teased.

"Let's keep that as our backup plan. We should try to humor your family."

Sue suddenly became aware of Becky and Jimmy standing discretely off to one side, trying to contain their giggles of excitement. She rushed up to them and let them gush about the ring and offer their best wishes.

"This has to be kept secret among the four of us until we tell out parents," Sue said.

"Let's all go out for dinner to celebrate," Jimmy said.

"Maybe they'd rather celebrate by themselves," Becky said.

"I'd like to share with our friends. Let's call Phil and Steve and make it a party," Sue said.

"Cool. Becky and I'll treat everyone," Jimmy said.

Becky pulled Jimmy off to the side. "We can't afford that," she said quietly.

"We'll never get a chance to do something like this again," Jimmy said.

"But what about money? I'm broke," Becky said.

"There's a bit of money put away from our Montreal trip," Jimmy said.

"I thought you were broke by the time we got home."

"I was."

"Okay, then explain where the money came from."

"When Sue's dad gave me back my Rolex, I told him there had been some other unexpected expenses."

"What expenses"

"There weren't any. I just wanted to get back at him for what he did to Jay."

"What did he say?"

"He said he didn't want to talk about it. He just handed me a wad of bills and said he didn't ever want to hear about it again."

"You're telling me you totally ripped off Sue's dad?"

"He had it coming."

"Once a con man, always a con man, I guess," Becky said.

"You mean him or me?" Jimmy asked.

"I'll have to get back to you on that one."

~ 22 ~

FAMILY TIES

As previously arranged, Sue and Jay pulled up in front of the Red Dragon, driving Helen's BMW. "You stay here and a look after the car. If anything were to happen to your mom's car, your dad would kill me," Jay said. "I'll go in and get R.B.'s things."

Jay was back in a few minutes with three cardboard boxes tightly tied with twine. "If we put one of our suitcases on the floor in the back seat," he said, "we can get these into the trunk."

"Do I sit in the front or back?" Sue asked.

"Maybe it would be best if you sat in the back, if you don't mind. There's not as much legroom in the back and it's a little awkward getting in and out. I expect R.B. isn't as flexible as you. I'm going back to get Arrow."

240

R.B. came out, walking tall and proud, his steps slow but firm. Sue hopped out and held the front door open for R.B.

"*Miigwech*," R.B. said, graciously accepting Sue's gesture as his due.

Sue climbed into the back seat.

When Jay returned with Arrow in his arms, she opened the door and greeted Arrow with the comment, "I guess we share the back seat."

Sue looked at Jay and said, "I don't have to hold him, do I?"

"He'll be fine lying on the seat."

"We go past Thunderbird House. I have not been there, yet," R.B. said.

"Would you like to stop there?" Jay asked.

R.B. nodded. "I have not seen it."

"I could have taken you there before now," Jay said. "You should have asked."

"It is not our way to ask. We do not push our wishes onto others."

"If I'd been more aware of your needs, I would have thought to offer long ago."

"The white man asks for what he wants. You live in his world."

"I try to live in both worlds. I'm sure it can be done but I need more practice."

"You are wise beyond your years," R.B. said.

"For our trip, I hope you can pretend to be a white man and tell me when you want to make a stop along the way. I'll be too busy driving this magnificent car to think about rest stops."

Jay parked in the area beside the Thunderbird House.

"I'm ashamed to say I've never been inside," he said. "My native spirituality is important to me, but keeping food on the table and clothes on my back takes up all my energy. I can't be spiritual and practical at the same time."

Thunderbird House rises from a previously deserted lot at the corner of North Main and Higgins, in a crumbling section of the city. After many years of moral decay and feelings of hopelessness in this core area, it serves as a symbol of the rebirth of first nation spirituality. The styl-ized Thunderbird, towering above the struggling neighborhood, serves as an inspiration to the community, and as a spiritual center for the first nation people of Winnipeg.

They entered through the west door. Inside, the laminated wood ribs support the walls, reaching to the windowed ceiling like the poles of a tepee, creating a round open expanse in the middle. A small sign advises that shoes are not to be worn.

Jay and Sue removed their shoes at the door and went in stocking feet. R.B. slipped the provided plastic covers over his moccasins.

They walked respectfully around the outside edge of the circle in a clockwise direction, looking at the pictures on the wall as they went.

Jay paused in front of one. "This was donated by the Winnipeg *Bahá'í*," he pointed out to Sue.

"Jamie said there are a lot of first nation people who are *Bahá'í*. Their philosophies are surprisingly similar in many ways."

"Like what?" Jay asked.

"They both believe in the oneness of the world, and the equality of all people," Sue said, pointing to the inscription beneath the picture. It read: "The earth is one country and mankind its citizens."

Preparations were being made for the performance of a native dance. Folding chairs for spectators had been set up around the Sundance Area in the center of the building.

As they walked around the circular building, they could see into the offices, meeting rooms, and the eatery. R.B. guided them to seats, taking care to approach them from a clockwise direction as required by native custom.

They stayed for an hour until the ceremony was over. At the door, Jay left a donation of money. R.B. left a donation of tobacco as well. It was, as R.B. said, a *Wacipi* time.

They walked to the BMW with the beat of the drums echoing in their heads. Arrow was sleeping peacefully, stretched across the back seat.

Sue held the door open and looked at Jay. "Would you move him, please? I don't want to hurt him."

R.B. stepped forward and slid easily into the back seat, shifting Arrow onto his lap in one smooth, effortless motion. "I will spend this time with my brother."

"You said he wasn't flexible," Sue whispered. "That was easier for him than for me."

"I guess sitting cross-legged all day keeps him in shape," Jay said. "Surprise. Yoga works."

"Why did you call Arrow your brother?" Jay asked R.B.

"The wolf was brother to our ancestors. There are no wolves in the city, so the dog has become brother to us."

"Does it make me an awful person that I'm happier with him in the back seat?" Sue asked Jay quietly.

"Not at all. I'm happier with you up here, too. Besides, he said he wanted to be with Arrow."

"So they can commune with each other?" Sue asked.

"They have a lot of love to share."

"You did say we're leaving Arrow here, didn't you?"

"For the trip, at least. Phil said he'd look after him."

"And after that?" Sue asked.

"Let's cross one bridge at a time. Things have a way of working out."

"Sometimes I think you leave too much up to fate."

"I try to create good karma. That's the best I can do," Jay said.

"I hope Arrow doesn't get carsick before we get to Phil's place," Sue said.

"It was good of your mother to loan us her car. Your Mustang would have been a bit awkward."

"It wasn't designed for the two of us, and old man, an old smelly dog and a pile of luggage," Sue muttered to herself.

Jay pulled up in front of Phil's place. He said to Sue, "I'll take Arrow up to the apartment. There's no need for you to come unless you want to."

"I'll stay and keep R.B. company," Sue said. "I want to tell him how much his dreamcatcher has meant to me."

R.B. lifted Arrow up and put him into Jay's waiting arms. "*Gigawaabamin naagaj*, my brother."

"Does that mean goodbye?" Sue asked.

"*Anishinaabe* has no word for goodbye. I said I will see him later."

"You mean in the Happy Hunting Ground?" Jay asked.

R.B. smiled gently. "Those are your words. We do not limit our spirituality with words."

"What about bad people? Don't they go to…you know…the other place?"

"There are no bad people. We are all made in God's image. Everyone goes to the place you call heaven. It takes some people longer to get there than others."

"How can you say there are no bad people?" Jay asked. "There is so much crime and violence in the world."

"There are people who do bad things. They must spend time in a misty place for maybe fifty years or maybe a hundred. Or a thousand years before they move on."

"We'll talk more about this on our trip," Jay said, heading for the door with Arrow in his arms.

Jay carried Arrow up the stairs to Phil's apartment and gently knocked on the door with his foot.

Misty opened the door to Jay's knock.

"Hi, man…and dog," she said.

"I hope you were expecting us," Jay said.

"Phil's not in right now but we're ready for Arrow. We've even set up a nice blanket for him over there in the corner."

Jay carried Arrow over to the blanket and set him on it. Arrow stood up and started turning in slow circles, scratching and sniffing in typical dog fashion as he made a nest.

"I wonder why dogs always do that?" Jay mused.

"According to the pet experts, it's a *feng shui* thing," Misty said.

"He's arranging his furniture?" Jay asked.

"He's aligning himself with the Earth's magnetic field. They say that when an animal has his head pointing north, the circulation improves, his heartbeat slows, and metabolism improves."

"You've got to be kidding."

"No. They say it's their sensitivity to the Earth's magnetic field that enables animals to find their way home, too."

"Now I've heard everything," Jay said. "*Feng shui* for dogs."

"They say it applies to humans as well. You should sleep with your head to the north."

Jay shook his head as if to clear out the cobwebs. "I'll give you a call when we get back. Be good to my dog, eh?"

"Don't worry. He'll be fine."

The drive to the White Earth reservation was three-and-a half hours of grain fields, evergreen forests, and bush bordering the two-lane highway. Frequent road signs warning of deer crossings kept Jay alert. Sue tried not to look at the assorted animal victims littering the paved shoulders. Jay carefully avoided driving over their remains.

"If I hit a deer with this Beemer I'll be dead meat when I get back," Jay thought to himself. He was unaware of an eagle flying high above the car, acting as a telepathic relay to warn the deer and other wild animals along the way.

The conversation was relaxed with long periods of comfortable silence. Jay and Sue communicated in the silent language of lovers. One would indicate a point of interest and the other would smile in unspoken understanding.

R.B. told Ojibwe legends and stories, interspersed with humor.

"You know our saying about respecting other people?" R.B. asked.

"That you shouldn't criticize a person until you've walked a mile in his moccasins?" Jay said.

"Do you know why it is such a good rule?"

"I think so but tell me," Jay said.

"Because then when you criticize him, you are a mile away from him."

Jay and Sue smiled.

"And, besides that, he is barefoot," R.B. concluded with a chuckle.

The traffic was light on the two-lane highway that sliced its way through the forest. On several occasions the Beemer exceeded the speed limit.

"Aren't you afraid of getting a ticket?" Sue asked.

"Steve taught me how to avoid things like that."

"He didn't suggest obeying the speed limit, did he?"

"It was more along the lines of how to avoid getting mugged, but it applies to most things in life, including speeding."

"This I've got to hear."

"He said there are two things to consider. You need to avoid attracting attention to yourself. And you need to make sure there is a more vulnerable target obviously available."

"I don't get it," Sue said.

"I always follow someone who is going at least as fast as I am. He will draw the policeman's attention."

"How do you avoid being vulnerable?"

"If I can, I travel in the middle of a group of cars all going the same excessive speed. The police won't pull someone out from the middle of the pack to give them a ticket, no matter how fast they are going."

"Like the wolf, they pick off a straggler from the herd," R.B. said.

"You two are really scary when you agree on something," Sue said.

Highway 59 leads directly to the Shooting Star Casino and Hotel, a favorite entertainment spot for Winnipeggers.

"This must be the White Earth reservation," Jay said.

"Only a very small percentage of the reservation is tribally owned anymore," R.B. said. "My people live in small rural communities. We go to the one called *Naytahwaush*."

"How do we get there?"

"The highway continues south. My nephew and his family live fifteen miles down County Road 125. When we cross Wild Rice River we are close," R.B. said. "They harvest maple syrup and wild rice in this region."

"This reservation is huge," Sue said.

"The guide book said it's as big as Rhode Island," Jay said. "However big that is."

"Big enough to get lost," Sue said.

"You think we're lost?"

Sue studied the road map. "Just kidding. I think we're doing okay."

They pulled over and parked a short distance from the house R.B. pointed out as belonging to his nephew. The house overlooked a wooded area that sloped down to a meandering creek.

Jay turned and looked sadly at R.B. "I'm going to miss you. Our time at the Red Dragon was the beginning of my new life. It'll never be the same without you, my friend."

"You'll look after Arrow, won't you?"

"I'll always try to do what is best for him. But he'll never replace you."

"You don't need me. Your eagle spirit will guide you if you put your trust in it."

"I don't know how to thank you. You've been everything to me."

R.B. looked at Jay without speaking. For several seconds their gaze locked.

Jay felt tears springing to his eyes. "I guess this is goodbye."

"Not goodbye, my friend," R.B. said. "*Gigawaabamin naagaj.*"

"Do you mean that I won't see you again in this life?"

"We will meet again."

"You mean in the Happy Hunting Ground?"

R.B. chuckled. "Before then. Close your eyes and let your mind go blank. Then you will know."

Jay closed his eyes. After a few moments he said, "Yes. I did feel that we'll meet again. How do you do that?"

R.B. smiled. "I do not do it. There are some things a person can know if only they will put their mind at rest."

"It's like a piano player doesn't really begin to play until the fingers can move with out needing his brain," Sue said.

"You're beginning to sound like your mother," Jay said. "But you're right. I'm always amazed when I see a piano player in a bar carrying on a conversation with someone while they are playing the piano. It's like they're on automatic pilot."

"Now who's sounding like my mother?"

"I must go to join my family," R.B. said. "I will think of you until we meet again."

"Whatever happens, I'll never forget you," Jay said.

Jay drove up to the house. Children ran out of the house and dogs barked as they drove up. Sue and Jay carried R.B.'s belongings into the house, with R.B. leading the way. There was a spring in his step and a smile on his face.

"Do not look back. Your future is ahead of you, not behind you," R.B. said, as Jay left.

After a leisurely drive to Bemidji, Jay and Sue took pictures of each other beside the massive statues of the mythical lumberjack, Paul Bunyan, and his blue ox. A walk along the lakefront beach, an intimate restaurant dinner, and Jay and Sue were ready for the motel. Jay's sleep was filled with dreams of minor car accidents involving BMW's.

In the morning they loafed on the beach, looked through stores and did touristy things.

"Should we stay here another night or head home?" Sue asked.

"Let's head home. I don't sleep well in strange motels," Jay said.

That night, after an uneventful drive, they were back in the apartment.

"What about Arrow?" Sue asked.

"I'll phone Phil tomorrow."

"Don't we need to talk about this?"

"I know you don't feel the same about Arrow as I do," Jay said.

"Then we need to talk about it."

"R.B. said for me to trust in my eagle spirit to guide me."

"If you think…" Sue started to say and then stopped abruptly.

"Trust me. At least until tomorrow."

"You're right. Let's sleep on it," Sue said.

Jay was relieved to have the BMW home uninjured. His sleep was
restful and dreamless.

Early the next day Jay phoned Phil:

"Hi. We're home."

" . . . "

"Yes. It was a good trip."

" . . . "

"He was happy to be with his family again. How're you making out with Arrow?"

" . . . "

"You're kidding."

" . . . "

"I promised R.B. I'd look after him. Would that count as my
looking after him?"

" . . . "

"Sue would like that."

" . . . "

"It'll give me an excuse to visit you more often."

" . . . "

"Thanks for everything. See you later."

As Jay hung up the phone, Sue asked, "What did he say Sue would like?"

"Phil wants to keep Arrow. He's fallen in love with the mutt."

Sue smiled. "Now I'm a believer. Karma does work."

"Hard work and planning sometimes help," Jay said.

"Now that we have R.B. and Arrow looked after, when am I going to get to meet your family?"

"As soon as you want. I'm sure they'd like to meet you. After all, you're my fiancée now."

"Would they come here to see the big city or would we go to their place?" Sue asked.

"I'd rather they came here."

"You're not ashamed of your place back home, are you?"

"Maybe a little. There's no hotel or anything like that, so we'd all have to stay together."

"I wouldn't want to put your family out," Sue said.

"I'm sure they'd be happy enough to share the space. It's our way. However, there wouldn't be much room for us there. We have only two rooms. My mother and her current friend would have one room. Then the four of us would have to fit into the other room. It has only one bed."

"What about the two who don't get the bed?"

"We'd sleep on the floor."

"You say that as if you were often the one on the floor."

"I'm the oldest. It was always easier for me to be on the floor than for the little ones."

"You're such a sweet guy."

"Don't say that. I'm supposed to be the tough macho guy who looks after his wife, remember?"

"I like it when you're soft and gentle."

"Maybe I'm only pretending to be soft," Jay said.

"If you are, you're doing a good job. We should tell my parents about our engagement."

"I thought you'd have told them by now."

"There never seemed to be a good time."

"Let's announce it to them when my family is here," Jay said.

"I hope Dad doesn't flip out over our getting married. He's sure to have all kinds of imaginary problems for us."

"And he has a way of making them real."

"He means well."

"We've never talked about our cultural differences," Jay said.

"Have there been any problems so far? I thought we were getting along well."

"We get along great. However, there are some things we need to deal with."

"Are you referring to my dad? I know he can be difficult sometimes."

"I can handle whatever he throws at me. There are a lot of people like him in the world. I've learned a lot about handling prejudice and verbal abuse from Steve."

"Then what is it?" Sue asked.

"I've had to make adjustments. When we are married I might not be able to keep it up."

"Like what?"

"I've avoided my own people. I have no native friends," Jay said.

"Why is that?"

"You might not have wanted to accept their lifestyle."

"I think I can learn to accept anyone. Maybe I can't accept all their behaviors but I can accept them as people," Sue said.

"Behaviors are the problem. Suppose we had two TV's and my native friend had none. He'd expect us to give him one of ours because his need for the second TV is greater than ours."

"So we'll only have one TV. No problem."

"If we have a car and aren't using it, and my friend needs to go somewhere, I should let him have it."

"Loaning it, I could accept. I draw the line at giving it to him because then we wouldn't have one ourselves," Sue said.

"The extended family thing could be tough."

"How do you mean by that?"

"It's not unusual for children to be raised by grandparents, aunts or even close friends. We learn that the whole native society is our family."

"How would that affect us? We'll raise our own children ourselves, won't we?"

"We will. It's other people and their children who could be a problem."

"They'd want to live with us?" Sue asked.

"If a street kid needs a place for the night, we'd be a possibility in his mind."

"There aren't many aboriginal street kids anyway, are there?"

"You just don't see them as much because they don't use the shelters. They find a friend or relative to take them in for the night or for a meal. We look after our own people."

"That could be a problem. Our family has always been close."

"And closed," Jay said.

"We can work things out when the situation occurs."

"Money is a tougher issue. If we have money and my friend needs to pay school tuition, then I should give it to him."

"As a loan, I assume."

"That's where it gets tough. You can't count on loans getting paid back. Could you live with that?"

"I'm willing to try. However, I'd expect you to limit your generosity to actual friends, not the whole aboriginal population."

"There do have to be limitations," Jay said.

"Getting back to your mother and family," Sue said. "When do you think they could visit? I'm anxious to meet them as soon as possible."

"It might be a bit of cultural shock for you."

"I'm willing to take that chance."

"Where would they stay?" Jay asked.

"They should stay here. We'd get to know each other better that way."

"We have only the one extra room. Are you sure you want to get to know them that well?"

"We could make it work. There's the sofa and I can always borrow sleeping bags if necessary," Sue said.

"At most there would be the three of them."

"What if your stepfather comes as well?"

"He's not an actual stepfather. I don't want to have some strange man coming to stay here. Whoever my mother's current friend is, he won't be invited to stay with us."

"What if he comes anyway?"

"Then he'll have to find a friend somewhere to put him up."

"Okay. Let's do it. You'll look after inviting them?"

"I'll send out smoke signals right away."

"While we're on the topic of your family, have you contacted your father?" Sue asked.

"I phoned him in California."

"I thought my dad said he was in Ohio?"

"That was just a red herring from one of his many private eyes. He's still in California."

"How did it go?"

"He said he'd received my letter. However, he didn't want to talk to me," Jay said.

"Not at all?"

"I told him who I was and said I'd like to meet him."

"How did he take it?" Sue asked.

"He said he didn't want to meet me and that we had nothing to talk about. Then he hung up."

"I'm sorry."

"At least it wasn't an expensive call."

~ *23* ~

MAYBE THE TWAIN CAN MEET

It was a typical warm and sunny summer day. Birds and young lovers busied themselves with their nesting instincts. People's spirits were filled with joy in anticipation of the rebirth of the world as it began to unfold.

However, Jay and Sue were indoors, pacing up and down in the waiting room of the Bus Depot, looking alternately at the clock and then at each bus as it pulled into a parking lane.

It was the day Jay's family was to arrive in Winnipeg. Finally, the scheduled time arrived and an eastbound bus pulled in.

"That might be the one," Jay said.

"Let me see if I can guess which ones they are," Sue said.

As the passengers got off the bus, Sue looked intently at each one.

"You said your mother was slim and pretty. Darren is fifteen and Corinne is thirteen."

Sue mentally compared people with her expectations as they stepped off the bus.

"They'll all get off together," Jay assured her. "Darren and Corinne are terrified of the big city. I told them all about it."

"Just like an older brother to tell horror stories and…wait! Is that your mother?"

"You bet. And there's Corinne at the end of the line. She's always been one to wait for everyone else to go first."

Sue hustled over to Jay's mother. "*Boozhoo*, Mrs. *Maytwayashing*."

Jay's mother beamed in pleasure. "You must be Sue. Call me Doreen. You've been practicing our language. Many people find my name hard to remember."

"Jay told me to think of a Maytag washing machine. He said if I could remember Maytagwashing, I could fine-tune it from there. Or I could just say if fast and mumble a bit."

"Jay always was one to play with words. He should become a lawyer."

"Where's Darren?" Jay asked.

"He's fifteen," Doreen said.

"I know how old he is. I asked where he is."

"Where were you when you were fifteen in the spring time?"

"Fishing, I guess," Jay replied.

"He and Maurice left last week. They will have returned by the time I get back."

They climbed into Sue's Mustang and headed west along Portage Avenue.

"If this is a big city, where are the tall buildings?" Corrine asked.

"They're down the other direction, toward Portage and Main. You'll get to see them soon enough," Jay said, pulling into a Tim Hortons parking lot.

"Why are we stopping?" Doreen asked.

"I thought you might like a bite to eat after your long bus ride," Jay said.

Doreen fidgeted in her seat. "Some other place would be better."

"This is a good place," Jay said.

"It doesn't look right," she said.

"What's bothering you, Mom?" Corinne asked.

"There are three police cars. There must be big trouble."

"They're probably there on their coffee break. There's no need to fear the police," Jay said. "Unless, of course, you have a guilty conscience."

"You can sit and have coffee with them there?"

"Why not? Doughnut shops are one of the safest places to be. There are usually lots of cops around."

"Back home, a policeman means there is big trouble."

"We like to see the police. It makes us feel safer," Sue said, as they walked into the shop.

"You guys sit over there while I get us some coffee and doughnuts," Jay said. "Unless you'd like soup or a sandwich."

"Black coffee," Doreen said.

"I like Coke," Corinne said quietly, as if speaking to herself.

"It's so great to finally meet you," Sue said. "You'll be staying at our place, of course, and we'll show you all the highlights of Winnipeg."

"Be easy with us," Doreen said. "This is not like where we come from."

"People are all the same. It's just that we have more of them in one place than you do," Sue said.

"A lot more," Doreen said. "There are as many people in this room as in our whole community back home."

"You'll get used to it. You learn to ignore the people you don't know," Sue said.

"That is not our way. We respect all people equally."

"I try to respect everybody but sometimes it is hard when you don't have a chance to get to know them," Sue said.

Jay set down the tray.

"What do you want to see first?" he asked.

"Your apartment. I like to know where I will sleep," Doreen said.

"And then what? Do you want to see the sites of the city? Or meet my friends?"

"You decide," Doreen said.

"What about you, Corinne? You're very quiet," Jay asked.

"I will do what Sue likes."

Sue smiled. "In that case, we'll go shopping."

"I have no money to shop," Corinne said.

"You don't need money. I have an Amex card."

"But you will still have to pay sometime."

"You're here as our guests. We'll look after everything for you," Jay said.

"If it isn't rude to ask," Sue said, "what is the meaning of the name *Maytwayashing*?"

Doreen smiled. "Do you know a place where there is a deep valley filled with tall trees, and the wind whispers gently through them?"

"I can imagine it, yes."

"That is what it means."

"Ojibwe is a picturesque language."

"We can't spend all day sitting around in a doughnut shop, "Jay said. "There's a whole city here to see, and friends to meet."

"And shopping to do," Sue added.

"For you, there's always shopping to do," Jay said. "Let's take a drive around Assiniboine Park first."

"It'll give us a chance to relax a bit," Sue said. "And maybe we could go to see that painting of Pooh."

"What's that?" Jay asked.

"You know. The famous Pooh bear. As in Tigger and Eeyore. They're setting up a pavilion for him at the park. I'd love to see that painting they bought to put on display."

After a leisurely time in the park, and lunch at the Conservatory, they went to Sue's apartment. Doreen and Corinne were impressed by the amount of space as they looked around.

"This is for you," Jay said, pointing to the spare room. "You'll be able to have some privacy if you want to rest."

"There are two sleeping bags, and there is also the sofa if you prefer," Sue added. "We'll leave it up to you to work the sleeping arrangement."

"We will be fine here with the sleeping bags," Doreen said.

"Mom invited us all over for dinner tonight," Sue said.

"I'm nervous about meeting them," Doreen said.

"Don't worry. My mom is eager to meet you. I know you'll like her," Sue said.

"She's really a super lady," Jay said.

"Nobody speaks of your father," Doreen said. "Will he be there?"

Jay and Sue exchanged looks.

"Try not to take him too seriously," Jay said. "Sometimes he doesn't mean everything he says."

"We have a couple of hours. What should we do until then?" Sue asked.

"Maybe we could split up. You and Corinne can go shopping. I'll take Mom over to see Phil. Then we'll meet back together at your place."

Sue gave Jay a kiss on the cheek. "About four-thirty. For cocktails, as usual."

This was the beginning of five hectic days of activities and meeting people. Up to now Doreen and Corinne were unaware that Jay and Sue planned to be married, and didn't suspect that they were on the brink of planning a major wedding.

Friday:

Helen ushered Sue and Corinne into the living room. George put down the Financial Post long enough to say, "Welcome. You are Jay's sister."

Corinne smiled shyly. "Yes."

"We've been shopping, Daddy," Sue said.

George muttered, "Whatever," and returned to his newspaper.

"Did you buy anything?" Helen asked.

"Corinne had them put a few things aside for us."

"I wanted Mom to see them before we buy anything," Corinne said.

"We should serve refreshments," George said. "It's four-fifteen."

"What would you like, Corrine?" Helen asked.

"I like Coke."

"Diet or regular?"

Corinne looked shocked. "I am not overweight."

"Heaven's no," Helen said. "Not at all. A lot of people prefer the taste of Diet Coke, that's all."

"I will have Diet Coke."

George went to the sideboard and poured himself a tumbler of Scotch with ice.

"Could you get Corinne a Diet Coke, George?"

George and his drink disappeared into the kitchen.

"Tell me what you plan to buy, Corinne," Helen said.

"It's a skirt and sweater," Sue said.

"I do not have a skirt," Corinne said shyly, looking at the floor. "I only have jeans."

"She looks smashing in it," Sue said.

George returned with a glass of cola in one hand and his glass, empty except for ice cubes, in the other.

"For you," he said, handing the cola to Corinne and then returning to the sideboard. He returned with his glass full, and with a glass of Amarula on ice for Helen.

The doorbell rang. Jay poked his head through the doorway. "I hope we're not late. Phil got telling stories and we forgot the time."

George muttered under his breath, "Indian time, obviously."

Jay introduced his mother to Sue's parents.

"Please, call us George and Helen. Come and sit here beside me, Doreen," Helen said. "We need to get to know each other."

"What can I get you to drink?" George asked.

"I'll have what Corinne has, thank-you," Doreen said.

"You'll have your usual," George said to Jay, more as a statement than a question.

"Thank-you," Jay replied, wondering to himself what his usual might turn out to be.

George poured a glass of Amarula on ice for Jay.

Jay forced a smile. "Thank-you, sir," he said, setting the glass on the table, being sure to have a coaster under it.

"We had a nice time with Phil," Doreen volunteered. "He is so interested in our people."

"He's been a good friend to Jay and me," Sue said.

Sue, Corinne and Helen chatted about stores, clothes and life in Winnipeg.

Jay tried to initiate a conversation with George. "How's the Real Estate business these days?"

George looked over the top of the newspaper. "I don't invest only in Real Estate."

"Oh. What kinds of investments do you do?"

"All kinds," George said, returning to his newspaper.

Jay shifted his attention to his mother. "How do you like Winnipeg so far?"

"It's very big," she said. "There are a lot of people."

"Would you like to live here?" Jay asked.

"If I were near you, I could learn to like it," Doreen said.

"Maybe that can be arranged," Helen said. "It would be so exciting to have you right here in the city. It would be like having you as part of the family. It would be like…"

George looked up from his paper. "We have more than enough family as it is," he said, looking pointedly at Jay.

"We have a surprise," Sue interjected. "We wanted to wait until everyone was together so we could make our announcement to everybody at the same time. Jay and I are engaged to be married."

Sue went around the room showing everyone her ring, and smiling broader with every compliment and offering of good wishes.

"What a lovely setting," Helen said. "It's like the diamond is on a nest of gold twigs."

"Jay had it custom made," Sue said with pride.

"The diamond is like an egg and…" Helen began to say.

"The diamond is bigger than I would have expected," George cut in. "Is it paid for?"

As often happened, George's comment was ignored, but he didn't seem to care.

"Has a date been set?" Doreen asked.

"June 21st," Sue said, smiling at her mother. "Just like I'd planned."

"I meant to ask your permission to marry Sue before we got engaged," Jay said, "but there never seemed to be a good time."

"Whatever," George grumbled to himself.

"Do we have your permission to get married?" Jay asked.

"Would it make any difference if you don't?" George asked

"It would make a difference as to what kind of wedding we'd have," Jay said.

"You'd still get married?"

"Yes, sir. We have to lead our own lives."

George headed back to the sideboard. Jay eyed his glass of Amarula, now with the ice melted.

Helen leaned over to speak quietly to Jay. "Leave the drink if you don't want it. You can get a beer or whatever you want from the kitchen."

"I don't want to insult him."

"He won't notice."

Jay took his glass to the kitchen and returned with it full of beer.

"Now that we are all together, this would be a good time to discuss wedding plans," Helen said.

"The father of the bride pays for the wedding," George said. "There's nothing else to discuss."

"Jay and I should have some say in it," Sue said.

"I don't see how the wedding concerns either you or Jay," George said.

"We're the ones getting married," Sue said.

"It's my wedding. Your getting married is just an excuse for the party, but it's my party."

"Relax, George," Helen said. "Everybody can talk about it. It should be a family event."

"That's what I'm saying. My family expects certain things from me as the host. The ceremony will be at our church and the reception will be at one of the prestige hotels, maybe the West Inn. It is what my family expects. What else is there to talk about?"

"What about the guest list," Helen asked.

"We'll have our friends and relatives. At my brother's wedding there were one hundred and fifty. We will have two hundred," George said.

"You mean your niece's wedding, don't you?" Helen prompted.

"Same thing."

"What about the groom's side of the family?" Helen asked.

Jay's brow furrowed in thought. "There would be my mother, Corinne, and my brother."

"Maurice would come," Doreen interjected.

"Who's Maurice?" George asked.

"He's Mom's special friend," Jay said.

"Oh. He's like her…" Helen started to say.

"Yes, Helen. We know. Like her husband, only not married." George said.

"We have six other relatives. There are a dozen close friends. Would two dozen guests be too many?" Doreen asked.

"We can manage that," George said. He forced a smile in an effort to appear friendly.

"I'd like to invite Winston, even though I don't think he would come," Jay said.

"Who's Winston?" George asked.

"My father."

"Is he Indian, too?"

"I've never met him. Would it make a difference if he were first nation?"

"He's European," Doreen said softly. "Do you want to have him there, Jay? You haven't met him."

"Please try to remember not to say Indian, George. It's not politically correct these days," Helen said.

"Whatever."

"I'd like him to be there," Jay said. "Is there a reason you don't think we should invite him?"

"I haven't seen him for twenty years," Doreen said. "He is a stranger to me."

"He's my father. It would be disrespectful not to invite him without a reason," Jay said.

"It is your wedding, and your day. You will do what you feel is right," Doreen said.

"Speaking of names, is Sue keeping her name?" George asked.

"Were we talking about names?" Helen asked, looking around the room in momentary confusion.

"We haven't talked about it," Sue said. "Maybe I'll hyphenate it. How does Parkington-*Maytwayashing* sound?"

After a short but awkward silence, Helen asked, "What about the wedding invitations? Do we put Winston's name on the invitation? Or should it be Maurice?"

"Jay and his mom should decide that," Sue said.

"I don't think Winston should appear on the invitation," Jay said. "He's never been a father to me."

"Maurice wouldn't be appropriate," Doreen said. "He's a friend, not a family member."

George looked sternly at Jay. "What do we use for your name?"

"Is there something wrong with what it is? Japheth Winston *Maytwayashing.*"

"Japheth? I thought it would be Jason. Is Japheth a real name?" George asked.

"Japheth was Noah's youngest son. It got tiresome explaining how to spell it, so I started using just the first letter as my name."

"I hope we don't have to pay by the letter on the invitations," George muttered as he went to refill his glass.

"You'll have to choose a best man," Sue said.

"That won't be easy. Phil's been like the father I've never had. He always pointed out the right path, but then let me make my own mistakes. I owe him a lot for that."

"Your brother would be appropriate," Helen suggested.

"Darren wouldn't care one way or the other," Doreen said.

"All in all, I feel closest to Steve," Jay said.

George gave his head a shake in disbelief. "Let me get this straight. You're suggesting that my daughter is going to marry a half-breed who'll have a faggot for his best man? Is there anything else you can do to ruin this wedding for me?"

Everyone studiously ignored George's outburst.

"I could let my hair grow. Would you like it in one braid or two?" Jay said quietly enough that no one except Helen would hear.

Helen suppressed a giggle.

Jay caught Helen's eye and mouthed the words, "With a headband."

Helen chuckled out loud. George glared at her.

"You seem to have way too many best men," Sue said. "That could be a problem."

"I'll talk to Phil and see how he feels about it. I think it would be more important to Steve."

"You could have Phil, Darren, Jimmy and Maurice all at the front with you. What do they call them when you do that? Isn't it outriders or something like that?" Helen asked.

Jay frowned. "This is beginning to sound like a Wild West show. What are outriders?"

"Like bridesmaids, only on the groom's side. They're called grooms-men," Sue said.

"That way there's room for as many as you want at the front with you," Helen said.

"Just don't have more than I do," Sue chided. "I'd be embarrassed if it looks like you have more friends than I do."

"I'll keep that in mind," Jay said.

"I believe dinner is ready to be served," Helen said.

The group moved into the dining room where the solid oak table was set with a lace cloth, cut crystal glassware and solid sterling silverware.

Helen guided people to their seats, putting Doreen and Jay on one side and Sue and Doreen on the other. George took his customary place at the head of the table and Helen at the other end.

The meal consisted of roast crown of lamb, oven roast potatoes, and Brussels sprouts, with lemon meringue pie for desert. It was all prepared by a professional chef, and impeccably served by the butler hired for the occasion.

"The lamb's excellent," George said.

Corinne gave Jay a distressed look. "Try some of the mint jelly with it," he suggested.

"Yes," Doreen said. "I like the mint jelly."

The conversation was sparse and centered mainly around food, weather and events taking place in Winnipeg.

Following dinner the group returned to the living room for the offer of liqueurs, which everyone declined except Helen and George. After a few desultory attempts at conversation, Jay and his family said their good-byes and returned to Sue's apartment.

Doreen and Corinne were happy to retire to their room early so they could share their observations about Sue's parents, and to rest from their long day of unaccustomed travel.

Jay had made up a schedule for each day of the visit, designed to include only a couple of their friends at a time. He knew that too many strangers at once could be stressful, even though not all their friends would be as overwhelming as Sue's parents.

Saturday:

Doreen and Corinne slept in until almost noon.

"Here's our plan for today," Jay said to them. "We'll pick up Troy and Misty and do the touristy sites of Winnipeg."

"Troy and Misty are friends from California," Sue explained. "He works with making movies."

"You make friends easily," Doreen said to Jay. "And such nice interesting people."

"Speaking of interesting, we should stop in and say hello to Steve," Jay said.

After lunch, they drove around the city. Jay concentrated on his driving and Sue gave a running commentary on all the buildings, their history, and which ones her dad owned or had sold at one time or another.

"Dude. This is one awesome tour," Troy said. "It would take me years to learn this much by myself."

"I'm so glad you and Corinne came to visit," Jay said to his mother. "I'd never thought about the history of the buildings, especially in the Exchange District. I'd always thought of them as funny old buildings."

Eventually, they arrived at Steve's apartment.

"Try not to be shocked by any of Steve's pictures or anything," Jay warned as the door opened.

Steve smiled and said a formal, "Hello," to Doreen and Corinne. He smiled and shook hands politely as Jay introduced them. He was dressed in black slacks and a plain white T-shirt.

Jay couldn't keep his eyes from straying to Steve's chest to check for the usual telltale bulges of the Montreal barbells. He noticed with surprise that they were not evident, nor were his earrings or any other of his body jewelry. As they walked to the living room, he noticed that the pictures on the walls were of pastoral scenes and portraits of people who could have been his ancestors. The suggestive statuettes, which used to grace the living room, were no longer in evidence.

"Let me introduce my friend, Taylor," Steve said.

Taylor was quite thin, shorter than Steve and wore slightly tinted wire rim glasses. The jeans and sweater, as well his the manner, were casual and relaxed.

"Am I in the right apartment?" Jay asked Steve while they were in the kitchen getting drinks.

Steve laughed. "I'm used to putting on an appropriate image. I didn't want to scare your family away on their first visit."

"Thanks," Jay said. "I appreciate that."

As they were serving the drinks, Steve noticed the ring on Sue's hand, and just about dumped the drink onto her lap. He grabbed her hand and peered at the diamond.

"Wow. Diamonds are a gay's best friend, and that is one great friend," he said with enthusiasm. He shook Jay's hand with enthusiasm and said, "Well done."

"I'd better ask you while you're still in shock," Jay said. "Will you be my best man?"

"For the wedding?" Steve asked inanely.

"That is what I had in mind," Jay said apprehensively. "What else could I have meant by that."

"You caught me by surprise, that's all. I don't get a lot of offers for public appearances," Steve said. "I'd be honored to stand up with you and Sue."

Taylor moved over to Sue, reached for her hand, and asked, "May I?"

"Certainly," Sue said, holding up her hand.

"Best wishes to both of you," Taylor said, as he examined the ring from every angle.

"You're invited to the wedding, of course," Sue said. "Any friend of Steve's is a friend of ours."

"Thank-you," he said. "I'd be honored to attend."

Sunday:

Sue and Jay arrived early with Doreen and Corinne at the United Church they had attended on two previous occasions.

"Cam and Jamie should be here any minute," Jay said.

"That new sweater and skirt look really nice on you," Sue said to Corrine.

Corinne smiled. "I like my hair, too. That's the first time I've had it done by someone other than Mom."

"I like this new dress," Doreen said. "Will I wear it for the wedding?"

"When you come to visit us at Christmas we'll find something else for you then," Sue said. "The color has to match with my dress and Helen's so they won't clash in the photos."

"There are so many things to think about," Doreen said. "I don't know what I should be doing."

"Just leave it up to Sue," Jay said. "She'll look after you."

"*Miigwech*," Doreen said. "You tell us what to do, and we will do it, won't we, Corinne?"

Corinne smiled and nodded in agreement.

In due time, Cam and Jamie arrived and the entourage went into the church.

After the church service, they went for brunch at Altos, one of the restaurants connected to the Canad Inns chain of hotels, which special-izes in buffets and one of Winnipeg's ubiquitous electronic slot machine rooms. They carried on a spirited discussion of the sermon, then branched off into discussing various religions and the importance of a spiritual basis for marriage. They didn't come to any conclusions other than that neither the *Bahá'i* Faith nor native spirituality was going to provide them with a minister to officiate at the wedding.

Monday:

Although Phil had really wanted to throw one of his big dinner par-ties, Jay convinced him to pare it down to just his group, Steve, and Taylor.

"Doreen already knows me, and she's met Steve and Taylor," Phil had said. "Having a few more new people wouldn't be too much, would it?"

"I think it would be nice if she and Corinne could just enjoy a nice meal without having to try to remember more names."

Jay and his "gang" arrived a bit early so that Phil would have a chance for an uninterrupted look at the ring and to discuss details of the upcoming wedding before Steve and Taylor arrived.

When they arrived, Steve was dressed in a sports jacket and open neck shirt. Taylor was gorgeous in high heels, and a long, periwinkle skirt with a slit up one side. A sash, draping softly from shoulder to waist, accented the matching bodice. Her nails were polished. Diamond stud earrings, pearlized nails, and matching high gloss lipstick com-pleted the stunning image of an attractive young woman.

"Hi, Phil," Steve said. "You haven't met my friend, Taylor."

"Hi, Taylor," Phil said. "Make yourself comfortable anywhere. Steve said you would know everyone here."

Steve sat in Phil's recliner. Taylor sat, with demurely crossed legs, on the sofa beside Jay and gave him a mildly suggestive smile.

Doreen and Corinne looked at each other. "Do I know Taylor?" Doreen asked quietly.

Corinne shrugged her shoulders and looked puzzled.

Doreen caught Jay's eye and gave him a questioning look.

Jay turned to Taylor. "Could I see you for a minute, please?" he asked.

Jay and Taylor disappeared into the kitchen.

"That really is you, isn't it?" Jay asked.

"Yes," Taylor said. "Nice to see you again."

"I wasn't expecting you to dress like that."

"Sorry. I didn't bring many clothes with me. This is the nicest outfit I have."

"It's certainly not what I expected," Jay said.

"I wanted to look nice for your family."

"That's not the problem," Jay said. "You were a man the first time you met them. Now you're a woman."

"Is that a problem?" Taylor asked.

"How am I expected to explain this to my mother and my sister?"

"I don't know. Can't you just tell them I'm a pre-operational male transsexual?"

"You've got to be kidding. They won't have ever heard of such a thing," Jay said. "I'm not even sure myself what that means."

"I don't suppose you'd want me to explain it to them," Taylor suggested.

"Trust me. They don't want to hear anything about your identity crisis," Jay said.

"I didn't intend to cause you any embarrassment," Taylor said. "I could just make up some excuse to leave."

"Maybe that would be the best thing for everyone."

"Okay," Taylor said, through clenched teeth. "Sorry to have upset you."

Taylor returned to the living room and went over to Phil. "I was just talking to Jay. I think it would be better if I were to leave now."

"Because you're in drag?" Phil asked.

"I'm not in drag," Taylor said. "Drag is when you dress up to be someone else. This is what I wear when I'm being myself."

At this point, Jay came over and joined the conversation.

"Hang on. You shouldn't leave."

"I don't want to upset you or your family," Taylor said. "It won't be the first time I've had to leave a party because of who I am."

"I'm the one that was out of line," Jay said. "Come with me."

Jay guided Taylor over to Doreen and Corrine.

"I bet you didn't recognize Taylor. I hardly recognized her myself," he said. "She looks different without her glasses."

"I'm wearing contacts," Taylor explained.

Doreen and Corinne smiled and murmured pleasantries. The dinner party continued without further confusion.

Tuesday:

The gang, as Jay had taken to calling Sue, Doreen, and Corinne, spent a "do nothing" morning at the apartment. It gave them a chance to discuss the events of the week. Doreen and Corinne appreciated the opportunity to get all people they had met sorted out, and, where necessary, explained.

In the early afternoon, they went downtown to do a bit of shopping before going to visit Jimmy and Becky. Jay assured everyone that there would be no surprises with Jimmy and Becky. "You don't need to dress up for them. They're casual people."

After a pizza dinner at Corinne's request, they decided to go to a movie at one of the multiplex theaters. Jimmy was surprisingly agreeable in the choice of the movie they decided to see. He pretended to be perfectly happy to go along with their choice of a lighthearted movie even though it obviously wouldn't have any explosions or violence. "You don't plan to skip out on us and go to a different movie when we get to the theater, do you?" Jay had asked jokingly.

They bought their tickets, and were standing at the concession stand trying to get Corinne to make a decision, when Becky announced, "There's Tanya."

Jay suppressed the desire to look. Instead, he leaned over to Sue and asked quietly, "What do we do now?"

"She's your friend," Sue said.

"Do you mind if we speak to her?" Jay asked. "We can pretend we don't see her, if you'd rather."

"That would be rude," Sue said. "Besides, it gives me another chance to show off my ring."

They joined Tanya, made introductions all around, and showed her the ring. No mention was made of Montreal.

"I'm so happy for you, Sue," Tanya said. "And it's so nice to meet your family, Jay."

"What movie are you seeing?" Jay asked. He was relieved to find out that it wasn't the one for which they had tickets.

Later that night, Sue and Jay talked about Tanya and the Montreal fiasco for the first time. They both felt better afterwards. Sue agreed that Tanya should be invited to the wedding.

Wednesday:

Doreen and Corinne caught an early morning bus heading north. They had two new suitcases crammed full of purchases (mostly clothes), and their heads full of wedding plans and their hearts filled with excitement and happy anticipation of the wedding.

~ 24 ~

COUNTDOWN TO HAPPINESS

Nine months may be enough time to create a baby, but eleven months is barely enough time to prepare for a wedding. As soon as the initial decision has been made, the lines of demarcation must be established, the key players identified, and areas of responsibility delineated. Reservations must be made, suppliers contacted, and guests invited.

At some point, maybe around the time that the invitations are sent out, the main players in the wedding network sense a subtle change. No longer do they need to make phone calls; other people call them. No longer do they have the initiative in making plans; people ask them if such and such has been done yet. The wedding is no longer under anyone's control; it has taken on a life of its own.

From this point onward, nothing short of outright termination can deflect the game plan from running its predestined course to fruition. Each activity choreographs another. The most one can hope for is that he, or more likely she, will react to the unending demands of the monster with proper protocol and decorum. The only solace at the end of each hectic day is the prospect that, yes, it will be beautiful and memorable. Dare one even dream that it may be fun?

August 10th:

Jay and Sue were lying in bed talking about their usual topic. The wedding.

"Are your folks going to be all right with the wedding party?" Jay asked.

"Mom is. Dad will have a problem with Steve as best man."

"Because he's gay?"

"He says his church doesn't accept gays in their congregation," Sue said.

"Is that true?"

"Probably not. You know he's homophobic. He probably assumes everyone else is, too."

"What if we use a different church?"

"He'd never agree to that. His family has always belonged to that church."

"Then what's the alternative?" Jay asked.

"As far as he's concerned, you'll have to get a different best man."

"I won't agree to having him choose my best man for me. I'm trying to be cooperative but Steve is going to be my best man."

"What if he refuses? After all, he is paying for the wedding and reception," Sue said.

"Then we go to Las Vegas."

"You're saying you'd elope with me?" Sue asked.

"In a minute. This whole wedding thing is for your family, not mine."

"Mom and Dad would be devastated to miss out on the wedding."

"They could watch it on the Internet," Jay said.

"What do you mean?"

"Cam told me about a chapel in Las Vegas that shows the wedding live over the Internet. They could watch the whole thing as it happens."

"Like all three minutes of it?"

"Maybe five," Jay said. "There must be a better solution. Does it have to be a church wedding? My side of the family isn't going to feel all that comfortable in a church. They don't have churches where they live."

"Could we do it outdoors somewhere?"

"Would that mean we'd have it done by a justice of the peace?" Jay asked.

"I want us to be married by a minister."

"Me too."

"There must be ministers who are flexible about the location."

"We could talk to the United Church minister where go to church sometimes, if your dad's minister doesn't want to do it."

"What about in the park? Where we got engaged," Sue suggested.

"Could we do that?" Jay asked. "My family would love having it close to nature."

"I'll have to talk to Mom about it. She's a sucker for romance."

September 7th:

"How are the wedding and reception plans going?" Jay asked.

"Dad's accepted the idea of having the wedding in the park. However, it messes up his plan for my dress."

"How's that?" Jay asked.

"He wants me to be a vision of beauty in a dress with a long train."

"And that's a problem because…"

"If the wedding is outside, I can't be dragging ten feet of train over the grass."

"He'll have to accept you in a short train. Unless he plans to pave a path through the park for you," Jay said.

"Don't suggest it. He just might do it."

"I thought he was staying as much out of the planning as possible."

"He likes organizing things so long as he's in total control. He hates surprises."

"And the reception?" Jay asked.

"That will have to be at some fancy place. It's his chance to show off for his friends and relatives. He'll want lots of expensive liquor, an elaborate meal and a dance. With a live band."

"He gave in to me on the wedding location. I'll let him have his reception wherever and however he wants it."

"I'm betting it'll be the Country Club. That would be more elegant than any our relatives have had."

"And I'm guessing, the most expensive," Jay said.

October 15:

Sue's dad was called into action to reserve The Leo Mol sculpture garden at Assiniboine Park for the wedding.

"We're not taking any more reservations for that area for next summer," the park manager said. "Perhaps another location?"

"Take me to your supervisor," George said.

An hour later the garden area had been reserved for the wedding.

November 10th:

"We have to talk," Sue said.

"That sounds serious," Jay said.

"My dad says we need a prenuptial agreement."

"We did agree to get married the way he wanted. I don't suppose that's what he means."

"He means we have to sign a paper saying that if we get divorced we each get to keep whatever we had before the marriage."

"Neither of us has any money now," Jay said. "We barely make it from one payday to the next."

"On paper somewhere I'm worth a lot of money. It's invested where I can't get at it until some lawyer says it's mine," Sue said.

"It isn't my money, anyway. Why would I get it if we got divorced?"

"The laws are funny that way. Without an agreement you'd get half of my money."

"I wouldn't want it. It's yours, not mine," Jay said. "It's you I want, not your money."

"My dad would like that in writing."

"That's easy. Have him draw up whatever papers he wants and I'll sign them."

"I was hoping you'd understand. Mom was afraid this would be a big argument between you and my dad."

"That's the nice thing about not having any money. There's not so much to worry about," Jay said.

December 27th:

All of Jay's family, including Doreen's significant other, Maurice, and her son Darren, came to Winnipeg for the Christmas festivities and to shop for wedding attire.

Maurice deigned to have his measurements taken but that was all. Darren felt the same way about fancy clothes. New jeans, of course, were a different matter.

"Don't expect me to go around trying on clothes," Maurice said. "You buy them and I'll wear them for the ceremony. That's all. And I'm not making any speech."

Doreen and Corinne more than made up for Maurice and Darren in their enthusiasm for shopping. Between the two of them they managed to exhaust both Sue and Helen. However, it was worth the effort. Outfits for the whole family were elegant, coordinated, and put onto Helen's Amex card.

"I haven't had so much fun in years," Helen said. "We should do this more often."

Sue and Jay groaned at the thought of it.

January 17th:

"Mom picked up the invitations today," Sue said.

"How do they look?" Jay asked.

"Impressive."

"You don't sound happy about it. Is there something wrong with them?"

"It depends on your point of view. Have a look."

Jay studied the invitation and then read out loud: "the marriage of Susan Eleanor Parkington and Jason Winston May."

He looked at Sue. "Who's this Jason May you're marrying? Anyone I know?"

"It could be the printer's error?" Sue asked hopefully.

"Why do I think I see your father's hand in this? He could at least have left me with Jay. I'm not a Jason. I'm Japheth. He could at least have made it Jayson, with a 'y.'"

"I'm sure he'd change that."

"You mean to put in a 'y' or to use Japheth?"

"I don't know," Sue said. "I'm just trying to think positively."

"What happened to *Maytwayashing*, anyway?"

"He probably doesn't like the native sound of it. He'll be afraid his business associates and relatives would find it off-putting."

"Did you say 'off-putting'? That doesn't sound like a word you'd use. It sounds like one of your dad's words. Have you been talking to him about this without consulting me? I'd resent that."

"I talked to Mom. I hoped she and I could work this out ourselves."

"Your mom's okay. We understand each other."

"I didn't want to upset you with these problems unless I had to," Sue said. "I know this whole wedding business is stressful for you."

"Well, I'm afraid you'll have to upset me. This is my identity we are talking about. I don't care what Shakespeare said, I wouldn't smell as sweet as a Jason without a 'y.' It's got to be either Jay or Japheth."

"What about Jayson with a 'y' in it?"

"Give me some time to think about this. It's beginning to make my head spin."

"I'll talk to Mom and we'll get the invitation fixed up any way you want it."

"Thanks. By the way, what name do you plan to use after we're married?" Jay asked. "Will I still know who you are?"

"I'd like to drop mine and take yours," Sue said.

"But?"

"I didn't say there was a but."

"There is no but?" Jay asked.

"Well, yes. I guess there is."

"What is it?"

"*Maytwayashing* is a bit more of a mouthful than I'm comfortable with. It's your decision, however. I can learn to live with it," Sue said.

"Actually, I've been thinking about *Maytwayashing* myself. I'd rather have people pay attention to me instead of my name. That's why I usually avoid using it."

"And?" Sue asked.

"If I'm going to change it, this would be a good time to do it."

"What about your native heritage? You've been working so hard at learning Ojibwe. You're not going to throw that away, are you?"

"I'm more than my name. I'll follow my native language and spirituality no matter what my name is," Jay said.

"I'm glad to hear you say that. I need a spiritual basis for my life. I'd want you to have one, too."

"I hope we can find a faith that is good for both of us," Jay said.

"Getting back to the invitations. All you have to do is choose the name you want to use."

"Your dad's idea of shortening *Maytwayashing* to May isn't all bad."

"Wouldn't your mother be upset if you gave up her name?"

"If she gets married, she'll take her husband's name. She's traditional that way."

"Is she planning on getting married? Sue asked. "Maybe we could have a double wedding."

"I don't think so," Jay said. His face betrayed the shot of panic that the idea of a double wedding caused.

"Relax," Sue said. "There's no way we could do a double wedding."

"I meant that if my mom can give up the name, I don't think she'd mind if I did. Besides, I'd still have the first part of it. Sort of like a nickname."

"So then you'd be called Jay May?"

"Oh great. I can see it all now. I get introduced as Jay May. And then the guy says, what's your last name, Jamie?"

"Let's sleep on it," Sue said.

"I'd never be able to go by Jay. I'd have to always be Jayson. I've never been Jayson. I'm Jay."

"Come on the bed, whoever you are."

The next day, Jay agreed to have his name legally changed to Jayson May, and started the necessary bureaucratic processes. "Well," he mused, "I guess that keeping the 'y' counts as a victory of sorts."

February 2nd:

Jay phoned Malabar's tuxedo rentals:

"This is Jayson May. I'm phoning about the tux rentals for June 21st."

" . . . "

"Oh, sorry. It will be under Jay Maytwayashing."

" . . . "

"Yes. That's the one."

" .. "

"I thought I wanted the tie and vest in white, but I was mistaken. I found that I want them in ivory."

" .. "

Thanks.

April 17th:

Jay and Sue were talking about, what else but, the wedding.

"I think I have an idea," Jay said.

"I hope you're not planning on changing anything," Sue said. "Helen is happy with the dresses and flowers. Dad is happy with the Leo Mol garden for the wedding and the Country Club for the reception. He's chosen the wine and champagne and Mom's looking after the dinner menu."

"Don't worry," Jay said. "I wouldn't want to change anything. I was thinking we could have a professional video made of the wedding."

"We have a photographer booked. Do you think we need a video?"

"It might be nice."

"If you want to set it up, go ahead," Sue said. "I'm sure Dad would be happy. The more impressive the better, he always says."

"I'll talk to Troy. I bet jaycee wouldn't mind the job. And maybe Troy would do the editing."

"Tell him to take it easy on the special effects. It's a wedding, not a video extravaganza."

June 19th:

Sue, the female side of the wedding party, Steve, and Taylor were doing last-minute beauty preparations. Now was the time for saunas, facials, massages and mud baths.

June 21st: 8:30 a.m.

There was much to be done. Hair salons had been reserved for the entire morning starting at 8:30 a.m. and running through until noon. Everything had been organized, reorganized, checked and rechecked to ensure the perfection of the well-oiled wedding machine.

A professional photographer was on hand to record every moment from the opening chords of the portable keyboard to the final departure of the newly married couple. Troy was enjoying his dual role as usher and director of jaycee's videography.

George had ordered two thousand dollars worth of flowers in spite of the florist's concern that there was no place to put them in an outdoor setting which consisted of flower gardens, a decorative pool with water lilies, trees, and life-size metal sculptures. Fortunately, the Country Club is large and would be able to hold the overflow.

June 21st: 1:30 p.m.

"It's going to rain. I just know this wedding is going to be a disaster," George said. "What will we do if it rains?"

"It's not going to rain," Helen said.

"You can't know that."

"There's not a cloud in the sky."

"I think it's going to rain," George said.

"It's like if you expect the worst, then that's what will happen. If you have faith that things will work out..."

George interrupted Helen. "Yes, yes. We know."

Helen continued. "What is it the poet said? The coward dies many times before his death; the valiant dies but once."

"What's that have to do with anything? We should have a tent set up in case of rain," George said. "Where can we rent a tent?"

"Don't worry. We can always go into the pavilion if it rains."

"I never should have let you arrange this. We should have hired a professional to look after everything. Then it would have been done right."

"Trust me, George. This will be a memorable wedding."

"Memorable isn't what I want. Impressive is what I want."

"Believe me. This wedding will make more of an impression on your relatives than any of those others your family has had," Helen said.

Folding chairs had been set up on the grass among the tree trunks and the sculptures of bear cubs and deer. A path through the center led to a small podium under an archway of flowers. The guests were seated with the fourteen guests of the groom at the front on the right, and the guests of the bride filling the rest of the seats except for a block of twelve empty reserved seats at the very back.

June 21st: 2:05 p.m.

The minister stood at the front with Jay and Steve. Jay looked handsome but somewhat uncomfortable in his black tuxedo with ivory vest and tie. Steve luxuriated in his image, looking as if he were a model on display for a roomful of his adoring fans.

Bouquets of flowers were everywhere. Two freestanding horseshoes of flowers, not unlike what one might expect to see in the winner's circle at the racetrack, flanked the podium on either side.

The strains of Clarke's Trumpet Voluntaire began, and as the stirring notes of the trumpet soloist resounded through the trees, the wedding procession began.

Sue's dress (from Paris, of course) was ivory, with a fitted bodice and a princess waistline to accent her trim figure. The short train fell from her shoulders to gently brush the grass.

Tiffany, as always, was exceptionally radiant as the maid of honor.

George, with a sigh of relief took his seat beside Helen.

The bridesmaids and the groomsmen took up their outrider positions at the front.

Out from the trees at the side, a stately native figure complete with full headdress, beaded doeskin jacket, moccasins and leggings, walked majestically over to stand beside the minister. Cam's eyes widened with admiration. He leaned over and whispered to Steve, "I'd kill to have an outfit like that to wear to the Club."

Jay immediately recognized R.B. and turned his head to look at Helen. She gave Jay a smile and a thumbs-up. The unmistakable aroma of a sweetgrass smudge wafted over the wedding party. High overhead an eagle carved lazy circles in the sky. A group of native people, varying in age from seven years to seventy, all dressed in full fancy dance costumes appeared from nowhere to fill the reserved seats at the back.

R.B. stood motionless and silent while the minister performed the ceremony. Just before the invitation for the couple to kiss, R.B. stepped forward.

He loosely knotted a banner around their clasped hands. The banner was made from two pieces of cloth stitched together, symbolizing the traditional Ojibwe custom of stitching the hems of the married couple's jackets together. Looking out over the heads of the gathering he delivered a brief prayer for the wedded couple in the rhythmic monotone of the Ojibwe language, followed in English by:

> "You will share the same fire and hang your garments together.
> You will help one another as you walk down the same trail of life.
> You will look after each other."

R.B. removed the banner.

"Be kind to one another. Be kind to your children," he said as he stepped back.

The minister gave the signal, "You may now kiss the bride."

The keyboard began Handel's Watermusic. The native dancers formed a silent honor guard for the newly married couple as they walked down the makeshift aisle.

Official wedding pictures were taken around the sculptures, after which the wedding party was transported by limousine to the Country Club for more pictures and the receiving line.

June 21st: 4:30 p.m.

At the Country Club, waiters dispensed quality champagne, liquors and sparkling fruit juices from portable bars. Servers with white gloves moved among the guests offering hors d'oeuvres on silver trays.

The native dancers, joined periodically by R.B., danced energetically amid the crowd to the beat and singing of four drummers. George studiously ignored the dancers. He concentrated his attention on small talk with groups of his relatives.

Jay left Sue for a minute to talk to Helen. "How did you plan all this?"

"Phil and I set it up with R.B. before he left. He wanted to do something spiritual for you."

"That must have been before Mom and Corinne came here. We weren't even engaged then."

"R.B. knew you'd be getting married. I knew when because every year Sue chooses a date, just in case. It's been sort of a joke between us ever since she was in junior high."

"So you both knew all about the wedding long before I did?" Jay asked. "You could have warned me."

"We thought it would be better to have it come as a surprise," Helen said. "We didn't want to scare you away."

"Where did you find the dancers and drummers?"

"They're a few of R.B.'s closest friends and relatives. It was their idea to throw a little powwow for you."

At 6:15 the guests were ushered inside for the formal five-course dinner. Most of the guests, and George, were unaware that the food was
totally vegetarian, specially prepared with Phil's advice

June 21st: 7:45 p.m.

The wedding dance was nicely underway. While Sue was freshening
up, Jay wandered around and then leafed idly through the guest book.
There were dozens of names he didn't recognize. Suddenly, one name
leaped out at him. Winston McNabb. Jay rushed around until he found
Sue and brought her to see the entry.

"My Dad was here," Jay said. "He signed the guest book. Did you
know about that?"

"No way," Sue said. "Let's check with Becky. She was looking after the
book."

They found Becky and Jimmy in the middle of the dance floor. Jay
caught her eye and waved them over.

"My father was here and signed the guest book. Did you see him?
What did he look like? Is he still here?" Jay asked.

"There were so many people. I didn't even notice their names when
they signed the book," Becky said.

"You don't remember anything?"

"I wish I did. Maybe he's still here."

"I'll check with Helen," Jay said. "She'd notice a stranger here. "

Jay worked his way around the crowd, making slow progress because
everyone wanted to shake his hand and offer congratulations. Finally he
found Helen. "My father was here and signed the guest book. Did you
see him?"

"I did see a middle-aged man who seemed to be all by himself. He
wasn't anyone I knew so I assumed he was a friend of one of the guests.
Maybe that was your dad."

"Did he say anything?" Jay asked.

"I didn't talk to him, although I'm sure he left a gift. Maybe I can find it for you."

Helen searched through the table covered with wedding gifts. They all looked generically similar with their elaborately elegant, professional wrapping.

"Wait a minute," she said. "This one didn't come from one of our bridal registry stores."

She picked up a shoebox-sized gift, wrapped in plain silver paper decorated by a single white Christmas bow. A card was taped to the wrapping.

"Here it is," she said, picking up the plainly wrapped package and its attached card.

Jay's hands shook as he undid the wrapping and opened the box. A single wooden goblet with two wooden rings trapped on the stem nestled on a bed of crumpled facial tissue.

"It's beautiful," Sue said. "Hurry. Read the card. Is it from your dad?"

Jay read the card to himself and then handed it to Sue. It read:

My dearest Jay and Sue,

Please accept my apologies for not introducing myself to you. I know it was rude of me to leave so quickly, particularly after you so kindly sent me a ticket to get here. However, I've never brought happiness or success to anyone whose path I've crossed. I didn't want to be a jinx at your wedding.

I had no money to buy you a present, so I made this little gift for you from a single piece of wood I found among the trees behind my trailer. With every wood chip that I carved out, and every speck of dust as I sanded it, I offered my prayers that you will find the happiness with each other that has always eluded me.

On each anniversary, please share a drink from the goblet, and pledge your love to each other.

Try not to judge me harshly. I know I shouldn't have come here after I was rude to you on the phone and ignored your letter, but I had to see you this one time. It's better for you that I stay out of your life.

With all my love and my sincere wishes for your happiness together,

Winston.

"That was nice of you to send him a ticket," Sue said, after reading the note.

"I didn't send him a ticket," Jay said.

"Then who did?" Sue asked. "You don't suppose…"

"Who else?" Jay asked. "He probably put Winston on the payroll so he could claim the trip as a business expense."

"I wouldn't be surprised. He manages to claim everything else."

"I guess he finally got a detective to do something right for him," Jay said.

"He never was one to give up easily," Sue said.

June 21st: 11:35 p.m.

Mr. and Mrs. Jayson May arrived at the bridal suite of the Holiday Inn West. On the table there was a complimentary basket of fruit, biscuits and cheese, a chilled bottle of champagne in an ice bucket, and a bottle of Amarula.

A few miles outside Winnipeg on the highest branch of an isolated tree a lone eagle sat with its eyes closed in restful sleep.

June 22nd: 11:35 p.m.

Sue and Jay left from the Winnipeg airport for their honeymoon in Hawaii, all expenses paid, compliments of George.

Jay was pleased when he checked the tickets to note that they were for a return trip.

About the Author

Charles (Bill) Shirriff resides with his wife Wilma in Portage la Prairie, Manitoba, in their home overlooking Crescent Lake.

Their son Ken is a computer engineer with Sun Microsystems and lives in California with his wife Kathryn and daughter Sydney.

Their daughter Anita is married to Henry Borger. They currently live in Illinois with their daughter Emma while Henry finishes his MBA program at Kellogg University.

His teaching career spanned thirty-five years and took him west to British Columbia and north to Swan River, Cranberry Portage, Flin Flon, and Norway House. Most of his teaching years were spent near

Winnipeg in the city of Portage la Prairie where he held positions as teacher, school counselor, Special Education coordinator, and consultant for the Gifted & Talented.

A brief foray into the field of Meteorology provided him with the opportunity to live in Moosonee, on the tip of James Bay, doing research on the upper atmosphere.

After graduation from the University of Manitoba with a Bachelor of Science in Mathematics, Physics and Chemistry, his love of learning and a penchant for new experiences led him to obtain a Master of Science in psychology from the University of North Dakota, and a B.A. degree from the State of New York. Additional courses in a variety of subjects were taken at the University of Toronto, University of British Columbia, University of Connecticut (Storrs) and Stanford University in California.

www.cwshirriff.homestead.com   SHIRRIFF@MTS.NET

Appendix
The Universality of the Golden Rule

(My thanks to the various Internet sites, too numerous to mention, from which this information was gleaned.)

Over some thousands of years of recorded history, versions of "The Golden Rule" have appeared with surprisingly similar messages.

HINDU:
—This is the sum of duty: do naught to others, which if done to thee would cause thee pain.

JUDAISM:
—What is hateful to you, do not to your fellow man. That is the law: all the rest is commentary.

SUFISM:
—If you haven't the will to gladden someone's heart, then at least beware lest you hurt someone's heart.

BUDDHIST:
—Hurt not others with that which pains yourself.

ISLAMIC:
  —Not do to others that which would anger you if others did it to
  you.

JAINISM:
  —A man should wander about treating all creatures as he himself
  would be treated.

SIKHISM:
  —Don't create enmity with anyone as God is within everyone.

CONFUCIAN:
  —Try your best to treat others as you would wish to be treated yourself, and you will find that this is the shortest way to benevolence.

ZOROASTRIAN:
  —Whatever is disagreeable to yourself do not do unto others.

SHINTO:
  —The heart of the person before you is a mirror. See there your own
  form.

TAOIST:
  —Regard your neighbor's gain as your own gain, and your neighbor's loss as your own loss.

ROMAN PAGAN RELIGION:
  —The law imprinted on the hearts of all men is to love the members
  of society as themselves.

SOCRATES:
  —Do not do to others what you would not wish to suffer yourself.

SENECA:
—Treat your inferiors as you would be treated by your superiors.

THALES:
—Avoid doing what you would blame others for doing.

ARISTIPPUS OF CYRENE:
—Cherish reciprocal benevolence, which will make you as anxious
  for another's welfare as your own.

NIGERIAN SAYING:
—One going to take a pointed stick to poke a baby bird should first
  try it on himself to feel how it hurts.

WICCA
—As in it harm no one (including oneself), do what thou wilt.

FIRST NATION (North American Indian)
—Grant that I may not judge my neighbor until I have walked a mile
  in his moccasins.
—Respect for all life is the foundation.

CHRISTIANITY:
—And as ye would that men should do to you, do ye also to them
  likewise.

HUTTERIAN BRETHREN:
—What's mine is yours. What's yours is mine.

BAHA'I
—Breathe not the sins of others so long as thou art thyself a sinner.
—Choose thou for thy neighbour that which thou choosest for thyself.

STANDARD MODERN:
   —Do unto others as you would have them do unto you.

CYNICAL MODERN:
   —He who has the Gold, makes the Rule.

Notes on Illustrations

Chapter 1: An aerial view of Winnipeg.

The CanWest Global Park is shown in the foreground beside the Red River.

Winnipeg, being situated on the Assiniboine and Red Rivers, takes advantage of them in the summer as an environmentally friendly transportation system. The "Splash Dash" is an everyday, inexpensive shuttle service operating between six docks along the two rivers at a speed of about 40 km/hr and no traffic lights. During the winter, the docks become changing areas for skaters and cross-country skiers.

Chapter 2: A Manitoba Winter Scene

This is a typical winter snowstorm scene in Manitoba. It isn't a blizzard. If it were you wouldn't be able to see the trees at all for the blowing snow.

Chapter 3: Summer at Portage and Main in Winnipeg, Manitoba

This intersection has the reputation of being one of the coldest places in Canada on January days when the winter wind blows down from the north. The tall buildings funnel the wind from the lake to produce an astonishingly high wind chill factor.

Winnipeg is sometimes referred to as the "Chicago of the North." Opinion differs as to whether this is because of the Chicago-style architecture in the Exchange District or the similarity in wind between of the corner of Portage and Main, and Chicago that is known as The Windy City.

Chapter 4: Wall art in Winnipeg

A few years ago Winnipeg was a finalist in the Canadian "Prettiest Painted Places" competition with more than 100 murals on buildings throughout the city.

By October of 2001, 125 murals had been completed by the "Take Pride in Winnipeg" program alone and at least as many more by other groups and individuals. Winnipeg could soon become the wall art capital of Canada.

In 1998, a man named Stephen Wilson recognized the wasted artistic talent of those who were vandalizing buildings in the city with their illegal graffiti. Investing his own money, he rented space and enlisted talented youth for what he called "Graffiti Art Programming (GAP)".

Within a month they began selling their paintings and getting contracts to paint murals on walls throughout Winnipeg. Of the eleven who originally signed up with him, seven are now studying fine arts at the University of Manitoba.

Murals continue to appear on blank walls and fences throughout the city as a viable way of beautifying the city while at the same time discouraging vandalism and graffiti.

Chapter 5: Exchange District in Winnipeg

In 1881, the arrival of the railroad in Winnipeg began a four-decade economic boom that marked Winnipeg as "The Gateway to the West."

There are thirty-three blocks of terra cotta and cut-stone buildings built over a hundred years ago under the influence of Chicago architects. These buildings are now the sites for restaurants, antique shops, nightclubs, and entertainment facilities.

Most recently, some of the heritage buildings are being converted into fashionable living quarters in spite of the problems encountered in meeting modern building codes.

An additional new campus for the Red River Community College is being planned for this area.

Chapter 6: First nation shaman implements

The native drum and rattle are used to provide rhythmic stimuli that create sensory overload and stop the rational thought patterns of the participant. This stimulus is helpful for the novice participant to achieve a receptive mental state.

Yogis achieve this same effect through rhythmic mantras, breathing patterns and postures. They refer to it as "stopping the oscillations of the mind."

The true shaman does not require the assistance of external stimuli because he/she is able to enter the alternate reality at will while always remaining in complete control. This is not the case with psychic mediums who enter a deep trance and lose control of their conscious processes.

Chapter 7: Dreamcatcher

Ojibwe legend has it that many years ago an old native woman stopped her son from stepping on a spider as it wove its web. As thanks for saving its life, the spider taught the woman how to weave a web that would catch and hold bad dreams.

The spider instructed that the dreamcatcher must be made with at least seven points—one for each of the sacred teaching of the grandfathers.

Chapter 8: Winter hoar frost

Moist winter weather conditions, coupled with rapid temperature drops, create hoar frost on the Canadian prairies. For a few days every winter the cities and countryside are turned into three dimensional Christmas cards.

Chapter 9: The annual Fringe Festival

Winnipeg is rated number one, just after Montreal and ahead of Edmonton, for having the most vibrant Fringe Festival.

Amateur writers and performers put together shows that are on the cutting edge.

You might ask, "The cutting edge of what?" If you have to ask, then you've never attended a Fringe Festival, and you really should.

Chapter 10: Summer in Winnipeg

Street vendors provide an opportunity for office workers to enjoy their lunch hour in the warm sun and fresh air.

Noon hour outdoor concerts take place throughout Winnipeg during the summer. It's common to have small concerts in parks and plazas around the city. Larger organizations, such as The Winnipeg Ballet or The Winnipeg Symphony, perform on the stage of the Lyric Theater in Assiniboine Park or in Market Square.

Chapter 11: A Hutterite colony north of Saskatoon, Saskatchewan

A group of school children is standing on a hill with some of the colony buildings in the background.

The buildings, facilities, and grounds are immaculate in every respect as is typical of all Hutterite colonies. Agricultural facilities and equipment are modern and state-of-the-art.

Chapter 12: A classroom in one of the more progressive Hutterite schools

Not all colonies have schools that are as modern and free in philosophy as the one shown, although many have computers for school use.

Where computers are available they are used primarily for computer-assisted learning, and not extensively for the Internet.

The schools on many colonies still favor the formal desks and the strict discipline of a more rigorous, traditional curriculum.

Chapter 13: The Stovel Building in the Exchange District

This Victorian style building was the built for the Stovel Printing & Lithographing Co., which printed many newspapers, including the Winnipeg Telegraph.

In 1997, the Winnipeg Exchange District was designated as a National Historic Site (one of only 17 such districts in Canada), in recognition of its many historical buildings in one location which share a common history.

Chapter 14: Window sign

Sometimes people try too hard to be inclusive. Or maybe it only seems that way.

Chapter 15: Bahá'i House of Worship, Wilmette, Illinois

The world headquarters for the Baha'i Faith is on Mount Carmel in Haifa, Israel.

It took half a century for the Temple at Wilmette to be completed, financed solely through contributions from Bahá'i believers.

Similar Houses of Worship also exist in Frankfurt Germany, Uganda, Sydney Australia, Panama, New Delhi India, and West Samoa.

The first Temple was built in Russia but was taken over by the communist government and eventually destroyed.

The next one to be built is planned to be in Peru for the continent of South America.

Chapter 16: Native justice

By the year 2001, Manitoba had 70 justice committees which dealt with seventeen hundred young offenders. 22% of the young offenders charged were sent to Community Justice Committees rather than the regular court system.

Winnipeg's Aboriginal Ganootamaage Justice Services, and a variety of other processes, dealt with twelve hundred adult offenders (5% of the total charges).

Sentencing Circles consist of trusted community members, with the participation of the victims being voluntary. This system of restorative justice, as opposed to punitive justice, is rooted in aboriginal traditions.

Chapter 17: The Crypt clothing boutique in Osborne Village

The Crypt is a basement store in Osborne Village that offers a wide range of subculture streetware clothing, shoes, and accessories for bold-spirited modern young people.

Chapter 18: Montreal's Lachine Canal

Thanks to Michael Wu for permission to use this picture and the one of the Montreal Olympic Park.

More beautiful Montreal pictures are shown on his web site: www.geocities.com/TimesSquare/Labyrinth/3565/1.html

Chapter 19: Montreal Olympic Park

Built for the Summer Olympic Games in 1976, this park now houses the Biodome, which is a museum devoted to promoting awareness of the world and the interdependence of all its inhabitants.

There are four different ecosystems in the Biodome: a tropical forest, a Laurentian forest, the St. Lawrence marine environment, and the polar region.

Chapter 20: The Forks

The junction of the Red and Assiniboine Rivers made this area an important gathering place for First Nations peoples and then for the early settlers.

More recently the area has been developed to attract tourists to the upscale restaurants and unique stores as well as outdoor skating and dancing depending on the season.

Chapter 21: Leo Mol's Europa

The sculpture, Europa, is based on the Greek Myth. It portrays Zeus, who has assumed the form of a bull, abducting a Phoenician princess.

Leo Mol is known around the world for his bronze sculptures. The Leo Mol Sculpture Garden in Assiniboine Park displays many of his works.

This section of the garden also displays sculptures entitled Lumberjacks, Standing Bears, and Polar Bear and Cub.

Many churches in Winnipeg showcase his work with his stained glass windows.

Chapter 22: Thunderbird House on North Main Street in Winnipeg.

The building, also called The Circle of Life, was officially opened on March 21st, 2000. The four entrances open to the true compass directions: north for the white race, south for black, east for the yellow, and west for red. Thus, all races from all parts of the world are symbolically welcomed to come and join with each other in the universal experience of spiritual contemplation.

Chapter 23: Pooh and the honey jar

The citizens of Winnipeg raised $285,000 towards the purchase of E.H. Shepard's painting of Winnie the Pooh so that it could become the focus for a $6 million "Poohseum" to be built in Assiniboine Park.

During the First World War, a Winnipeg soldier rescued a lost Black Bear cub in Ontario and later donated it to the London Zoo. He named the cub Winnie, after the city of Winnipeg. The bear later inspired A.J. Milne to write his famous stories for his son.

Chapter 24: Powwow dancers in 'fancy dance' costume
Long Plain First Nations hosts an annual powwow in August that attracts some 250 contestants of all ages from across Canada and the U.S.A.

Powwows are popular throughout the United States, with many dancers following a summer circuit.

Bibliography of WebSites

(For your convenience all these sites are listed as direct links from my book site at: www.cwshirriff.homestead.com)

Pets
- www.petsmart.com
- www.animaltalk.net

Hutterian Brethren: www.hutterites.org

Native Peoples: www.turning-point.ca

Sentencing Circle
- www.realjustice.org/Pages/vt99papers/vt_bushie.html
- www.usask.ca/nativelaw/jah_circle.html
- www.nanlegal.on.ca/sentencingcircle.html

print references – www.usask.ca/nativelaw/jah_scircle.html

Restorative Justice
- www.sgc.gc.ca/epub/corr/e199810b/e199810b.htm
- www3.ns.sympatico.ca/icjs/core.htm

Adult Education
- www.gedonline.org
- www.acenet.edu/calec/ged

Bahá'i: www.bahai.org

White Earth reservation: www.startribune.com/spirit

New Age:
- www.newageinfo.com
- www.religioustolerance.org/newage.htm

Hasidic Jews

                    –   www.jewishtours.com
                    –   www.chabadofwestmount.com
                    –   www.chabad.org
Kabbalah: www.kabbalah-web.org
Parents & Friends of Lesbians and Gays
                    –   www.pflag.org
                    –   www.outproud.org/brochure

Talk to Your Kids
    menu of topics –   www.talkingwithkids.org
    drugs –   www.talkingwithkids.org/drugs.html
The Crypt: www.cryptclothiers.com
Wedding Plans
    Overview –   www.theknot.com
    Advice –   www.weddinggazette.com
    Ethnic Ceremonies–   www.askginka.com
    Handmade Stationery–   www.custompaper.com
    Your Web Site –   www.weddingidea.com
    Ceremony –   www.weddingchannel.com
                    –   www.vivalasvegasweddings.com
    Speeches/vows –   www.ultimatewedding.com
    Honeymoon trips –   www.whereintheworld.co.uk
                    –   www.rcrusoe.com

0-595-20626-3

Printed in the United States
135940LV00001B/131/A

9 780595 206261